JOURNEY THROUGH LONELINESS

A Search for Life's Purpose

Dennis McTighe

Story Pocket Books
4724 Fairway Pointe Ct
Louisville KY 40241

ISBN:978-0-9969900-2-8

CHAPTER ONE

Trapped In Darkness

Every morning, we would put on our heavy equipment and descend into the earth's belly. It was just us and our headlamps cutting through the darkness, winding through tight tunnels where the air was thick with the smell of hard work and the earth's grit.

My pickaxe whistled through the space, chiseling out chunks of earth in a rhythm as steady and familiar as the thrumming bass at a music festival. The hazy light painted my silhouette against the rough-textured walls of rock, my sole companion in this dusty dance-off.

In the dimness, dust particles came alive like fireflies caught in the beam of my headlamp, blurring my vision and leaving a gritty residue on my tongue with every breath I sucked in. With each swing of my pickaxe, chunks of earth cascaded down around me.

My body moved instinctively, its motions honed through hours of laboring under the weight of the slabs above me; thinking was a luxury I couldn't afford. Despite the burning ache in my muscles and overwhelming exhaustion, I kept swinging my arms, each strike breaking through solid earth and consuming the energy reserves I never knew existed inside me.

As I trudged ahead, my worn boots dragging along the ground, every step grew more burdensome, as if the earth conspired to trap me. The handle of my pickaxe, worn smooth from countless hours of toiling, felt foreign in my grip, while the ceaseless labor rendered my hands numb, almost as if they belonged to another person entirely.

The deafening roar of machinery echoed through the never-ending tunnels, vibrations shaking the ground beneath our feet. The air was thick with the smell of oil and metal, a constant reminder of the harshness of our surroundings. We walked in almost complete darkness, headlamps guiding us as we navigated the labyrinthine corridors.

Every step felt like descending into a forgotten world where light struggled to reach and darkness reigned supreme. In this underground realm, dreams of life beyond the machines and oppressive darkness felt as distant as the surface.

In the earth's belly, it felt like the mine was slowly chipping away at us, piece by piece. You'd lose track of the days because they all blended into one long, unending night. Even when we surfaced, blinking against the setting sun, it was like we were just shadows of ourselves, hollowed out and stretched thin.

But it wasn't just the physical toll; it was how the mine seemed to take over your thoughts too. You'd dream of those dark tunnels even in your sleep, the sound of your pickaxe striking stone echoing in your dreams. It was as if the mine gripped your soul, pulling you back no matter how much you longed for the sun and the sky.

The mine was a relentless beast, sapping every ounce of strength from my body. My bones felt like they were being twisted and pulled in different directions, and my muscles screamed with each movement. The constant grind and strain had turned my once smooth hands into a rough terrain of calluses and scars.

But I endured, driven by an unbreakable determination to provide for my family. Every strike of my pickaxe was a testament to this unwavering resolve imbued with a deep sense of purpose. Each swing brought me closer to my goal despite the physical toll it took on me.

I could almost hear their laughter echoing through my mind with each swing. My wife's gentle voice and my children's boisterous giggles were the fuel that ignited the fire in my weary bones. Like a candle in the suffocating darkness, their love and the promise of a better future shone brightly before me.

I pushed myself beyond what I thought I could handle. It wasn't a choice. It was a necessity. As time slipped away like the dust I worked in, each grain represented precious seconds lost, moments away from those I had toiled so hard for. But my determination outweighed the exhaustion in my bones. I couldn't ignore the ticking clock, the narrowing window to secure the future I longed for my family.

The extra hours stretched into what felt like endless nights beneath the earth, the darkness outside mirroring the one I worked in. But it was more than just coal I carried on my shoulders; it was the weight of hope, the burden of dreams yet to be realized.

In the depths of the mine, amidst the soot and the sweat, I found a strength I never knew I possessed. Love fueled it by the vision of my children's future, brighter and unburdened by the hardships I faced. This vision, this unwavering goal, propelled me forward, pushing me to endure, work those extra hours, and carry that additional load. For them, I would brave the darkness repeatedly, determined to emerge into the light.

I kept my head down, and my eyes focused on the task at hand, never allowing myself to be overwhelmed by the darkness. I had become numb to the pain of my existence, resigned to the fate that life had dealt me.

The conveyor belt's roar filled the narrow space, a constant, thunderous growl that seemed to vibrate in my chest. Around me, shadows moved in frantic haste, hands and shovels blurring as we heaved chunks of coal onto the insatiable metal beast that snaked through the tunnel. Each piece landed with a metallic thud, a chorus of clanks and clangs that set our pace, urging us on faster and faster.

The belt didn't care for tiredness or aching muscles; it always demanded more, its appetite reflected in our determined, grim faces. We didn't just move to its rhythm; we raced against it, each of us silently vowing not to be outdone by a machine, our breaths coming in sharp gasps as we pushed our limits, driven by the unspoken promise of a better tomorrow.

With every shovel of coal, every heave and haul, we weren't just moving earth; we were fighting against the ticking clock of our daily quota. The air was tense, making me aware that falling short was not an option lest we face the boss's sharp rebuke. His presence loomed over us even in his absence, a specter of authority and demand.

The fear of reprimand loomed like a dark cloud in the dusty, sweltering atmosphere. It was a tangible force, pushing us to dig deeper and work harder despite the harsh conditions. Every time we heard a faint rustle at the entrance, we all darted our eyes toward it, momentarily silencing the clamor of work in anxious anticipation.

The air was thick with palpable tension as if everyone was holding their breath, dreading the supervisor's arrival. His looming presence felt like a heavy weight on our shoulders, his voice a sharp blade that cut through the intense hum of labor.

As the company whistle pierced through the oppressive air, its shrill cry brought a wave of sweet relief washing over us, like a soothing balm to our weary souls. We moved as one, a slow procession of shadowed figures emerging from the earth's embrace.

Our steps were slow and laborious, like wading through a sea of thick molasses. Our boots, caked with mud and dirt, dragged us down with each heavy step. The weight of exhaustion hung over us, pressing down on our chests and making breathing hard. The well-trodden path that led us to our ride showed evidence of the countless souls who had trudged along this same way.

Our eyes were heavy as we approached the designated pickup spot. We saw some of our friends already gathered there, their weary expressions mirroring our own. And then we saw the approaching tram that promised a much-needed break from our exhaustion. Seeing it renewed our energy, and we quickened our pace to reach it.

All I could think of was my bed’s warmth, comfort, and serenity after this long, draining day. Then I heard Dan’s voice echoing through the mine, shattering the darkness with its sharpness. It broke through my daydream, my weariness forgotten in an instant.

"Collin, did you forget something?" he shouted.

In that moment, it hit me like a bolt of lightning, I had left my pickaxe behind. It was more than just a tool; it was my lifeline in this relentless job, and it would cost me a week's pay to replace it.

“Crap!” The word burst forth, a raw exclamation borne of desperation as I spun, my boots digging into the ground, propelling me back into the darkness I had all too eagerly fled just moments prior.

Approaching my abandoned post felt akin to stepping into a courtroom, the scene eerily silent save for the quiet indictment of my negligence. There, leaning with an air of indifference against the wall, was my pickaxe, its presence taunting my oversight. With a swift motion, I reclaimed it, turning to flee, the burden of my mistake amplifying the gravity of each step.

When I arrived back at the designated pickup spot, a crushing realization hit me. The shuttle that took me back to the surface had disappeared into the distance. Its red taillights slowly faded into the darkness, leaving me completely stranded and alone in this lonely prison.

As the tram moved away, my heart dropped to my stomach. I could feel the vibrations of its engines fading into the distance, leaving an overwhelming sense of loneliness. I stumbled on the uneven ground, desperately trying to keep up with the departing vehicle.

I shouted for it to stop, but the tunnel's echoing darkness drowned my voice. With each passing second, the small red light from its taillight grew smaller until it disappeared completely, leaving me alone in the underground depths.

A red-hot fury coursed through my veins, boiling and bubbling like molten lava. With a primal scream, I heaved my pickaxe with all my might, watching it sail through the air before landing with a resounding thud on the ground.

My anger reverberated in my ears as I cursed under my breath, my feet dragging heavily along the path created by the departing shuttle. My heart raced with fear and desperation, praying that this path would lead me back to safety before it was too late.

The walls closed in with each frantic heartbeat, squeezing the breath from my lungs. I scrambled through the narrow passage, darkness swallowing me whole. How long could I endure this claustrophobic tomb before the oppressive abyss claimed me forever?

With panic rising in my throat, I fought against the darkness. There had to be a way out somehow. I just needed to keep moving. The ghostly fingers of isolation clawed at my mind, shredding any last vestiges of hope. I pressed on desperately, plunging into the unknown. I told myself one step at a time…just one more step.

Out of nowhere, the ground beneath me gave a profound, grumbling warning. Everything started vibrating, from the tips of my toes to the pit of my stomach, making it feel like I was standing on top of a ticking time bomb.

Then, a sudden, jarring vibration tore through the silence. The ground beneath me trembled with a force that seemed to come from the depths of the earth itself. Before I could even process the change, a deafening roar filled the space, more felt than heard, as if the very air had ignited.

The earth shook violently as if being ripped apart at its core. The deafening explosion echoed through the mine, reverberating off the walls and causing the ground to tremble beneath my feet.

A thick cloud of dust and debris filled the air, engulfing me in a suffocating haze. Stinging rock particles rained upon me like tiny glass daggers, slicing through the darkness in sharp shards. I could barely hear myself think over the constant roar of destruction that surrounded me.

The sound of splintering beams, once sturdy protectors of the mine's stability, punctuated the chaos, now breaking like fragile bones in the face of the relentless explosion. Every crack echoed through the turmoil, a reminder of the crumbling world I was trapped in.

Wide-eyed and horrified, I watched as the solid walls of the mine began to bend and sway, succumbing to the relentless pressure of the expanding devastation. I stumbled blindly through the maze-like network of tunnels rapidly falling apart.

Amid the loud destruction, I desperately clung to a flicker of hope for survival. My heart pounded in sync with the thunderous symphony of collapse. However, as I witnessed wooden beams breaking and snapping around me, I suddenly realized that the collapsing mine sealed my fate within its suffocating grip.

A suffocating fear gripped me as I frantically tried to make sense of the madness that surrounded me. Each breath felt labored, my chest tightening with each panicked inhale. Was this a mine collapse, an earthquake, or something more sinister?

My mind raced, overwhelmed by terrifying scenarios, each more menacing than the last. With every passing moment, the weight of the fear seemed to press down on me, suffocating and paralyzing. I felt trapped in a nightmare, unable to escape the grip of terror that threatened to consume me.

Surrounded by an oppressive darkness that swallowed every

hint of light, my senses heightened, trying to cut through the blanket of black. My ragged breathing and the occasional distant echo of falling debris punctuated the silence. It felt as if I were the last soul left in a world that had suddenly shrunk to the size of this mine.

My heart hammered in my chest. Standing still wasn't an option, yet every potential move felt like a gamble. Do I push forward, blindly groping my way deeper into this labyrinth, or do I risk retracing my steps, hoping to find a sliver of light, a way out of this nightmare?

I cautiously stepped forward, my boots crunching on the gravel path as I deliberated which fork to take. Before I could decide, a loud explosion shook the ground beneath me, and debris rained down. The left passage was completely blocked off, so I turned and quickly went down the right one. As I hurried along, something hard collided with my head. My helmet light flickered before going out, plunging me into pitch-blackness.

It was like suddenly being blindfolded. You could almost feel it pressing against your skin. I panicked for a second, my hands shaking as I tried to find the light switch on my helmet. It felt like ages before my fingers finally stumbled upon it. The moment I flipped the switch back on and the light cut through the darkness, I couldn't help but let out an enormous sigh of relief. It was like finding my way back from being lost in a nightmare.

But that moment of relief evaporated as soon as my eyes adjusted and focused on the path ahead. The way out, my flicker of hope in this underground nightmare, was cruelly cut off by an avalanche of rubble. A solid barrier of rock and coal stood between me.

I shouted into the void, “Hello? Is anyone there? Please, I need help!”

I stood there, feeling paralyzed, as I slowly realized the gravity of the situation. I found myself trapped in this dark mine with no one around me. The walls seemed to squeeze in on me, adding to my unease.

My mind was exhausted, urging me to give up and just collapse. My body struggled between the desire to give up and the necessity to persevere. It was a constant battle, and I didn’t know if I had the strength to keep fighting it.

CHAPTER TWO

A Desperate Plea

Surrounded by darkness, I felt a whisper amidst the thumping of my heart, urging me to find a way out of the fear consuming me. The endless blackness ahead offered no comfort, only quiet terrors lurking in the shadows, intensifying my growing terror.

The cold walls scraped against my skin as I navigated through this maze of fear, the icy chill making me shiver with panic taking over every part of me. Each breath I took filled with a sharp bitterness that seemed almost palpable.

As I moved forward in this nightmare, it felt like a blend of darkness and dread fueled by the insecurities of youth. Each moment felt like a battle against impending disaster, threatening to unravel my fragile sanity bit by agonizing bit.

My heart raced against my ribs, overwhelmed by countless

thoughts. I prayed for clarity, straining to see through the dense fog that encased me. But it was like trying to grasp smoke; the more I reached out, the more elusive clarity became.

"God," I muttered, my voice trembling with desperation. "If you're there... I need to know I'm not alone in this..." The silence that greeted me was far from reassuring.

I shook myself, attempting to summon a sense of courage. "You've faced worse than this before, Collin," I muttered into the darkness and to myself. "You've stared fear in the eyes and triumphed." But my words only echoed back, a weak pep talk that fell flat.

Blind and vulnerable, like a newborn, I stumbled around, reaching out desperately for an escape. My fingertips screamed in pain as they scraped against sharp rocks. Each step felt like a rebellion against exhaustion and agony, a test of both body and mind. Yet I forced myself to keep going, tapping into the last vestiges of strength within me.

"I won't give up!" The declaration tore from my throat, a primal roar reverberating in the vast emptiness around me.

It hung in the air as a testament to human resilience in the face of adversity, a plea projected into the void of the universe. Fear and defiance intertwined as I continued through oppressive darkness, grappling with invisible foes, fighting for survival.

After hours of crawling desperately, wearing down my body and sanity, I stumbled around a lonely corner and found salvation, an abandoned mining cart. It was like a perfectly placed piece in the terrifying puzzle of my escape from whatever nightmare I was running from.

The sight of tracks vanishing into a narrow, unforgiving shaft sparked a glimmer of hope within me, or maybe it was just my desperate mind creating illusions of salvation. But the human will to survive can make us see beacons even in the faintest flicker.

I hoisted myself into the mining cart, my hands slick with sweat, gripping the cold metal handle. My palms collected tiny grains of rust that clung like tragic reminders of time's passage and decay. On the brink of uncertainty, I could feel my heart pounding in my chest like a wild drumbeat.

Grasping the flaky metal handle of the brake lever with trembling hands felt like clutching onto life itself. Every fiber of my being stood poised for this one decision that held such weight. The loud snap resounded through the tunnel as I yanked back on it with all my might, a desperate cry for survival reverberating through every cell in my body.

The cart surged forward, hurling me into a black vortex. The wind whipped against my face, its icy sting jolting me awake. In response, I let out a scream of terror, an untamed animalistic howl swallowed by the ghostly roar of the wind and haunting creaks from ancient wheels.

Clinging tenaciously to the rusty edges of the cart, I willed myself not to let go, at least not yet. My knuckles paled against their will as fear dictated my grip. My mind danced in a somber tango between stoking the flames of survival and accepting the chilling possibility of an end.

The gravitational force embraced me in an intensity that defied words, thrusting me back into my seat as if waging war on every breath I owned. The cart, hurtling at an incomprehensible speed, became my only anchor.

I felt like an insignificant speck caught amidst the cosmos while honing my focus on surviving this relentless trial. This fearsome venture was overwhelming, scattering my thoughts like stardust in the wake of its speed.

Fear etched into my trembling hands as they fervently grasped the harsh metal. It threatened to engulf me, freezing my heart mid-beat. Still, I regarded the cart as my refuge, a ticket to escape from this chaotic labyrinth that had trapped me.

I wanted it to move and carry me away from the complex tribulations that had entrapped me. But nothing comes easy in life or mines, as it turns out.

Smash! The force of impact thrust me against the cart's metal frame, causing my teeth to clack together. My shoulder throbbed in pain, but I clenched my teeth and endured it. The collision made me feel nauseous, and I could sense warm blood trickling down my cheek from a slight cut above my eye. The pain was unbearable.

Desperately, my fingers dug into the grooves and ridges of the metal as if trying to pull myself up. Colors blurred together as the world spun around me. Flashes of reds, oranges, and yellows formed an endless kaleidoscope. I struggled against dizziness, determined to remain upright even though everything felt out of control.

As I stood there, figuratively and emotionally, at the end of the line, a wave of terror crashed over me like an impenetrable storm. The fear that had once only whispered in my ear now roared like a voracious beast, ravenous for every bit of my being. The path that had once seemed to lead to safety had disappeared, leaving me stranded and hopeless, with no chance of rescue or escape.

Regret clawed at my soul, its bitter sting piercing every inch of my being. I cursed my foolishness for forgetting my pickaxe - a single oversight that plunged me into a treacherous abyss of unfathomable peril and unrelenting torment. Each step forward only served as a brutal reminder of how my recklessness had brought upon this dreadful plight. How could I have been so utterly irresponsible?

Finally, after what felt like an eternity, I stumbled upon a hidden alcove nestled deep within the tunnel. The entrance to this enclave, carved into the worn rock, caught my attention.

I cautiously directed the trembling glow of my lamp into the space, casting a light on an old metal ladder clinging to one side. The ladder climbed upwards towards a steel door, its disfigured appearance hinting at untold tales.

As I carefully climbed up the shaky ladder, I stopped to make sure it could hold my weight. The cold feel of the metal brought comfort to my tired hands, filling me with excitement as I made my way up step by step towards the mysterious heights ahead.

Crawling out from the pitch-black maze, my arms and legs shook like leaves in a storm while soot tattoos blemished my skin. I found myself blinking rapidly into an ocean of sunlight that pierced through me like a scorching laser.

I yearned for a break from the dense thickness of underground air. Taking deep breaths, it felt like breathing in pure freedom, cool, wild, and filled with life's essential magic, oxygen.

Even after breaking free, the gnarly reek of poisonous smoke stubbornly stuck to me, stinging my weary eyes. Desperate for some sort of ease from it all, I squeezed them shut tight before cautiously lifting my eyelids. What greeted me was a scene straight out of a nightmare, one that sent chills rocketing down my spine.

The flames towered above me, roaring with a ferocity that seemed to shake the very ground. Their voracious appetite devoured everything in their wake, the once serene coal yard now a sea of angry orange and red.

Shadows danced and flickered around me, taunting me with

their sinister intensity. I gazed upon the swirling bedlam before me. It was like standing on the edge of hell itself, captivated yet terrified by the power of the inferno.

The murky sky emitted a sickly, greenish light, which cast an eerie glow over the ruins. The silence was intense. Not a living person could be seen.

I walked unsteadily amidst the ruins, feeling my stomach churn with disgust at the sight of lifeless bodies strewn everywhere. Their faces bore expressions of terror and hopelessness, leaving me haunted by thoughts of their last moments. The longing for eternal peace was evident in their motionless eyes, creating an atmosphere that resembled a graveyard.

Thick black smoke rose ominously, blending with fiery orange flames that streaked across the expansive, darkened sky. The loud crashes echoed through the air, bouncing off shattered buildings nearby. Once sturdy structures now lay in ruins, reduced to piles of bricks, splintered wood, and smoldering ash.

Confusion swirled in my mind as I struggled to comprehend the sheer force behind such merciless destruction upon this once-thriving landscape. Every inch of the scene bore witness to the terror that unfolded. In the distance, mournful sirens wailed, haunting reminders of lives forever altered by this cataclysmic event.

In this desolation, I yearned for answers and understanding in a world that seemed to have lost all reason. What force could unleash such devastation? What dark power wields such destructive might?

These urgent questions swirled in my mind, driving me to seek truth amidst madness and despair.

The gravity of the situation weighed heavily on me, making it hard to breathe. My eyes could not process what they had seen. Where once a place of vibrant memories stood, now only an empty shell remains.

Gone was the familiar hum of machinery and laughter that usually filled the coal yard, replaced by an eerie warning as a whistling breeze.

A pile of debris reduced the spot where workers once gathered every Friday, to pick up their pay checks. Absent were their conversations of plans for hard-earned weekends and the laughter that comes with the close of a week.

My hands trembled as I searched for survivors. I wept as I touched the face of a dead friend. I experienced a deep sadness that I had never known before. My heart ached for the lives lost, and I prayed for the strength to continue fighting.

"How... how did this happen?" "Please," I begged, my voice shaking with sorrow and terror.

The once lively streets now lay in ruins, their former grandeur reduced to mere memories. And there I stood, amidst the debris and devastation, a solitary figure bearing witness to the aftermath.

But as I surveyed the desolation, questions flooded my mind. What about my family? Could they be somewhere in this nightmarish landscape, hidden by the veil of destruction? I hurried towards what used to be our home. Each step felt heavy, burdened by the weight of uncertainty.

The trudge back seemed endless, with thick smoke filling the air from the remnants of our once sanctuary. My heart pounded in my chest, its rhythm echoing the chaos surrounding me. Eventually, I reached the place I once called home, only to be met with a sight that shattered my hopes.

In front of me yawned a deep hole that seemed endlessly hungry, like a starving beast swallowing everything in its path. I watched as smoke rose from the remains of my past life, spiraling upward like thick tendrils.

Fear gripped my heart as I desperately searched for any sign of survival in the emptiness that surrounded me. The silence was unsettling, echoing my pleas into nothingness. My family was gone, leaving only a void that felt unbearable to face.

Grief washed over me like icy waves, leaving me feeling weak and broken. Tears streamed down my cheeks as I mourned the loss of what was once a happy home, now reduced to debris. In that moment I realized I was utterly alone in this desolate world.

The life I once knew crumbled away, taking with it all that mattered to me, my wife, my children, and the love and laughter that used to fill my days, now just distant memories. Each breath I took felt heavy with sorrow, a constant ache that grew deeper with every passing moment.

The physical ruins around me were nothing compared to the devastation in my heart, a loneliness so intense it felt suffocating. In this new reality of emptiness, I was like a lost soul among wreckage, haunted by what was and mourning what would never be again. My grief was overwhelming, consuming me entirely, leaving me stranded in a sea of despair with no end in sight.

I felt as vulnerable as a fragile leaf caught in a wild gust, helpless against an unseen force that seemed to have taken control of my life.

Amidst my deep sorrow, I sensed a glimmer of inner strength or perhaps a stubborn determination to keep moving forward. I wondered about my survival, contemplating the meaning of my life. Looking up at the vast expanse of starlit sky, it felt like the universe was holding untold secrets, silently urging me to discover mysteries I couldn't quite grasp.

Slowly, I realized that maybe my survival was connected to something larger than myself and that others might have faced similar challenges and found resilience. This realization kindled a spark of hope, a light shining through the darkness around me.

As the moon hung high, casting a spectral glow over the landscape, I stood alone, my heart echoing with a desperate hope. I could not be the last person on earth, left to perish in obscurity. Somewhere in the vast expanse of the world, there must be others like me; there had to be answers. Thus, under the silent watch of the stars, my journey into the unknown commenced.

CHAPTER THREE

LonelyWanderer

I feel so isolated, like a ghost wandering through existence, yearning for someone to understand my pain. I long for a connection with another soul who can see past my surface and share in my sadness. Despite my relentless efforts, that profound bond remains elusive, leaving me adrift in an unyielding sea of despair.

Each passing day blurs into the next, ensnared in an unending spiral of desolation, desperately seeking an escape. Hope hovers on the horizon like a distant mirage, slowly dissipating, casting shadows on my quest for meaning. Today mirrors countless others, the sky cloaked in darkness and burdened by clouds, much like my own internal struggles. Even the sun's valiant attempts are thwarted, echoing my own battles within.

Silence surround me like a shroud, broken only by the solemn cadence of my footsteps upon the earth. The absence of birdsong and laughter leaves an eerie void, reverberating with emptiness. It feels as though I am treading through a cemetery of forsaken dreams, with naught but the echo of my thoughts to accompany me in this profound isolation.

As I walked, memories flickered through my mind like faded photographs, each frame revealing a glimpse of a bygone era. Once vibrant with life, the cobblestone streets now lay in silent disarray. Flashes of laughter and carefree moments danced before my eyes, vivid and fleeting, like ethereal specters of the past.

I imagined children playing in the narrow alleyways, their infectious giggles echoing off the weathered stone walls. The old bakery on the corner exuded the comforting aroma of freshly baked bread, its golden crusts tempting passersby with promises of warmth and sustenance.

And the bustling coffee shop, its tables spilling onto the sidewalk, filled the air with the rich fragrance of freshly brewed coffee, mingling harmoniously with the tantalizing scent of pastries.

But as these nostalgic images played out in my mind's eye, reality seeped back in, shattering the illusion of a time untouched by turmoil. The acrid smell of destruction hung heavy in the air, mingling with the bittersweet reminiscences. Charred remnants of buildings stood as solemn reminders of the havoc that had befallen this once-thriving neighborhood.

As I kept walking, a chill ran through my body, the wind picking up a little more with each step. My feet ached with every step, but I was determined to keep going. I knew that if I could reach the end of the road, I would find something or someone. I still hoped to find survivors. I couldn't stop. I had to keep going.

The smell of death hung in the air, making my stomach turn. I tried to take shallow breaths so I wouldn't have to smell it, but it seemed to follow me everywhere. I kept my eyes on the ground, not wanting to see the destruction surrounding me.

I had seen the horrors of war, but this was entirely different. I kept moving, not sure where I was going. I just wanted to escape the destruction and the memories that came with it.

At the end of the street, I could make out the blackened remains of a once proud train station. Its slate walls were coated in sooty film, leaving ghoulish silhouettes in its broken windows. It seemed strangely beautiful in its ruin.

In the silence, I felt a tug at my heart, and a wave of nostalgia washed over me. I stepped closer to inspect the building, and flashes of memories from years ago surged through me.

As I strolled down the long corridor, my footsteps echoed through the deserted station. The tiles in the corridor were stained yellow and cracked. And I could feel loose gravel beneath my boots with every step. The air was musty, and cobwebs decorated the ceiling like a distorted canopy above me.

I entered a musty room at the end of the hallway. Years of

neglect had left the old maps hanging on the walls tattered. But something about them still captivated me.

I peered at the maps, tracing my finger along their intricate lines and faded colors. They were like a window into the past, and I couldn't help but wonder what stories they held. As my curiosity grew, I focused on the train schedules on the walls.

I read their destinations and studied the names of the cities and towns they were heading to. I stepped away from the schedules, my fingertips still tingling from touching their worn edges. I felt a sense of warmth and connection to this place. I wished I could explore its history to uncover the stories behind these ventures.

I entered the next room. A large mural adorned one wall, depicting a bustling train station in its heyday. The vibrant colors and lively scenes depicted in the mural filled me with sorrow and longing. It reminded me of the life that once existed in this place, making the surrounding desolation seem even more cruel.

But what I really wanted to see was outside. I pushed open the tattered double doors. In front of me was a sea of dormant locomotives, each a unique sculpture in its own right. I almost felt like I could hear the trains' whistles echoing through the air.

I ran my hands over the cool metal of the locomotives, feeling the history of each one. I marveled at the intricate details of the engines, like the engraved lettering on the sides and the gold-plated accents. I even found a few old lanterns, their glass windows cracked, and the metal tarnished from years of neglect.

As I continued along, I felt something tugging at my heart. I knew that each of these trains had seen its share of adventures and held its own stories. I could almost hear them whispering, beckoning me to explore further. With a newfound excitement, I continued down the tracks and into the unknown.

The further I went, the more I felt like I was being transported back to a different era. It was a stroke of fate that brought me to this train station. I had been an Amtrak engineer for years before mining, and memories flooded back as I strolled through the yard.

I had visited countless cities and encountered hundreds of passengers, all of which reminded me of life's fleeting nature. A sense of joy and sadness overcame me. I cherished those moments, never thinking that someday they'd be gone. Life's fragility came to my mind at that moment. And the importance of cherishing people and moments.

I closed my eyes and allowed myself to be transported back in time, savoring the memory of my career as an engineer. The wheels clicking on the tracks were still fresh in my mind. I recalled traveling through bustling cities like New York, Washington, DC, Chicago, and Boston.

I could almost feel the weight of my engineer's cap resting on my head. The wind from the open window whipped around me as I stood on the deck, the sound of the engine humming beneath me. I remembered the feeling of the vibrations traveling through the soles of my shoes and the whistle of a train piercing my ears as it passed by.

In those days, I ferried hundreds of people across the country daily. As they shuffled onto the train, I noticed a few passengers dozing off in their seats. Others buried their heads in books and newspapers.

Further down the aisle, I saw women freshening their makeup with cotton swabs and lipstick. Men fussed and brushed out wrinkles in their suits and straightened ties that had become sloppy from travel.

Now and then, excited chatter would erupt near the bathrooms as travelers scurried to take turns for one last grooming session before the next station.

I imagined creating a story about each person. What were they hurrying to, and what were they rushing from? I was part of something more meaningful for a while, helping people reach their dreams and destinations.

Lost in my thoughts, I was abruptly pulled back to the present by a loud crash. A large metal pipe had tumbled from its place against a wall and landed on the floor with a loud noise. I looked up at the skylight windows and noticed the sun was setting. I gathered my belongings and searched for a place to spend the night.

After a few days had passed, I found myself inexplicably drawn back to the train station. I stepped lightly through the train yard in the early morning light and was astonished to find an intact Amtrak engine.

Its dark green paint shone like polished emeralds, with no signs of rust or weathering. I followed its length and found a luxurious compartment car coupled to it. Despite the layer of dust on the windowpane, the wooden panels still glowed in the morning light.

I couldn't believe I had never thought of it before. It was so simple, yet so brilliant. Using the train to travel across the country was the perfect way to find survivors. The idea consumed me, filling me with a newfound sense of purpose.

I could already see myself on the train, gazing out the window as the landscape flew by. I would stop at every station, searching for anyone who survived the apocalypse. I would offer them a chance to join me on the train, to travel together in search of a new home.

As I continued to ponder the idea, my excitement grew. This was my chance to make a difference in this desolate world. With the train as my trusty companion, I would bring hope to those who had lost it. And with each new survivor, my determination would only grow stronger. The train would become my lifeline, my hope in this dark and broken world.

I knew my adventure would start here. I opened the door of the compartment car. Inside was a world of comfort and luxury. Velvet curtains adorned the walls, plush velvet seats filled the compartment car, and the armrests were made of the most exquisite leather I had ever seen. I could easily imagine lounging with friends and colleagues in this space, laughing and talking about our travels.

I packed my bags, said goodbye to my old life, and stepped onto the train. The engine rumbled to life with a flick of a switch. I pushed the throttle forward. The train gradually increased speed as it moved down the rails, whistling in the wind.

As the train lumbered, I glanced out the window and saw the world passing by. I imagined all the possibilities of what could happen in the places I would go and the people I would meet. It filled me with excitement and anticipation.

The further I traveled, the more I realized how liberating the journey was. I was free from my worries and doubts and, for a while at least, free from my self-pity.

I embarked on this journey with a sense of trepidation, unsure of what I would find in the depths of my soul. But as the miles passed under my feet, I began to unravel the layers of my being, peeling back the facade I had built over the years.

With each passing day, fresh revelations came to light. I learned to appreciate the little things, the minor details that make life worth living. As I delved deeper into my thoughts, I saw how I could be a better father, companion, and human being overall.

This journey was not just a physical one but a spiritual and emotional one as well. It allowed me to understand myself and truly appreciate life's complexities.

Sure, I know you may think this idea is insane, but I had no other choice. If my journey were for naught, traveling the country solo would be a death trap and a fool's errand. But I had already lost everything in my old life. There was nothing left to cling to but this wild hope.

I left the engineer's seat and went to the VIP compartment one day. I couldn't believe my luck. As an engineer, I never thought I would experience such luxury. The VIP compartment of the train was like a dream come true. The soft velvet chair contrasted with the hard, uncomfortable seat I had been sitting in earlier.

As I gazed out the window, I couldn't help but feel a sense of guilt between the extravagance of my seat and the desolate landscape beyond my window.

The click-clack of the train's wheels on steel tracks echoed like a heartbeat, soothing my soul and strengthening my resolve. Each jolt and vibration of the car stirred something deep within me, as though awakened by some primal force urging me forward.

The scent of oil and metal mingled in the air, carried along by the whoosh of wind outside. I leaned forward in my seat to better see the countryside. It was all still so new, yet each mile traveled brought me closer to a time when I had no limits. And I couldn't wait to see what the future held.

Day after day, the locomotive trundled along the antiquated tracks. As I went by, deserted towns decayed increasingly with each mile. Nature obliterated houses and stores, leaving only moss-covered ruins. Yet each morning, I arose, reinvigorated, prepared to go onwards. The idea of a brighter future propelled me forward.

By chance, I stumbled upon a wondrous forest. The fact that it had survived amidst all the destruction only added to its allure. I couldn't resist stopping my train to explore the area. Stepping off the train, the peacefulness of the dense woods surrounding me immediately struck me.

Large trees rose into the sky, spindly branches reaching for the heavens. Streaks of sunlight shone through the crowns of trees, giving a sense of tranquility and satisfaction. The magnificence of nature and its capacity to bring serenity took me back.

As I meandered through the forest, my feet carried me along a winding path until twilight cast a magical glow over the trees. Finding a large boulder to rest on, I watched in wonder as the sun slowly dipped below the horizon, painting the sky in shades of pink and purple. The cool evening breeze brushed against my skin, carrying pine and earth scents. At that moment, I felt truly connected to nature and all its wonders.

Needing to get back to the train before dark, I started my descent. My feet skidded against the slippery rocks as I descended the boulder. I felt a sense of freedom as I moved, the wind playing in my hair and the trees swaying around me. I stopped at the base of the boulder, taking a few moments to admire the beauty of the landscape.

I could hear the river in the distance, its gentle rushing sounded like a lullaby. I could feel the peace and serenity of the woods, the secrets they would share with me.

Sitting by the campfire, I carefully arranged the kindling and logs to create a crackling fire that soon blazed brightly. I was captivated as I watched the flames dance in shades of orange and yellow, bewitching all my senses. In that flickering light, a sense of peace and calm blanketed me, easing the exhaustion from my bones.

Looking up, I gazed at the vast night sky spread out like an endless canvas. The wispy clouds drifted gracefully in the gentle breeze, moving as if in a choreographed performance. It was a magical sight that made me appreciate the wonders of nature deeply.

Though I knew my journey was far from over, in that moment, I allowed myself to feel grateful. Grateful for overcoming challenges, for learning valuable lessons, and for the precious memories that now resided within me. Every step had brought me closer to this moment of rest, this peaceful pause amid the wild surroundings.

As the night progressed and midnight approached, I couldn't look away from the tantalizing dance of the flames. The air seemed charged with an unseen energy, electrifying every corner of the forest around me. The ancient trees appeared to lean closer, their rustling leaves whispering secrets known only to them.

In that mystical hour, I felt a deep connection with nature itself. The woods emanated a tangible energy, as if they were alive and communicating with me in their mysterious language. A smile formed on my lips as I sensed they were sharing hidden stories with me, tales of forgotten civilizations, unknown adventures, and timeless wisdom.

The world felt suspended in anticipation as a sudden flash of light broke through the darkness. The landscape was bathed in an eerie glow, casting long shadows that danced upon the forest floor. My heart raced with a mix of excitement and nervousness as I tried to make sense of this enigmatic phenomenon before my eyes.

Was it a shooting star streaking across the sky in a brilliant display? Or maybe a celestial visitor, leaving behind its luminous trail as it graced our earthly realm?

Thoughts swirled in my mind like a turbulent storm, yet there lingered a subtle feeling of apprehension as if this unearthly spectacle held an element of mystery or danger waiting to be unraveled.

CHAPTER FOUR

Backyard Brawlers

Anticipation coursed through me, causing my heart to race as I tried to make sense of the extraordinary occurrence that had just taken place. Then I realized it was a meteor shower. The beauty of the sky and the gentle shower of sparkling stars intrigued me. I experienced a feeling of being transported to another world.

As I processed the breathtaking sight of the meteor shower, my racing heartbeat gradually slowed down, eventually finding a peaceful, rhythmic pace. As each celestial body traced its path across the night expanse, I felt an inexplicable connection with them, as if their journey across the cosmos mirrored my life in some obscure way.

Suddenly, one star shone brighter than the rest. It streaked across the sky before fading into nothingness, much like life itself. That spectacle seemed momentous; it held significant symbolism for me as though communicating something.

I couldn't help but stand there, neck craned to the night sky, as hundreds of shooting stars danced across the darkness. A rush of emotions overcame me as I witnessed the stunning scene unfolding before me, and I couldn't contain my amazement.

As the shower continued, I found myself lost in thought, pondering about the mysteries of the universe. It was a humbling experience, reminding me how small we were in the grand scheme of things. I couldn't help but feel grateful for this moment, for this opportunity to witness such a magnificent event.

As I gazed at the last meteor disappearing beyond the horizon, its ethereal glow fading into the night's darkness, a sense of wonder enveloped me. The celestial spectacle of light and motion left an unforgettable mark on my mind. It reminded me of the hidden beauty in our world.

Immersed in nature's embrace, surrounded by ancient trees whispering their secrets, I spent the next three days in this dense forest. Each moment here felt like a sacred connection with the earth's core rhythms.

One serene night, under the moon's silver light at my campsite, I set up my camping stove and arranged cooking utensils. Gathering twigs and logs, I ignited a crackling fire that flickered with warmth and light, mixing with the scent of burning wood in the crisp air.

Watching the flames dance eagerly, I felt anticipation building as I prepared to cook soup in my pot. The simmering soup's aroma filled the air, inviting me to partake in its nourishing essence. With each spoonful savored, I marveled at the interconnectedness of nature - from meteors in the sky to the crackling fire that warmed me and the comforting meal that fed my body.

As I breathed in the peaceful night air, memories of my ninth birthday flooded my mind. I could almost taste the chocolate cake and hear my family's laughter as I blew out the candles. But what I couldn't wait to do was open my presents. That's when my father's voice cut through the excitement, calling me outside for something important.

As my father extended his arm from behind his back, I caught a glint of orange leather and felt a surge of excitement. He presented an official NBA basketball with the league logo and textured grip. We rushed to the backyard, where he hung a basketball rim off the front of the garage. "Let's shoot some hoops," he said with a grin.

I still remember scoring my first basket. My friends cheered, and I was enthusiastic. I took one step and tripped over my feet, but I still made it to the basket! I was proud and sure I would be the next Michael Jordan. I got up and did a little victory dance, dancing around the court and high-fiving all my friends. I knew I needed to work on my balance, but it didn't matter. I had done it!

Ah, the Backyard Brawlers, as we called ourselves. It was the summer of 1999. Laughter, shouts of encouragement, and friendly insults lingered in the air as Bobby, Jim, and I ran up and down the asphalt court.

The sun beat down on us as we passed the basketball back and forth. We dribbled to the rhythm of our sneakers, slapping against the scorching asphalt. It was like a song with a percussive base that kept us going until we could no longer play.

Though I was a couple of inches shorter than most kids on the court, I still dominated. My jump shot from the corner was so powerful that the ball would rip through the cool air and arc into the net in a graceful swish. I had learned to spin the ball at varying angles, resulting in unpredictable trajectories that even surprised me.

Jim was tall and skinny, with thick, black-rimmed glasses perched precariously on his nose. He was like a string bean with a superpower: seeing clearly while playing sports. Meanwhile, I stumble over my shoelaces and call it a victory.

But Bobby stole the show. Ten years old and with a knack for basketball that surpassed us all, he was our golden boy, even if he had a mean streak. We all have flaws.

For Bobby, a combination of cockiness and temper rivaled a volcano. Bobby had a noticeable swagger in his step. It's like a peacock strutting its stuff, but with fewer feathers and more trash talk.

He was unstoppable on the court, and every time he scored or grabbed a rebound, he made sure everyone knew it with his boasting and trash-talk. I swear that kid could talk more smack than a politician during election season.

His mouth was like a never-ending spigot of insults and taunts. Occasionally, his temper led to a fistfight. And let me tell you, seeing nine-year-olds throwing punches is a sight to behold. It's like watching a brawl at the daycare center.

It feels like just yesterday when Bobby and I faced off in a one-on-one game. The sun beat down on us, casting harsh shadows as we moved across the asphalt court. Our competitive drive intensified with each passing moment, our breaths quickening and sweat trickling down our faces. The gritty particles of dirt clung to our skin, mixing with the salty taste of determination on our lips. Engrossed in a heated battle, we moved fluidly and with precision as we vied for victory against one another.

I could feel my heart pounding in my chest as I dribbled the ball past Bobby, dodging his attempts to steal it from me. The sound of our sneakers screeching on the court echoed through the empty streets, as if they were cheering us on.

"Is that all you got?" Bobby taunted, a mischievous grin plastered across his face. "I thought you were supposed to be the backyard king!"

I smirked, not letting his words rattle me. I had a trick up my sleeve that I had been saving for just the right moment. As Bobby lunged towards me, I quickly spun around him and launched myself into the air, releasing the ball with precision.

The basketball soared through the air, its trajectory guided by years of practice and determination. It seemed to hang there for a moment, suspended in time, before it gracefully swished through the net. The satisfying sound of the ball meeting its mark filled me with a rush of accomplishment.

"I guess that answers your question," I replied, a hint of triumph in my voice.

Bobby's jaw dropped momentarily before he regained his composure. "Beginner's luck," he grumbled, refusing to let his pride take a hit.

Jim watched from the sidelines, eyes shining with excitement. He had always been content to spectate rather than take part in our heated matches. But deep down, he admired our passion and skill. It was in moments like these that I saw a flicker of inspiration ignite within him.

As we continued playing under the scorching sun, time seemed to stand still. The Backyard Brawlers were more than just friends competing against each other; we were bound by a shared love for the game. In those moments, nothing else mattered except the swish of the net and the camaraderie that flowed between us.

No matter what happened on that court, win or lose, we were all winners in our own right. Our dedication and determination had molded us into better players, but more importantly, into better friends.

All that endless summer our laughter filled the air, bouncing off the nearby homes and mixing with the dull thump of basketballs on pavement and the occasional crash of a diving player. Suddenly, one misguided dive ended with a loud smashing noise and an apologetic cry of "Sorry, Mrs. Johnson!"

Childhood joy reverberated with the sound of the ball striking the asphalt. As we spun and jumped, we were carefree and free. We didn't have to worry about taxes, deadlines, or that our parents were probably filling out paperwork for a second mortgage to afford our home.

"Bobby, quit hogging the ball!" I yelled, my voice tinged with playful annoyance. It's great that Bobby has skills, but we all want a chance to shine.

Like the sunflowers in my grandma's garden, we also need sunshine to thrive. "Oh, come on. Don't be a crybaby. I'm just showing you guys how it's done," Bobby replied with a grin, moving the basketball smoothly between his legs.

Seriously though, who does he think he is? LeBron James? We're not playing at Madison Square Garden. We're playing basketball in the backyard.

Jim, usually the peacemaker, chimed in. "Come on, guys! Let's all have a turn. We're supposed to have fun, remember?" Jim, the voice of reason, always spreads peace and harmony like peanut butter on a sandwich. If only he could spread it on Bobby's bravado.

Bobby's smirk softened into a smile as he passed the ball to Jim. "Yeah, you're right. Let's keep it friendly." And with that, we continued our game.

Those summer afternoons were irreplaceable treasures whittling away faster than we'd have liked. Each hoop showdown unfolded as games and baptism by fire, leading us into adulthood, testing our skills, and shaping friendships to last under a relentless onslaught of trials and tribulations.

Drenched in sweat, we dribbled the worn-out ball with determination, the rhythmic thumping echoing in our ears. Each move we made was a testament to our growth, resilience, and hunger for victory.

But it wasn't just about winning; it was about forging bonds that would withstand the test of time. The challenges we faced on that court mirrored those in our lives, defeats, setbacks, and moments of triumph. We learned how to rely on and trust one another when the stakes were high.

We shared stories of our dreams and fears between exhilarating plays and expertly executed shots. We confided in each other, knowing that these conversations were sacred, seeds planted within the fertile soil of friendship.

Through the sweat-soaked jerseys and tired legs, we discovered that true strength lay in physical abilities, empathy, and understanding. We became each other's support pillars, lifting one another up when life's burdens seemed too heavy to bear alone.

And as dusk painted the sky with hues of orange and pink, we knew our time together was slipping away. We clung to those fading moments, cherishing every laugh, every high-five, every whispered word of encouragement.

But even as summer gave way to fall's arrival and our lives pulled us in different directions, the memories we etched on that basketball court remained eternally woven into the tapestry of our souls. The lessons we learned and our forged friendships will forever be a part of us.

So, when the sun set on another glorious summer day, we packed up our dreams and worn-out basketball. The court would remain silent until the next battle, but our memories would echo through the ages. Or at least until we all got old and senile and forgot where we put our dentures.

But for now, the Backyard Brawlers would disband our youthful spirits full of laughter and hope. We would go our separate ways, armed with the invaluable lessons we learned on that humble court. And maybe we would carry a bit of that childhood joy with us long after the final buzzer sounded.

I will cherish these memories in my heart, that no amount of time or distance can diminish. The bond between us is something I hold dear, and I vow to keep these special moments in my soul close and safe, like a priceless heirloom.

And who knows, maybe someday we'll gather again, middle-aged and slightly more out of shape, to relive those glory days. We'll attempt to dunk on each other, but our knees will creak louder than a haunted house.

We'll reminisce about our past feats, even if they were just nine-year-olds stumbling and falling. The Backyard Brawlers may not have made it to the NBA, but we had the skills to pay the bills. Or at least skills that could get us free ice cream sandwiches from Mr. Johnson's garage freezer.

We were the kings of our asphalt kingdom, ruling our small piece of the world with basketballs as our scepters. Our reign may have been short-lived, but damn, did we feel like champions.

I snapped out of my daydream, feeling a shiver run down my spine as the chill of the night air seeped through my skin. I rubbed my arms and made my way to my cot, pulling my sleeping bag up to my chin to ward off the cool breeze.

As I lay there, reminiscing about those precious moments, I couldn't help but smile. Despite the passing of time and the distance separating us, our bond remains unbreakable. Our childhood friendships have stood the test of time, and I know they will continue to hold a special place in my heart forever.

I am grateful for the memories we shared, the laughter and tears, the support, and the love. Those moments may have passed, but they will always be a cherished part of my life.

CHAPTER FIVE

Night Under The Star

As the train emerged from the dark tunnel, a loud screech sliced through the air, reverberating through the carriage and sending a jolt of adrenaline coursing through my veins. My heart raced, pounding against my chest like a wild beast desperate for freedom. Instinctively, I turned towards the window, my eyes widening in shock as they beheld an astonishing sight.

A massive tree lay before me, sprawled across the tracks like a fallen titan. Its gnarled branches reached out in all directions, like the skeletal fingers of some ancient creature. The sheer immensity of the obstruction made my breath catch in my throat. The train abruptly stopped, jerking me out of my seat and into action.

I dismounted the train with a sense of urgency, my footsteps echoing off the stillness of the countryside. The fallen tree stood before me like an impenetrable fortress, its twisted branches taunting my feeble attempts at progress. Exasperation gnawed at my frayed nerves as I realized this absurd tree thwarted my plans to search for survivors.

I had to devise an alternative plan, but how? Clearly, I possessed no superhuman strength to lift the colossal tree from the tracks effortlessly. Frustration welled within me like a storm, and I lashed out at the gravel stones with a forceful swipe of my hand, watching as they scattered through the air like shattered dreams. At that moment, I hoped the foolish tree would learn its place.

But alas, my less-than-impressive attempt at playing knight in shining armor yielded no results. Undeterred, I circled the enormous obstacle, whispering words of defiance to myself in a desperate bid to summon courage. Yet, the tree remained impassive, utterly uninterested in my superhuman efforts.

With every conceivable approach tried and failed, I resorted to tugging, pushing, heaving, and pulling. The rough bark scraped mercilessly against my palms, leaving them bloodied and raw, but I refused to surrender. Frustration mingled with determination as I pressed on, refusing to yield to the weight of defeat. The sweat dripped down my forehead, mingling with the dirt and dust of the tracks, a testament to my unwavering resolve.

But it was like pushing a boulder up a hill, or in this case, trying to move a stubborn tree. No matter how hard I strained and flexed my muscles, the tree remained unmoved. While I stood there, contemplating my options, it felt like the universe had once again conspired against me. It was as if everything tested my resolve.

Leaving the train behind also meant leaving my hopes and aspirations behind. It was hard to let go of that ticket to a new life, but I had to face the reality of an impossible situation. My heart and mind were in constant turmoil, urging me towards a different path. But ultimately, I had no choice. Life had once again put me in a no-win situation. The tree blocking the train tracks left me only one option, walking.

Well, universe, I accept the challenge! With immense sadness gripping my heart, I turned away from the toppled tree and returned to the train to collect my belongings. Each step felt like a humbling surrender to my circumstances, a reminder that sometimes we can't control everything.

As soon as I stepped back on the train, the smell of worn-out leather seats and musty air reminded me of how lonely my solitude had been. Maybe leaving the train behind wasn't such a bad idea after all.

I looked at the control panel, pausing at the buttons that once brimmed with endless possibilities. The memories of countless journeys flooded my mind, reminding me of all the adventures I had embarked on with the train by my side.

Farewell, old friend, you served me well. I walked away with a heavy heart and glanced back at the fallen tree. There it stood, solitary and unyielding, a mute protector watching over a defeated struggle. It had fulfilled its intended role, but now it was time for me to move on.

The tree may have blocked my path but it couldn't stop my spirit. It was time to embrace the unknown, to step outside the mechanical boundaries of the train and into the untamed wilderness. And so, I bid farewell to the train with every confident step.

I embraced the unknown journey that awaited me. It wasn't the ending I imagined, but perhaps it was the ending I needed. It was an opportunity to push my boundaries and discover an inner strength I never realized I had.

As the sun dipped below the horizon, painting the sky in hues of orange and pink, I couldn't help but notice the shadows stretching across the forest floor. The scene was beautiful, but it did little to ease the ache in my chest. Everywhere I looked, reminders of a past life lingered, highlighting what was missing.

Sitting on a fallen log, I watched as stars started to twinkle in the darkening sky. Their beauty was undeniable, yet my heart still felt heavy. Leaning back against the log, I found myself seeking encouragement in the shimmering stars above. Each one held a spark of hope that I longed for, but memories of the past continued to haunt me.

Closing my eyes, I let the sounds of the forest wash over me, leaves rustling, crickets chirping, a melancholic melody that mirrored my emotions. It felt like nature itself understood my sorrow, offering whispered comfort on the wind.

A gentle breeze brushed against my skin, carrying scents of pine and damp earth. The familiar fragrance took me back to happier times filled with laughter and carefree days. Homesickness washed over me, tugging at my heartstrings with bittersweet memories.

Rummaging through my backpack, I felt the smooth leather of a journal I impulsively took from a stationery store. A voice in my head had urged me to take it, and now, as I opened its blank pages, I knew why.

I made a promise to my wife before she passed away. She had always been my biggest supporter and had encouraged me to pursue my passion for writing. I knew what I had to do. And so, I wrote, and the words flowed effortlessly from my pen. My wife's laughter echoed in my mind, and her gentle touch guided my hand.

I made a promise to my wife before she passed away. She had always been my biggest supporter and had encouraged me to pursue my passion for writing. I knew what I had to do. And so, I wrote, and the words flowed effortlessly from my pen. Memories of her laughter and touch inspired me as I put pen to paper.

Words poured out like a waterfall cascading into a peaceful pool. Her laughter resonated in the quiet room, a beautiful sound that filled the space as I wrote on the empty page. I could almost feel her touch, soft and comforting, guiding my hand.

Ink spilled onto the pages. Each drop was a reflection of my heart's emotions. Every shared moment, promise, and goodbye found their place in the lines I penned. They captured the essence of our love and life together.

Her presence felt real to me, with hints of her lavender

perfume lingering in the air and the warmth of our shared morning routine bringing back memories. The taste of our last kiss lingered on my lips, pushing me forward whenever I felt lost for words. Clutching her favorite locket in my hand, I found contentment in the memories we shared.

As I wrote, a mix of longing, and grief washed over me. But within those emotions, a sense of healing emerged, a soothing balm to my pain as I continued to write tirelessly.

Every word I wrote helped ease the pain in my chest. My wife's spirit had given me the strength and bravery to keep going in this post-apocalyptic world. I promised myself that I would finish writing my story, creating a tribute to her memory. I was determined to do it justice and honor her with every page. It would be my way of saying goodbye.

CHAPTER SIX

Embers of Love

As the morning sun peeked through the cotton candy clouds, I felt a rush of excitement. I was filled with energy, eager to embark on an adventure. Thoughts from my recent writing session danced in my mind, leading me toward new sources of inspiration.

After packing my bag, I headed out on the trail. The forest greeted me with a friendly gesture, its lush greenery welcoming me with open arms. The trees swayed gently to the tunes carried by the wind as if nature was rooting for me to explore its hidden treasures.

The cool fall air invigorated me, filling my senses with the scents of damp leaves and earthy soil. It felt like an invitation to delve deeper into the secrets of Mother Nature. Amidst this vibrant world of wisdom, the trees seemed likewise mentors offering lessons in their way.

Guided by the breeze rustling through the leaves, I felt like a student navigating a magical maze, with nature subtly imparting its teachings at every turn.

Even on days like today, when the rain poured down upon me with an unforgiving strength, I still felt a sense of tranquility. After the final pitter-patter of raindrops faded, I trudged forward in search of shelter.

My backpack weighed heavily on my shoulders, and my fingers ached from clutching my soaked map. As I spotted a clearing in the trees, I quickly set up camp, arranging my sleeping bag, tarp, and meager supplies neat and organized.

Exhaustion washed over me as I finally settled down for the night, grateful to have found a dry and comfortable spot in the wilderness. I sank into my familiar worn camping chair. The crackling of the campfire provided a gentle lullaby.

I watched the enthralling dance of the flickering flames, delicate tendrils of smoke ascending and whispering secrets into the night air. The tranquility of the evening stirred up memories of the past, tugging at my heartstrings with an emotional blend of joy and sorrow.

In the echoing halls of my mind, I submerged myself in the watercolor memories of my only love. The scent of pine from the crackling firewood, the sharp, sudden sound of a log splitting under the heat, and the warmth that radiated from the dancing embers each became a key, unlocking a vault of emotions both bitter and sweet.

My eyelids knotted in concentration, her image seared across my inner sight like light through stained glass. The gentle curve of her cheekbone, the familiar scent of lavender interwoven in her hair that I used to bury my face in during stolen moments. And the melody of her laughter, all these took form in my mind's theater, sketching out an artwork that time could never fade.

A sigh escaped my lips, one that carried warmth and unspoken words. And as if she were there beside me by our old and weathered hearth, her hand within mine, my heart echoed back with a throbbing rhythm. It was a rhythm that whispered her name; it was a rhythm that sang our song.

On a beautiful July afternoon, Michelle and I found ourselves on the stage of a local performance of the musical Godspell. We were both sixteen and fate had brought us together. I played the drums, entirely captivated by watching Michelle effortlessly strumming the guitar with her slender fingers.

Her connection with the audience was enchanting. Our music reached a thrilling climax, and our communication was so natural, with just shared nods. Looking out at the crowd, I could tell our performance had left them breathless, time standing still for a moment.

I knew that day marked the beginning of something extraordinary for us. As we mingled with the audience, excitement filled the air, mixed with chatter and praise for our performance.

Michelle's radiant smile was like a lighthouse, its warm glow illuminating my heart, her vibrant energy buzzing like an electric current that I couldn't resist. Our conversation flowed effortlessly, touching on simple pleasantries and shared praises intertwined with the melody of our voices.

As we walked out of the music venue, the cool night air surrounded us, carrying the distant sound of laughter and chatter. Michelle glanced over at me, her eyes sparkling with excitement.

Excited, I suggested, "I'm part of this band, and we really need a lead guitarist. Are you interested?"

"So, tell me about this band of yours," she inquired, slipping her hands into the pockets of her leather jacket.

I grinned, feeling a rush of enthusiasm. "Well, we're called 'The Mystics,' and we mainly play rock with a hint of blues. We've been looking for a lead guitarist to complete our sound for weeks now."

Michelle nodded thoughtfully. "That sounds like my kind of music. I've always loved experimenting with different genres and styles on the guitar."

With a shared passion for music igniting our conversation, we strolled down the bustling street lined with cafés and taverns. The neon lights cast a warm glow on our faces as we chatted animatedly about our favorite bands and musical influences.

As we entered a cozy diner, the aroma of freshly cooked food greeted us, making our stomachs rumble in unison. Michelle scanned the menu with interest before looking up at me with a mischievous grin.

"You know," she began playfully, "I have a weakness for burgers and fries. What's your go-to order?"

Chuckling, I replied, "A classic cheeseburger with crispy bacon and a side of loaded fries is my usual choice. How about we share both?"

Michelle's eyes lit up with delight as she nodded in agreement. "Perfect! I'm all in for some indulgence tonight."

As we sat there, our laughter mingling with the cheerful ambiance of the diner, I couldn't help but feel grateful for the magical connection we had stumbled upon that evening.

I suggested more food as we finished our meal, but Michelle's satisfied smile said it all. Stepping out into the night breeze under the moonlit sky, we continued our journey on foot, teasing each other and laughing until we reached the park.

Sitting under the starry sky, we shared dreams and aspirations openly as if they were old friends. Our hearts connected in moments of vulnerability against a backdrop of haunting beauty.

I offered to walk her home. Gratefulness and farewells exchanged painted a bittersweet picture of departure, yet the anticipation of reunion kindled within us.

Summer unfolded, promising more adventures ahead, our hearts beating in harmony as we navigated through band practices and spontaneous escapades.

But looming military duties threatened to separate us for two long years, casting a shadow over our budding relationship.

However, at that moment, we both knew we had finally found the love we had been searching for. Our hearts and souls were in perfect alignment, and we promised never to let each other go.

Fresh out of my time in the army, we said our vows on a cool October Saturday, promising never to be apart. I was so happy and excited, my heart beating with the hope of a loving future.

Our honeymoon took us to a cabin off the grid, deep in the Smoky Mountains. Surrounded by the beautiful sight of golden and scarlet leaves swaying in the wind like a puzzle, with wildflower meadows as nature's mesmerizing artwork and breathtaking views that showed the untouched beauty of the earth, it felt like a sanctuary from a fairy tale.

The crickets sang their familiar lullaby each night while stars lit up our little wilderness home like specks of magic. The sweet scent of dewy moss and pine brought a sense of peace to our hearts.

Michelle and I had much in common, having experienced the

same upbringing. Neither of us was born into wealth, though we weren't entirely poverty stricken, except in terms of the dwellings we lived in. Michelle had the most challenging time.

Growing up in a crowded household, Michelle rarely had the luxury of privacy or solitude. She shared two small bedrooms with seven siblings, and the kitchen was minuscule. And don't even get her started on the constant arguments over who got to use the bathroom first.

The air was often tense as they argued over who got the top bunk or the biggest slice of cake. Her brothers and sisters were creative in their bickering, creating increasingly innovative ways to one-up each other.

And yet, during all this chaos, there was joy. Michelle's home stood as a place of love and warmth amidst the laughter and disputes, and they would forever remember it with fondness.

The guitar was Michelle's escape, a way to express her feelings and to break away from the hustle and bustle of her busy home. She would sit in the middle of the night, strumming away and letting the music flow through her. She could relax in the moment, letting her worries and anxieties escape with each chord.

I once told Michelle how lucky I was that she'd chosen to marry me, and she replied amusingly, "Don't flatter yourself. I was going to marry the first man who promised me my own bedroom!"

Michelle was a natural hostess. Her friends and family admired her energy and enthusiasm and often sought her out to plan parties and events. But Thanksgiving Day was extraordinary.

It was the one day of the year when her entire, and I mean entire, family would gather at our cozy home.

At 4 AM on Thanksgiving morning, Michelle was excited to start cooking. As the sun reached noon, the solid wooden table was loaded with an array of delicious side dishes and indulgent desserts.

The aroma of slow-cooked turkey wafted through the house. Each dish was meticulously arranged, resembling a masterpiece fit for a high-end restaurant. Excitement filled the air as everyone's mouths watered and stomachs rumbled.

Each dish made with love and attention to detail, tempting even the most selective eaters. It felt like a feast fit for kings and queens, yet it was shared among close friends and family, creating a cozy and happy atmosphere for everyone gathered around the table.

Still, things got competitive when it was time to sit down at the table. Everyone wanted a prime seat, leading to a lively scramble. Eventually, they found their spots, some perched on borrowed chairs or well-loved cushions. Laughter and playful banter filled the room as they eagerly dug into the feast.

While we enjoyed our meal, we exchanged stories, strengthening the family bond. The essence of Thanksgiving was evident, bringing us together in a shared experience. With each delicious bite of candied yams or creamy mashed potatoes, we found comfort and tradition that only this holiday could offer.

As the last guest stumbled out the door, a scene of devastation greeted me. Red plastic cups and empty soft drink cans littered the floor, and a mountain of dirty dishes covered the kitchen counter.

Michelle approached with a sly smile and sparkling eyes that glimmered like diamonds in the fading light. She wrapped her arms around my waist and leaned in close, her breath warm and sweet against my cheek. Her flowing hair carried the scent of blooming lilacs that filled my senses with wonder.

"I love you," she whispered. I felt her words resonate as I ran my fingers through her hair, forgetting everything else.

Michelle was a devoted mother whose love for her children was beyond measure. You could find her cheering for her children in the stands at every game, helping them with their homework, and providing a shoulder to cry on when things got tough.

She was the Mama Bear who always had their backs, no matter what. She was the anchor that kept them safe, and her unwavering support was the most precious gift she could give her children.

Like the ebbs and flows of a timeless melody, our bond grew stronger each day. Our love remained steadfast even when the world howled and raged with discordant noise. We embraced and clung to each other, sheltering from the storm.

Our connection was so powerful it seemed like the sun was rising in our hearts, burning away the world's darkness. We were a shining beacon of hope in a sea of despair, a song of love that could never be silenced.

But life has a cruel way of testing us, and as the years went by, we could feel Michelle's health slowly slipping through our fingers like sand. Even with her ever-present optimism, we couldn't ignore the subtle signs that something was amiss.

Her once vibrant energy began to dim, like a candle flickering in a breeze. Every day felt like a battle against an unseen enemy, and we held onto hope with every breath. But deep down, we all knew that something was gravely wrong.

We tentatively entered the doctor's office, sweating, palms revealing our fear, hearts racing with unease. Perching on uncomfortable chairs, we avoided eye contact, lost in our thoughts. The heavy atmosphere was filled with fear, each passing moment bringing more anxiety. A knock broke the silence.

"Michelle, may I come in?" Dr. Johnson's gentle yet authoritative voice filled the room. I glanced at him briefly, feeling exposed by his gaze.

Anxiety consumed me as we waited for his words that could change everything. Dr. Johnson sat beside Michelle, her body tensing for what would come. His reassuring hand holding hers did little to ease the tension.

My heart sank as I watched their hands connect, sensing the bad news to follow. The silence stretched until it was unbearable, and then he spoke, each word heavy with regret.

“Michelle,” he started, his grip on her hand tightening, “I wish there was an easier way to say this…” A pause filled the room with dread. “Your results are back and... I’m sorry to say we didn’t get good news.” His unwavering gaze met hers. “You have cancer.”

The room grew colder as the words sank in. I had anticipated this news but hearing it out loud was a harsh blow. The world blurred as I closed my eyes, fear lingering on my tongue. A silent plea for a miracle lingered in my mind, hoping this nightmare would fade away.

Michelle's heart plummeted as the words fell from the doctor's lips, each syllable like a hammer striking her chest. "Cancer? No, it can't be!" she choked out, her voice trembling with disbelief and fear.

The doctor's grave nod confirmed her worst fears. "I'm sorry to say," he replied gently, his eyes brimming with understanding. "All of our tests point in that direction. I know this is difficult news to hear, but I want you to know that we are here to support you every step of the way."

Tears instantly welled up in Michelle's eyes, blurring her vision as she struggled to process the reality of her diagnosis. "I... I can't believe this," she whispered, her words laced with emotion. "How did this happen?"

The doctor's tone softened as he explained the various potential causes of cancer. Michelle's mind was racing, unable to focus on anything except for the word that had changed her life forever - cancer.

After a few moments, Michelle gathered her courage to ask the next question. "What treatments are available?" she asked, trembling with hope and terror. "Is there a chance I can fight this?"

Meeting her gaze with unwavering assurance, the doctor said calmly, "There are several options for treatment that we can discuss after your surgery. But right now, it's important to hold onto hope. Many people have faced cancer head-on and emerged victorious."

Overwhelmed by the gravity of her diagnosis, Michelle couldn't hold back her deepest fear any longer. "I... I don't want to die," she confessed through sobs, her voice wrought with fear and desperation. "There's still so much I want to do in life - my children, my grandchildren... so many experiences ahead."

The doctor's expression softened in response to her raw pain and vulnerability. "It's completely natural to feel scared and overwhelmed right now," he said tenderly. "But please know that you are not alone in this fight. There are support networks, counseling services, and loved ones who can offer strength and comfort. We will guide you towards resources that can help you navigate this difficult journey."

Michelle's tears flowed freely as she struggled to come to terms with her diagnosis. "I don't even know how to handle all of this," she admitted, her voice full of vulnerability. "Everything feels like it's spinning out of control."

With empathy in his eyes, the doctor offered her a reassuring hand on her shoulder. "Take your time," he encouraged softly. "Allow yourself to process this information at your own pace. It is normal to experience a range of emotions right now. Please do not hesitate to reach out if you have any questions or need anything from us."

Michelle now completely sobbed, "Thank you, Doctor Johnson, for being honest with me. I know this won't be easy, but I appreciate your support and guidance through this challenging time."

"You're very welcome, Michelle. Remember, we're here for you, and together, we'll devise a comprehensive treatment plan to tackle this head-on. You're not alone in this fight, and I believe in your resilience."

Every day, we surrounded her with all the love our hearts could muster, holding onto a sliver of hope that, somehow, she'd make it through. With each new treatment, we'd pray a little harder and a little stronger, believing against all odds that she could beat this. But as the days slipped by, her pain grew, and so did the shadow in our hearts.

We all put on brave faces, trying to be the strength she needed, but watching her fade away was a torture no pretense could ease. Every night, as she lay struggling, I'd sit by her side, painting pictures of a future filled with laughter and light, promising her that I'd always be there no matter what.

But as powerful as they are, promises and love couldn't fend off the inevitable. Seven years of fighting and hoping led to a quiet room where her gentle breaths no longer filled the air. Holding her hand, so cold and still, I watched the last spark of her spirit flicker out. It was a silence that screamed, a pain that no words could ever capture.

In those final moments, as I whispered goodbye, every memory and every hope we shared was a testament to a love that even death couldn't erase. But it also left an emptiness that echoed with the beauty of what once was.

My heart shattered into a million pieces, unable to escape the anguish that consumed me. Though every part of me screamed for her to return, no miracle could break death's finality, and the harsh truth of her absence.

The music of our love still echoes in my soul, each beat of my heart aching for the rhythm of our days. I can still hear the harmony of our love, even if the notes are now silent. My heart still aches for those moments that have gone and will never return. But I know I haven't forgotten our love, and it will stay in my heart until the end of time.

CHAPTER SEVEN

Bridge of Self-Discovery

You can't get lost if you have nowhere to go. So, I decided to take a new approach today. After what felt like hours, I came across an old bridge. The sun-weathered wood creaked and groaned. I carefully tested its strength, felt the floor flex, and felt a sharp splinter dig into my foot.

I couldn't help but marvel at the bridge's weathered beams standing strong against the river below. It was a testament to the enduring power of our engineering, yet humans could not find such strength within themselves.

Wars, poverty, inequality, and injustice continued to plague societies despite our ability to construct magnificent structures like the old bridge. As I gazed at its majestic arches, I couldn't help but wonder when humanity would harness the same resilience and unity to overcome these persistent challenges.

It was a hard truth that we were so caught up in our differences that we couldn't find common ground. Our stubbornness and pride prevented us from building a bridge that could connect us. Instead, we found ourselves stuck in our separate worlds, unable to unite. Just as this river below fiercely separated one bank from the other.

I asked myself, what if we had chosen a different path? What if we had used these differences to create something beautiful, to build bridges that connected us? We could have learned from one another and grown together, creating a world where acceptance and understanding flourished.

I could have gone on for hours questioning the failures of humanity but for what purpose now? I knew I had to get to the other side. I stood on the bridge, my fingers shaking as I peered down into the darkness below.

The fear of one misstep taking me into the river made my heart beat fast. As I hesitated at the edge, thoughts of surrender and danger raced through my mind. With each step across the old bridge, I couldn't ignore the gaps between the planks that seemed to challenge me.

The sound of the creaking wood added to my unease, hinting at a possible collapse. Feeling the wind around me, I felt like it was trying to push me towards the edge. I froze in fear as the roaring river below seemed to wait for me.

The trees by the shore moved with a sense of foreboding, their rustling leaves whispering eerie truths. The air and water felt wild, creating a scene of desolation and power, with only nature's sounds breaking the stillness.

"Why did I decide to go this way?" I muttered to myself, questioning my life choices. "Why did I have to be so stupid? Why did I have to rush?"

I took a second to compose myself and prayed for strength and courage. I knew I had to make the best of this situation to survive.

I wiped away the sweat drops that ran down my forehead, smearing a thick layer of dirt and dust across my face. The bridge groaned and creaked beneath me, and I felt the vibrations travel through the wooden boards to shudder through my body. I shivered involuntarily, my heart racing with fear.

"I should have taken another route. I should have inspected the crossing." I was becoming my worst enemy, questioning my every move.

The bridge swayed back and forth, rattling with laughter at my attempts to cross it. My fingers wrapped around the beam so tightly that it was almost painful.

"Please, just let me make it across this bridge. I promise I'll change. I'll be a better person!"

I shut my eyes and felt the sun's heat on my face. I thought of my family and friends, their smiling faces filling my imagination. No matter how hard things got, I knew I had a family who cherished me and whom I loved deeply. I had to make them my foremost thought. I had to keep them close and cherish my beautiful moments with them, and this structure wouldn't take that away.

I had come too far to turn back now, and I knew I had to make it all the way across. I could feel the tension building as I took each step, the creaking of the bridge growing louder and louder. I was so close, yet so far away. I could almost taste my freedom, but I knew one wrong move would send me to the depths below.

It's funny the thoughts that race through your mind when you believe death is imminent. It was an awakening, like a gentle reminder of what it meant to be alive. I thought of all the times I had taken life for granted, not stopping to appreciate the smallest moments that made up the day.

I remembered the laughter of my children when we were all together, the smell of the air after a summer rain, the taste of a perfectly cooked steak.

I thought of all the people I had known and loved and those I had yet to meet. I thought about my choices and the ones yet to come. I saw the possibilities of what could be and the dreams I had been too afraid to pursue.

As winds howled and battered against my body, I clung to the rusted steel beams of the bridge with trembling hands. The force was so strong that my muscles strained and quivered in protest, each gust feeling like a sledgehammer strike.

Dirt and dust swirled around me, stinging my eyes and coating my throat with a gritty film. Suddenly, my foot slipped off its foothold, and I felt my ankle snap with searing pain. It was as though I had been thrown into an inferno, every nerve in my body throbbing with fiery agony.

As the tempest raged on, my foot slipped off the beam, and a searing jolt of agony shot through my body as my ankle snapped beneath me. It felt as though I had been cast into a raging inferno, the pain burning hot and fierce.

Tremors of torment coursed up my leg, igniting my insides with an unbearable sensation of fiery torture. The intensity of it all was so consuming that I could not contain the agony any longer. A guttural scream tore from deep within me, my voice intertwining with the howling wind in a symphony of pain and anguish.

Every heave and strain of my muscles was met with a burning ache as I clung desperately to the edge of the bridge. One leg dangled precariously in the air, defying gravity's pull. With each futile attempt to inch my way up, nature's power seemed to mock my feeble efforts. The weight of fear intensified as it coursed through me like a jolt of electricity, making my ankle quiver in protest.

The roaring river and howling wind made my spine tingle. My lips tasted of salty sweat, and the coarse bridge surface scraped against my hands, reminding me of my vulnerability.

My lungs burned with each ragged breath, my muscles quivering with exhaustion. I clung to the edge of the bridge, feeling my grip weaken as sweat dripped into my eyes. My mind screamed to give up, but I couldn't let go.

With a surge of determination, I dragged myself hand-over-hand back onto the bridge, gritting my teeth against the pain coursing through my body. My limbs sprawled out on the rough, weathered surface, my body fighting for oxygen.

My forehead was slicked with sweat, and searing pain shot through my ankle with every movement. I dragged myself forward, taking heaving breaths that burned my throat. My body trembled as I finally reached the end of the bridge. An indescribable surge of relief flooded through me like a raging river.

“Yes... I made it,” I whispered, mustering a feeble smile.

My heart pounded as I savored the moment. I had done it. I had conquered my fear and pushed through the doubt. I felt elated, experiencing a sense of pride in myself and my accomplishments. I stood tall on the bridge, savoring the victory. I was a conqueror of my fears and doubts, and my bravery had paid off.

I felt free, liberated from the chains of my anxieties and insecurities. My victory empowered me filled with a newfound sense of courage that I would carry with me for the rest of my life.

My journey across the bridge had been a long one. Full of self-doubt and fear. But in the end, I found the courage to take the leap of faith and trust in my strength. I emerged victorious and wouldn't let anything stand in my way again. I was unstoppable.

Lying on the ground, I gasped for breath and felt my heart thumping wildly. I turned my head slowly to survey the mess behind me. Fear? It was there, but this time I embraced it.

This wise old bridge has been more than just a physical structure; it has been my greatest teacher, mentor, and guide. It has shown me the importance of delving deep into my soul and finding the bravery to confront my deepest fears.

A sense of gratitude washed over me as I reflected on the lesson I learned today. Venturing beyond the familiar and embracing risks had revealed unexpected opportunities and profound truths. It reminded me that my tendency to play it safe had been a hindrance in the past.

Looking around at my surroundings, I realized how much I had kept myself boxed in by fear. The people I surrounded myself with, the places I went, and even the thoughts that consumed me had all been a safe haven where nothing could go wrong. But today's experience has shown me that stepping out of our comfort zones could sometimes lead to tremendous growth.

I shook my head, wondering why it had taken me so long to realize this. Maybe it was due to my upbringing, as years of being taught to remain silent and obedient had made me inclined to avoid taking risks. But no more. Today, I marked a new beginning, embracing the unknown and all its opportunities.

CHAPTER EIGHT

Longing for Connection

As the clock ticked away in the quiet stillness, I realized that there was a special magic in sharing moments with another heartbeat. It was more than just conversations and laughter. It was a connection that filled the void of loneliness and brought understanding to my soul. But as I sat alone, the weight of solitude deepened like shadows over my heart, intensifying feelings of isolation.

I searched desperately for a remedy to fill the emptiness within me. Keeping busy with activities seemed like a solution, but even in busyness, solitude echoed persistently.

Yet, amidst despair, I found pockets of joy in simple things - painting my soul with dazzling sunsets, listening to birdsong melodies that danced through the air, and savoring morning coffee as if it were a comforting melody to awaken my senses and soothe my restless mind. The world may have been devastated, but I found solace and contentment within myself in those peaceful moments.

And so, I would meticulously lay out my supplies each night for the next day's journey. I filled my backpack with non-perishable food items, and a water canteen hung from the side. As I drifted to sleep, my mind ran through potential routes and where I might find shelter or resources. I always focused my plans on survival, constantly seeking sustenance and a safe place to rest my head each night.

Today has been grueling. The unforgiving sun beat down relentlessly, forcing me to shield my eyes with a hand. The scorching heat seemed to drain every ounce of energy from my body, leaving me drenched in sweat. I longed for a cool breeze to relieve the oppressive weather.

Each step felt like walking on hot coals, my feet throbbing in protest. My parched throat burned with each painful breath, and my body trembled from exhaustion. Every muscle screamed for relief as I pushed forward, determined to reach the end of this grueling journey.

The vast sky sprawled like a canvas of hazy blues and confused yellows, with clouds streaked orange as they sunk low, draping the asphalt stretch. The scorching heat welled up from every tiny pit in the road, stinging my soles while squinting eyes battled the harsh sunlight.

As I walked on, I saw the silhouettes of bright neon lights and shop signs that once added life to the city skyline, bringing back memories of days gone by. I strolled along the sidewalks filled with memories, surrounded by old buildings now covered in dust.

The echo of shattered glass underfoot cut through the silence, betraying tales of brighter times. In front of what used to be an Apple store, I paused and looked up at the large logo still hanging on the facade. I finally understood the magnitude of my loss. A sharp reminder of the harsh truth washed over me, a reminder that what I had lost could not be regained as quickly as downloading an app from a store.

Anxiety was like a heavy fog around me. I did not know where to turn or what to do. So, I decided this would be my home for a while. As I wandered the streets of this new city, I noticed something that made me laugh. Its slogan was "Where shopping is a pleasure, not a chore!" I couldn't help but feel optimistic about this city. Shopping was a task I hated, so the thought of it being a pleasure was refreshing. I knew then I had made the right decision.

The sun's final, fiery bow was casting long shapes of shadows across the rough concrete. I sat on a timeworn bench in the park, feeling the scratchy texture of wood grazed by its age. Around me, a handful of solar-powered shops sparkled to life as day spun into night. They stood defiant against the encroaching darkness like tiny oases of radiance within an ocean of inkiness.

As I sat alone in the darkness, a sudden warmth flooded my chest, chasing away the chill of loneliness. The twinkling lights around me seemed to dance and twirl, their reflections bouncing off nearby objects and casting a mesmerizing glow. At that moment, I realized something important. Even when you feel alone, there is still beauty and comfort.

I laid down on the hard wooden bench, wrapping my arms around myself for warmth, and drifted off to sleep as the store lights served as my only companions. The soft sound of crickets in the distance lulled me into a peaceful slumber. And for a moment, my worries melted away in the magical glow of the surrounding lights.

An invigorating morning breeze kissed my cheeks, gently rousing me from my slumber. As I opened my eyes, the first thing I saw was the magnificent sunrise. The sky was a breathtaking blend of fiery crimson and delicate shades of pink like a painter's canvas come to life. I couldn't help but marvel at how the wispy clouds seemed to dance in perfect harmony with the vibrant colors, creating a stunning display of nature's grandeur.

I got up and stretched, feeling energized and refreshed. A yawn escaped my lips as I prepared for another adventure. Despite its desolation, the city called out to me, inviting me to explore its secrets.

The abandoned city beckoned me, its mysteries calling out like a siren's song. I stepped over the crumbling remains of a wall and entered the silent streets. My boots crunched on the cracked pavement, shattering the ghostly stillness.

Dust motes danced in the sunlight streaming through collapsed rooftops, mixing with the faint, musty scent of decay. The wind whistled through broken windows and stirred leaves that skittered across the ground.

The hinges moaned in protest as I pushed the door, but it opened. My eyes widened with awe at the sight that greeted me.

Shelves upon shelves, towering high with books of every genre. The atmosphere was heavy with the scent of vanilla and dust, and I couldn't help but think it was like stepping into a world lost to time.

My fingers danced over the spines of the books as I moved through the narrow aisles, each holding a unique story and world within its pages. Some books looked new and untouched, while others showed evidence of years spent gathering dust on the shelf.

A smile played on my lips as I imagined myself getting lost in each adventure and mystery these books held. As I continued down the aisle, I couldn't help but think about what each book held in store for me, stories of love, loss, friendship, vengeance, all waiting to be discovered.

For a moment, I closed my eyes and breathed in deeply, letting the musty scent consume me entirely. It was then that I realized this place was not just a library or a bookstore; it was a sanctuary for those of us who found comfort in words and imagination.

I spent hours lost in those dusty pages, immersing myself in tales of love, adventure, and triumph. It was as if the characters in those books whispered secrets into my ear, urging me to keep trying, never to give up. Their stories became my own, intertwining with my hope.

But right now, I needed more than inspiration. I needed food.

As I stepped out of the musty bookstore, I scanned the empty street for any sign of the supplies I desperately needed. I searched around a corner, and suddenly an old-fashioned butcher shop caught my eye.

The enormous window made of glass and the tattered sign swaying in the gentle breeze seemed to call out to me, luring me inside.

As soon as I stepped inside, the familiar aroma of homemade sausages greeted me. Memories rushed back to me, transporting me back to my grandmother's kitchen, where I would watch her skilled hands craft these delicacies just for me. The savory scent filled my nostrils, sending my mouth watering in anticipation. It was a comforting smell that reminded me of home and family.

In the corner stood an old refrigerator, its paint chipped and worn from years of use. And there, on a worn wooden table, lay the same knives and cutting boards my grandmother had used to create her mouthwatering sausages. It was as if time had stood still in this place, preserving the essence of my childhood memories.

I wrapped my fingers around the handle of the cumbersome metal door leading to the freezer. The cold metal felt refreshing against my skin but slippery from the frost that accumulated as air seeped through cracks in the store.

The hinges creaked, and a rush of cold air, scented with the sharp metallic smell of steel, escaped and made me shiver. I squinted in the darkness as my breath misted around me. My eyes adjusted, and I glimpsed several slabs of beef on the shelves. I grabbed a few steaks, tucking them into my bag.

I was looking so forward to returning home to enjoy a delicious meal cooked on the grill, feeling excited. But then reality hit me hard, and I realized my home was no longer there, and there was no sizzling grill to be found. Feeling disappointed, I put the steaks back in the freezer. Determined to find another way to satisfy my hunger, I left the store to search for something more practical.

As I walked down the street, my stomach grumbled while something inside me told me to turn around and go back. A pang of injustice hit me. Why should I miss out on those delicious cuts of meat?

With grit, I marched back to the shop and flung open the freezer door, grabbing the steaks with a victorious smirk. I couldn't help but feel a sense of satisfaction at my minor act of rebellion. After all, who could resist the temptation of perfectly marbled steaks?

I stumbled upon a few cans of beans and a case of bottled water at a small grocery store on the next street. For days, I had been searching for food with little luck. But today, the butcher shop and grocery store had just what I needed. With these supplies, I could finally satisfy my hunger.

The frayed shoelace cinched tight around my bulging canvas bag and chafed my palm as I lugged it down the cracked sidewalk. Cans of beans and bags of rice thumped against my leg with each step, my empty stomach growling in protest. Squinting against the harsh sunlight, I scanned the neighborhood until a familiar red sign appeared, YMCA.

My pace quickened, sneakers slapping the pavement. Bursting through the front doors, I searched desperately for any sign of electricity. And there, in the corner, a working solar panel. My sigh of relief echoed through the silent lobby. I got to work, laying out my sleeping bag on the hardwood floor and assembling my camping stove.

Clutching the frozen slabs of meat, I submerged them in hot water, hoping they would defrost faster. With that task taken care of, I returned to town for another errand

I stumbled upon a liquor store, so I stepped inside, escaping the chill. My fingers trailed over glossy wine bottles, pausing on a dusty Pinot Noir tucked away on the bottom shelf. I turned the bottle in my hands, tracing the intricate vines etched into the label. Bittersweet memories flooded back.

Shivering, I hurried to the abandoned YMCA, the cold air biting my cheeks. Kneeling on the cracked concrete floor, I arranged the spruce branches in a teepee shape. Striking a match, I watched the tiny flame catch and spread, bathing the room in a warm, flickering glow.

The fire crackled and popped, filling the air with the sweet scent of burning pine. I held my numb hands out, soaking in the heat.

I delicately grasped the bottle of wine, and a rush of anticipation coursed through me. With a gentle twist, the cork surrendered to my efforts, emitting an echoing pop reverberating through the room.

Instantly, memories of joyful family gatherings flooded my mind, transporting me back to the warmth and laughter that enveloped our home.

Pouring the velvety liquid into the waiting glass, I marveled at its rich, ruby hue reminiscent of a captivating sunset. Its enticing aroma wafted up, teasing my senses with promises of indulgence and relaxation.

Bringing the glass to my lips, I took a cautious sip, allowing the flavors to unfold on my palate. The first taste sent ripples of pleasure cascading through my taste buds. It was a symphony of sensations, bold yet refined, with hints of blackberries and a subtle trace of oak.

With each subsequent sip, the wine revealed new layers of complexity, like a tapestry woven with care and precision. Its smooth texture danced delicately across my tongue, leaving behind a lingering trail of satisfaction.

As I savored the wine's embrace, it felt like time stood still, wrapping me in a comforting embrace. It was more than just a beverage; it was a conduit for connection and reflection. I found cheer and companionship in its depths, reminding me of the cherished moments shared with loved ones.

At that moment, I reveled in the magic that a simple bottle of wine could conjure. It was not merely a drink; it was a vessel that transported me to a tapestry of memories and emotions, offering tranquility from the devastation outside.

The steaks were ready within minutes. The sizzling sound and savory smell of cooking beef brought back fond memories of family dinners. The aroma of wine and caramelized fat and the smoky steam from the grill created a mouth-watering symphony of scents.

I eagerly anticipated sinking my teeth into those juicy steaks; it was like a dream come true, and I felt on top of the world for a while.

As I set my fork down on the plate, the sound of its collision filled the room, reflecting how much I was craving this meal. The first bite of the tender meat, soaked in a flavorful marinade, exploded with taste in my mouth, making me yearn for more.

The fragrant herbs added a comforting warmth to every chew, bringing back memories of special evenings with Michelle. Each delicious mouthful made me appreciate this wonderful meal even more, leaving me wanting to savor every bit of this culinary experience.

As I sat amid the ruins, my mind drifted away from the terrors that had led me here. Instead, I found myself staring at the starry night sky, its glittering constellations offering a glimmer of hope in an otherwise lonely world.

I reached for my wine glass and took a sip. The taste brought back memories of when life was simpler when I didn't have to worry about fighting for survival every day.

But even in this moment of indulgence, I couldn't escape the grim reality of my situation. I was alone in a world devoid of all life, surrounded by rubble and decay.

Yet despite it all, a small flame of hope burned within me. Perhaps someday, somewhere, there would be signs of life again. Maybe even other survivors like myself had managed to cling to hope and overcome the unthinkable.

The thought made me smile briefly as I raised my glass in a silent toast to the world I had lost. And with that small act of defiance, I vowed to keep fighting for whatever scraps of happiness I could find in this lonely world.

As I drifted off to sleep, a subtle yet clear sound cut through the room's peaceful atmosphere. It wasn't like the usual house settling noises; this sound felt alive and purposeful. My heart quickened, and my breath caught as I tried to pinpoint where it was coming from. I couldn't shake the feeling that something was wrong.

Was it the rustling of clothes? A floorboard creaking beneath someone's weight? Or maybe it was all in my mind? While I shifted around in my sleeping bag, thoughts about the place's past consumed me. Who inhabited this space before me? What untold mysteries lurked behind these walls?

One thing was certain, I needed to uncover the source of that sound before my vivid imagination took control.

I carefully peeled back my sleeping bag, my feet feeling the cold floor as I inched around the room. My pulse quickened as I heard the noise again, and I strained my ears to identify its source. I knew it had come from somewhere outside my doorway.

My heart pounded as I cautiously approached the source. I could feel the surrounding air, heavy with anticipation, as I readied myself to confront whatever was outside.

A mysterious figure stood in the shadows by the curb, casting a looming presence. The night air suddenly felt colder, and a sense of fear washed over me as its silent gaze pierced through my body, leaving me frozen, unable to move.

CHAPTER NINE

A White Shadow in the Ashes

My heart pounded as the shadowy figure emerged from the darkness. I pressed my lips together, stifling the scream rising in my throat. Carefully placing one foot in front of the other, I crept toward the door. My eyes strained against the blackness, struggling to make out the shape slowly approaching. It moved with a graceful lope, its outline becoming clearer. Snow white fur shone in a sliver of moonlight streaming through the trees.

As the figure drew nearer, my heart rate quickened, and my muscles tensed in fear. But as it stepped into the light, my tension eased and was replaced by a sense of warmth and comfort. It was not a menacing presence but a furry bundle of joy. A Labrador retriever with matted fur covered in dirt and soot stood before me.

Her chocolate brown eyes were soft and welcoming, her tail wagging excitedly as if she had been waiting for me. I couldn't resist the urge to run my hand over her soft coat and feel the warmth radiating from her body. As I stroked her gently, a sense of calm overtook me, and all my worries faded away like snow melting under the sun's warm rays.

With gentle hands, I brushed the grit out of her coat and searched for any signs of injury. Although malnourished and exhausted, she wagged her tail when I stroked her face. Her warm brown eyes captivated me as I offered a reassuring smile and whispered comforting words.

Despite her hardship, she radiated joy and playfulness, as if her spirit remained unbroken by the chaos that consumed everything else. I looked down and saw a future full of possibilities and happiness. From that moment on, I knew my life would never be the same.

I knelt, extending my hand with a piece of steak resting on my palm. The dog stepped closer. Her nose twitched, and her tail wagged in anticipation as I offered it to her. With a snap of her jaw, she devoured the morsel. Her tail wagged gently in appreciation, and I watched her eyes light up joyfully.

Gazing into those kind, brown eyes, a wave of emotion washed over me. In this lonely, post-apocalyptic world, this bubbly dog stumbled into my life at just the right moment, bringing some light and hope into the darkness. I couldn't help but marvel at the coincidence of our meeting. It seemed like fate had brought us together, two lost souls seeking comfort in the midst of chaos.

In a swift motion, she leaped onto her hind legs and placed her front paws on my shoulders. I marveled at her strength despite her physical exhaustion from all she had been through. Like me, she was a fighter, and I could see my resilience mirrored in her. Our shared struggle against the forces united us. We shared a silent communication, our souls intertwining.

The following day, she was already by the door when the first rays of sunlight peeked in through the window. Her nails scratched against the wood as she pushed it open with her nose, and her tail wagged wildly behind her in anticipation. The cool morning air brushed against her fur, urging her to venture outside and explore the world that awaited.

We carefully made our way through the debris. She avoided obstacles like broken glass, tall grass, concrete pieces, and twisted tree branches. My trust in her was unshakable. She had a talent for spotting danger and leading us to safety.

At one point, she came to a halt and looked back at me with shining eyes and a wagging tail. It was as if she wanted to ensure that I was still by her side, united in this journey.

A warm smile curved my lips as I reassured her with a nod. Yes, I was with her to the end. And so we continued our journey, traversing desolate landscapes and barren wastelands. The world showed us the devastation of humanity, with only ruins and decay left.

During those quiet moments, amidst the rubble and wreckage, I found comfort in her presence. I confided in her my deepest fears and regrets, knowing she would keep them in her trusting heart.

My newly befriended companion listened closely, her gaze piercing mine as if she comprehended every syllable. Even if it was just a four-legged companion, having a dog by my side gave me relief and comfort. I no longer felt alone in the world.

Sometimes, in the night's silence, I would catch her staring intently at the moon, her head tilted to the celestial glow above. It was as if she understood the universe's vastness and fragility.

We searched through the empty houses, looking for anything we could use. She was a natural hunter, picking up subtle clues and quickly putting together the pieces of what used to be someone's home. Together, we hunted down food and supplies, returning to our campsite with a full bag slung over my shoulder.

The nights were long and filled with uncertainty, but there were also moments of peace and reflection. I marveled at our strength as we huddled under the starlit sky.

The world crumbled around us, but we did not. Instead, we rose from the ashes, more vital than ever. Amidst this new world, we discovered pockets of beauty that chaos hadn't ruined. Fields of wildflowers danced with the wind, their vibrant colors offering relief from desolation.

I watched as she ran across the field, her ears flopping with each stride while she grinned a toothy smile of pure bliss. The sun shone down on her white fur and highlighted her twinkle. With every jump, a sense of lightness filled my heart and lifted the world's weight away.

One day, we trudged through the dense wilderness, her nose twitching at each unfamiliar scent. She surged ahead with newfound energy, and I followed, curious about what captivated her. We emerged into a sun-dappled clearing and a crystal-clear lake glistening in the sunlight. The surface shimmered like a thousand diamonds.

Without hesitation, she plunged into the water, her movements graceful and fluid. Her head popped up, and she paddled towards me with a gleeful expression. Something about her in that moment, her wet fur glimmering in the sunlight, made me feel the pure bliss I hadn't experienced in years.

We spent hours in that hidden oasis, swimming and splashing, letting the water wash away our burdens. It was a rare moment of comfort, a reminder of beauty in this brutal world. And for those precious moments, we lived, reveling in life's simple joys.

I felt a renewed sense of purpose as we left the haven behind. The world had not yet fallen into complete darkness. In the chaos, we would continue to seek those hidden pockets of beauty and hold on to them with all our might. They kept us motivated, fueling our determination to survive.

As the days passed, I watched fall colors fade, and winter began. Snowflakes swirled and danced in the gray sky, filling the meadows and forests until everything was white.

I watched my companion move gracefully and quickly through the soft snow blanket. Joyfully whirling in circles, her barking echoed like music. I stood there captivated by her endless energy and enthusiasm.

During those long winter nights, I would find peace in her presence. We sought refuge in whatever shelter we could find. She became my anchor in this tumultuous world, a constant source of love and support when all else seemed lost.

We became more robust and resilient in the face of hardship as time passed. But we were also exhausted, with the weight of survival taking its toll. Yet, when I looked into those warm brown eyes, I knew we would get through it.

Finally, our trek brought us back to where it all began, the YMCA. We made camp inside and were ready for rest. The future loomed before us, dark and unforgiving. I knew that no matter what horrors awaited us, we would face them together.

CHAPTER TEN

Echoes of a Lost City

I felt pride as I strode down the deserted street, my heavy boots crunching shards of glass and rubble beneath them. Each step reminded me of my resilience and the mental fortitude it took to survive in this harsh world.

The only sound breaking the silence was the soft padding of Maggie's paws against the cracked pavement. My loyal companion stayed close, her presence offering comfort and companionship in a place where both were scarce. With Maggie by my side, I felt a sense of purpose and belonging, even in this desolate landscape.

As we rounded a corner, an enormous red sign with faded white letters declared "Pet Store." Maggie's excitement was palpable as she tugged eagerly on her leash towards the crumbling remains of the store. I followed, my heart racing, anticipating what we might find inside.

Broken glass and scattered chew toys littered the store entrance, but Maggie didn't seem to mind as she bounded over them, her nails clicking rhythmically on the tiled floor. Her nose worked furiously as she explored every nook and cranny, her tail wagging fiercely with each discovery. Leaning against a dusty shelf, I couldn't help but smile as I watched her joyful exploration.

Maggie burst through the debris, her nostrils flaring with excitement. Her tail wagged in a steady rhythm as she scoured the ruins for hidden treasures. She sniffed every nook and cranny, searching for anything of value. Suddenly, her nose caught a familiar scent, and she let out a joyful bark.

I followed her gaze and saw her pounce on an old stuffed squirrel. Her joy was evident in every wag of her tail. As she happily pranced around, she stumbled upon a squeaky ball, and her excitement reached new heights.

I couldn't help but smile at the sight of her pure joy. "Looks like you hit the jackpot, Maggie," I chuckled as she looked up at me with a mischievous glint. The rubble may have been a reminder of the destruction, but it was a playground filled with endless possibilities for her.

After our shopping day, I took Maggie to a park she loved. There was a chill in the air, but the sun's rays and excitement kept us warm. We ran around and laughed. It delighted Maggie each time she found another spot to explore. When we stopped to rest, Maggie snuggled on my lap and fell asleep. I smiled, content with our time together. We stayed there, enjoying the park's peacefulness.

We were basking in the park when a chill settled over us, like something was lurking in the shadows. I saw a wall of thick, gray clouds rolling towards us, blotting out the brilliant blue sky. The wind picked up, and I grabbed our things and started for home.

The sky shed tears like delicate snowflakes, starting with a few sparse ones drifting slowly. As time passed, more and more flakes filled the sky, creating a wall of white.

The wind was a banshee's scream, and the snow came down in such a torrent that our faces stung with icy pellets. Visibility dropped to almost nothing, but we stumbled forward, knowing that if we continued, the warmth of the YMCA would be waiting for us.

Maggie's pace quickened, an intuitive understanding that we needed shelter before the storm swallowed us whole. The park, usually a place of sanctuary and happiness, transformed into a battleground against nature's fury.

The weight of the snow blanketed the land, caused the trees to bow and break, and their limbs reluctantly surrendered. Each crunch of frozen grass and ice was a battle between us and the elements, as my boots quickly filled with heavy powder, and I labored forward.

It felt like time slowed down, seconds stretching into eternity as we fought against the relentless storm. We pressed on, two lone figures in a sea of whiteness, our determination fueling each step.

My breath crystallized in the cold air, like miniature clouds of steam, while Maggie's tongue lashed out in a mix of exhaustion and resolve. The wind whipped at our faces and stung my icy fingers.

The path ahead seemed treacherous, but we pushed on. "Hang on, Maggie! We'll make it back, I promise!"

Maggie's fur bristled with excitement, her ears twitching forward as she let out a sharp bark. Her tail wagged rapidly from side to side, its fluffy tip describing an arc in the air as if to signal her determination.

As we walked through the blanketed landscape, our feet sank into the freshly fallen snow, leaving deep imprints. The gusts of wind howled around us, drowning out any other noise. Each step felt like a burden, and the heavy snow weighed down our bodies.

Each step felt like a weight on my chest, and I gasped for breath as the frigid air clawed through my lungs. Ice crystals clung to my eyelashes, obscuring my vision, and my nose was raw and dripping from the freezing temperatures. My body begged me to stop, but then a faint sparkle of light appeared in the distance, promising warmth and shelter.

"I see something, Maggie," I said, my voice shaking from the cold and exhaustion.

Maggie's ears perked up, her pace quickened as if she sensed our destination drawing near. The YMCA loomed ahead, its doors welcoming sights amidst the swirling storm. We stumbled towards it, our bodies shivering from the cold, but our spirits high.

With one last burst of energy, we reached the entrance, collapsing onto the lobby floor. We were safe for now. "We made it, Maggie. We made it."

Maggie let out a contented sigh and pressed her wet head against my chest, her eyes shining with gratitude. We arrived battered, weary, and cold, but we survived. As I closed my eyes, huddled against Maggie's warm fur, I couldn't help but feel triumph.

The snow continued to fall outside, its relentless embrace transforming the world into a frozen symphony. But within the YMCA walls, we found comfort in each other's presence. We knew that as long as we had each other, we would always find our way home.

Mother Nature can be extravagant. A snowstorm is already impressive, but a blizzard. That's just her showing off. The snow had been falling all morning and continued into the afternoon, blanketing the city in a thick white quilt. Towering piles of snow entirely buried the entrance to the Y.

I stepped outside with my shovel in hand, feeling the quietness of the street. The only audible sounds were the crunching of snow as I walked and the groaning of tree branches burdened by their weight. The world around me had an enchanting feeling, yet the chill in the air kept me grounded. For this was no dream.

I stuck the shovel blade in and pushed against it with all my weight. However, it only sank an inch before becoming too heavy for me to lift. My arms were shaking after I scooped only a few shovels. I could feel sweat gathering on my forehead as I stopped to take a break.

While I caught my breath, I looked around. Snow had covered every surface, turning the world into a blank canvas. It was striking in its simplicity and a reminder of how insignificant I was in the grand scheme. A crisp breeze blew past me, startling a few snowflakes out of the sky that stuck to my coat like white crumbs. I sighed deeply and felt despair creep in.

I knew it was hopeless. Even if I could shovel the entire pathway, the snow would return in a few hours, burying everything I had worked so hard to uncover. I was so exhausted that I barely had enough energy to trudge back inside, let alone shovel.

I had thought the convenience of the Y would save me from the frigid winter temperatures, but it didn't. I knew I needed to find a new place to stay before it got too cold, but having a familiar and safe place felt reassuring. Part of me was eager to search for a new home, while another part wanted to delay and remain where it was secure.

After four long, dreary days of huddling in our makeshift shelter, the elusive sun finally broke through the heavy layers of clouds. I quickly stuffed our tattered belongings into my worn-out backpack, my heart overflowing with anticipation of what lay ahead.

My faithful companion, Maggie, stretched her legs and wagged her tail, content to be out in the fresh air. We did not know our future but were determined to face it together. Our mission was to find a new home that offered us warmth and safety.

As we wandered through the eerie towns, I felt overwhelmed by the emptiness. The silence was deafening and oppressive. Every home and shop served as a reminder of what we had lost. In all this sadness, Maggie's presence was the comfort that motivated me. But even her companionship couldn't stop me from being haunted by my doubts about our future.

I occasionally found a car parked crooked, its engine long dead. With a mixture of trepidation and hope, I would try to start it. I knew its convenience would be a valuable resource that could help me cover longer distances. But always, the vehicles remained stubbornly silent, their keys mocking me.

As I wandered the twisting path, I found ways to lift my spirits. I created stories about the little creatures that lived in the trees and bushes around me. I gave them silly names like Fizzlebottom and Tanglefoot and had them go on ridiculous adventures together.

I couldn't help but laugh out loud, which always brought a stern look from Maggie as I imagined their antics. In those moments, I realized joy could still find its way into my heart.

I had lost all track of time before I stumbled upon a new city.

As I gazed upon the majestic ruins of what used to be a vibrant cityscape, a frenzy of emotions, reverence, sadness, and rage swept through me. I stared at the towering buildings reduced to mere skeletons.

It was as if time had frozen them, preserving this tragic scene for future generations. The remnants of human greed and destruction were all too clear, their oppressive weight weighing heavily on my heart.

As I walked down the abandoned city streets, nature had reclaimed its territory with a vengeance. Ivy and vines infiltrated every crevice of the decaying buildings, their verdant growth contrasting starkly against the bleak concrete. A heavy silence hung in the air, interrupted only by the gentle rustling of leaves and the waves crashing against a forgotten shore.

"This, my friend," I whispered, "is the price of human arrogance."

But despite the devastation, humor bubbled up. I laughed at the thought of a tourist finding this post-apocalyptic paradise. "Sorry folks, no deep-dish pizza today," I mused aloud, a wry smile playing at the corners of my lips.

As I walked, the jagged pavement crunched and cracked under my feet. As I approached the lake's shoreline, I saw the towering condominiums in the distance. However, their formerly impressive façade now showed signs of decay and ruin, with balconies jutting out at odd angles like a toppled stack of blocks from a child's toy set. It was almost as if an angry deity had sculpted this abstract structure, creating an unsettling yet intriguing sight.

As I looked around, it was easy to picture people rushing past, their hurried footsteps adding to the city's symphony. I could almost hear the blaring horns of the cars and buses rushing up and down the crowded streets. Even in its ruined state, I could practically feel the energy and excitement that must have once existed here.

I climbed the stairs of one building, my heart heavy with the weight of the past. From the top, I could see the vast expanse of the lake, stretching out as far as the eye could see. It used to be beautiful and luxurious, but now it has become a ghost town. But even in its dilapidated state, it held a strange allure. A reminder that everything in life is temporary and that even the grandest of things can fall.

The wind picked up, carrying the echoes of a forgotten city. I closed my eyes and let it wash over me, feeling a sense of melancholy and peace all at once. This place had a soul, and I felt drawn to it like a moth to a flame.

I walked down the staircase and stepped out into the sun's warm embrace. I felt a sense of familiarity washed over me. I felt at home, even though I had never been here before. It was as if this place called out to me, urging me to stay.

I turned to Maggie and said, "Let's find a room with a view."

CHAPTER ELEVEN

Shoreline Serenity

The dry air had hovered still, and the only sounds had been my footsteps as I had inched forward, prepared for anything. A profound silence had hung in the air, broken only by the distant lapping of the waves against the shore and a light lake breeze that ruffled leaves and stirred up a dusk mist.

With each cautious step, uncertainty lifted off my shoulders as the devastated streets whispered stories of a forgotten era; the buildings stood like silent witnesses to the unfolding destruction. Yet, in the midst of chaos, I had managed to detect a glimpse of salvation—a high-rise condominium which drew power from solar energy.

The small brass elevator buttons gleamed under the sunlight cast by dozens of miniature glass chandeliers. I pressed the one marked Penthouse and took a stance on the metal grate floor. I shifted from foot to foot as the cables groaned overhead and set off the elevator on its descent through the shaft.

The elevator hummed as it rose, each floor passing slower than I thought possible. I grew excited in anticipation of what was to come. At last, the doors opened into the opulent penthouse and all my expectations were surpassed. Exquisite furniture, artworks, and sculptures adorned every corner, a breathtaking display of wealth and good taste.

The condominium sprawled before me, its regal presence magnified by the sun's rays streaming in through the windows. Its rooms and hallways were cozy and inviting, full of warmth. A sense of surprise and safety raced through my veins as I stood there, allowing me to forget for just a moment all the challenges I faced.

"Pretty nice digs, wouldn't you say, Maggie?" I said, turning towards my faithful companion, who wagged her tail.

It was a small victory, but in that moment, it felt like a triumph in the face of despair. I unpacked the modest supplies from my tattered backpack, a meager feast would sustain us for a while.

As I heated up a can of black beans for dinner, a jolt of emotion surged through my veins. Gratitude overwhelmed me as I realized the luck and privilege had allowed this moment to take place. The scent of the beans filling the room was a reminder of how far I had come and how blessed I was.

Sitting at the sleek, modern dining table, I savored each bite, gazing at the breathtaking lake view. Its pristine waters mirrored the pink hues of the sky, creating a serene image that washed away the weariness that had plagued my soul.

A contented sigh escaped my lips, a rare moment of peace amidst the chaos. In this secluded haven atop the world, I basked in the tranquility. I knew it was a temporary break from the trials ahead.

With a satisfied belly, I headed towards the master bedroom, drawn by the promise of a good night's sleep. And before me stood one of the grandest king-size beds I had ever seen, adorned with a thick-down comforter beckoned me closer.

The bed's allure was irresistible, and for a moment, I contemplated surrendering to its inviting embrace. But the responsibilities of survival urged me onward, knowing a deep slumber awaited once I secured our temporary sanctuary.

As I turned away from the bed, my heart heavy with the weight of the coming winter, a spectral veil of snow descended outside the window. The delicate beauty of the snowflakes reminded me of the long and harsh season ahead.

I turned my gaze away from the wintry scene, searching for peace in the comfort of the room. And there, in the corner, I found a loveseat adorned with fluffy pillows. This promised a place to curl up and escape the world's burdens.

Without hesitation, Maggie claimed the loveseat as her own,

snuggling up among the plush pillows. Her eyes closed, blissful sleep washing over her weary frame.

I couldn't help but envy her ability to find peace so effortlessly. I stroked Maggie's head with a wistful smile, grateful for her unwavering presence. In this barren world, she was my anchor, a reminder that love and connection could still be found amidst nothingness.

The snowfall outside intensified, a haunting reminder of the impending hardships of the coming winter. It was a bitter pill to swallow, realizing survival depended on enduring the harshest conditions.

"Maggie," I said, my voice breaking the uneasy silence. "What was the purpose of my life? What is the meaning of my survival in this useless world?"

Maggie lifted her head, her eyes staring back at me with a depth of understanding that transcended her canine nature. It was as if she comprehended the weight of existential questions that plagued my mind.

The heaviness in my heart lifted, replaced by a glimmer of hope. I took a deep breath, determined to find strength in adversity. I wanted to survive this winter that threatened to swallow me whole.

Nightfall encircled the city, casting long shadows that danced across the remnants of what once was. The solitude weighed on my soul, but in the quiet embrace of the condominium, I found comfort.

Lighting a few candles, their warm glow illuminated the space with a delicate ambiance, warding off the pitch-black darkness beyond the walls. It was a feeble attempt to reclaim normalcy, to push back against the encroaching void.

The world outside remained silent, holding its breath in anticipation of hardships ahead. Despite this, I clung to the flicker of hope that burned within in this forsaken place. This was a stubborn defiance to the despair that threatened to consume me.

Sitting at the edge of the bed, I let out a weary sigh. The weight of survival was heavy on my tired shoulders. But the luxurious bedding whispered promises of repose, urging me to surrender to its embrace.

I crawled into the bed, nestled in the soft comforter. A sigh of contentment escaped me as I sank into the mattress, feeling its plush warmth cover me. In that moment, surrounded by the silence of the night and the subtle hum of the condominium, I found a semblance of peace.

It was a fragile relief, but it ignited a drive within me. This resolve was to face whatever challenges the coming days would bring. I whispered a final prayer into the darkness as my eyes grew heavy. I asked for courage and strength in the face of the unknown.

As the world outside lay dormant, I drifted into a realm where hope bloomed and nightmares faded. It was a fragile sanctuary, a whispered promise in a world torn asunder. And as sleep claimed me, I clung tightly to the belief that, against all odds, survival was within reach.

Dreams intertwined with reality, each blurring into the other as the night passed. The boundaries between what was and what could be became hazy, allowing me to imagine a world filled with life and laughter again.

The winds howled outside, carrying a haunting symphony of forgotten echoes. But within the condominium walls, sheltered from the harshness of reality, I slept, finding peace in the darkness.

As each hour passed, I wrote another chapter of hope in the tranquil dream. My subconscious chose and forged paths of courage for me to confidently face what lay ahead.

The following day, I awoke to the glorious sunbeams shining through the grand window of the penthouse. Brilliant streaks of vibrant colors cascaded across the antique furniture and fine artwork. Luxurious velvet couches, beautiful landscape paintings, intricately decorated vases, and delicate porcelain ceramics. Everywhere I looked, sheer beauty and magnificence abounded.

A stunning chandelier hung from the center of the room,

casting light rays through delicate window patterns. They covered the walls in floral wallpaper with intricate golden tassels. I brushed my fingers against a vase that must have been centuries old and examined an elaborately painted ceramic plate displayed on a shelf.

I scanned my surroundings, pondering why the devastation spared it from destruction like me. A wave of bittersweet nostalgia washed over me as I remembered everything had an expiration date. And that perpetual permanence is just a fancy notion.

Photographs, decorations, and luxurious furniture held no significance in this empty existence. I walked over to the floor-to-ceiling bookshelf. There, I perused philosophy, science, and religion titles. Each book offered a glimpse into humanity's deep questions. However, I sought personal and relevant answers to my predicament.

"What is the purpose of my survival?" I murmured, hoping the books themselves would provide the answers.

The study was a warm, inviting space filled with the gentle scent of ancient leather and paper. They covered the walls with tall shelves filled with antique books.

I stepped inside and peered around the room. A fine layer of dust muted the sunlight spilling through the windows on the antique lamps. This created a dreamlike brilliance that beckoned me further into the chamber of secrets.

I saw a leather-bound journal wedged between two volumes on

a nearby shelf. The title, Daily Reflections of James Scully. I hesitantly ran my fingers along its spine, feeling the leather's softness against my skin.

I opened it and read the faded ink that filled the pages, words of wisdom, reflections, and diary entries. As I flipped through each page, my curiosity peaked, and I found myself quickly engrossed in the world within its words.

Sarah, my dear friend, in the darkest moments of our lives, we often find the brightest light. We've shared countless moments of joy, laughter, and love.

Those moments have shaped who we are and are imprinted on our souls. And now, as you face this challenging trial, I want you to carry those moments with you.

Let them be the strength that propels you forward. You are a warrior, Sarah. You have faced adversity before; you've always emerged stronger and braver.

This battle may be the toughest yet, but I believe in you. I have faith that your spirit will overcome. Do not be afraid of the unknown, my friend.

Life is a journey filled with twists and turns, unexpected joys, and heartbreaking sorrows. But these very challenges mold us into who we are meant to be.

Embrace this journey every step of the way. You are not alone in this, Sarah. We will walk this path together, hand in hand.

And no matter what lies ahead, have faith in yourself, life's beauty, and love's unwavering power.

I read the words over and over, my fingers tracing the lines as I searched for answers. My mind swirled with questions, each one more uncertain than the last. What gave him this insight, this hope? Was there something he knew I didn't know? Is there something secret that gave him the courage to believe? Something intangible that I couldn't quite make sense of.

Despite the turmoil and longing for an answer I couldn't name, I only saw a void. I slowly shut the journal with both hands, feeling its weight in my palms. My eyes stared out the window, and I sighed heavily, knowing there was no definite answer to my quest. My strength failed me as I realized I'd have to take a leap of faith and trust. I had enough courage and belief to carry on. With trembling fingers, I placed the journal back on its shelf.

James' writings made me question whether I could find my life in the ruins of what was once grand. Instead, it lay somewhere inside me. A mysterious and unfathomable concept that I couldn't quite make sense of.

The lavish surroundings suffocated me, while the loneliness and emptiness of the outside world haunted me. It scared me to leave the comfort of the walls, yet I felt trapped by the overwhelming extravagance. I couldn't bring myself to take a step forward or back, and I felt like I was being slowly suffocated.

I was battling with myself, weighing the risks of moving forward into the unknown against the safety of staying inside the walls.

I was desperate to find something to fill the void within me, but I feared the consequences if I made the wrong choice. I struggled to decide which route to take, and the pressure of making the right decision was crushing.

CHAPTER TWELVE

Radio Enticement

In this lonely world, my thoughts were the only constant. My voice echoed inside my head, a lonely symphony in a silent landscape. The weight of isolation was too much for me to bear, even with Maggie by my side.

As we wandered through deserted streets and abandoned buildings, I couldn't help but feel a sense of uncertainty. The world as I knew it had ended, and it seemed like there was no hope left. But I refused to give up. I knew that there had to be others out there somewhere.

Maggie was my steadfast companion, always by my side. Her warm fur and wagging tail were the only things that comforted me in this empty world. It was as if she understood my every thought, every feeling. Maybe she did.

As we searched for signs of life, I couldn't help but feel a sense of nostalgia for the world that once was. The cozy homes and bustling streets were now replaced with rubble and decay. But as bleak as our surroundings were, I refused to let go of hope.

And then we saw a small glimmer of light in the distance. A town untouched by time, beckoning us forward. It was a sign that maybe, just maybe, there was still something worth living for in this broken world.

The town emerged like an oasis, a mirage of life amidst the desolate wasteland stretching for miles in every direction. It stood as a stark contrast to the endless expanse of barrenness, its presence commanding attention. As we journeyed down the cracked sidewalks, the buildings rose like weathered sentinels, telling tales of grandeur and decay.

A mosaic of crumbling brick and gleaming glass adorned the structures, a testament to the passage of time and neglect. Each building stood as a silent witness to the town's former glory, now marred by the wear and tear of years gone by. Yet, there was an undeniable allure in their dilapidation, as if they held secrets whispered only to those who cared to listen.

Along the streets, trees stood tall and proud, their branches arched overhead, forming a verdant canopy that shielded us from the relentless assault of the blistering sun. The dappling light that filtered through the foliage danced upon the cracked pavement, casting delicate shadows that seemed to breathe life into the forgotten corners of this forsaken place.

Abandoned vehicles lay scattered haphazardly along the curbs, their once vibrant colors now faded and weathered by the unforgiving elements. Lifeless shells baked under the scorching sun, their metal frames groaning in protest. Faded and peeling paint offered glimpses of when these cars roamed the streets with purpose, now relegated to mere relics of a bygone era.

Spiderweb cracks adorned the windshields like intricate lace, fragile yet enduring. I couldn't help but peer inside each car as I passed, catching glimpses of remnants left behind by a vanished populace. Discarded coffee cups nestled in cup holders, their lids stained with rings of forgotten mornings. Faded receipts clung to dashboard surfaces, their ink barely legible, a ghostly reminder of forgotten transactions.

As we ventured deeper into the heart of the town, Maggie's nails clicked along the sidewalk beside me, her tail wagging with eager anticipation. Her senses seemed attuned to the mysteries that lay ahead. The police station loomed prominently in our path, its faded sign creaking mournfully in the hot wind, an invitation to explore what lay within.

Maggie's ears perked up at the sight, her pace quickening as if she sensed something stirring inside. I paused, instinctively reaching for her collar, a silent command to wait.

I strained my ears, hoping to catch any sound that might betray a presence within the station's walls. But all that greeted us was a overwhelming silence, as if the building held its breath, guarding its secrets until the right moment to reveal them.

I think she recognized the place as a shelter and a haven where broken souls had once found protection. I pushed open the creaky door, its rusty hinges protesting against the sudden intrusion.

The air inside was heavy with stale neglect, thick with the scent of forgotten years. Sunlight filtered through the cracks in the windows, danced with dust particles in a hushed ballet. It cast an ethereal glow on the deserted desks and chairs, adding an almost whimsical touch to their abandonment.

Faded posters of missing people lined the walls. Maggie moved around the room, her keen nose leading to every corner. It was as if she were searching for something, or someone. I wondered about the mysteries her senses would uncover.

The desks and chairs bore the weight of time, untouched for years and cloaked in a layer of grime that told its own story. Cobwebs stretched their delicate threads from wall to wall in corners shrouded in darkness, a testament to the room's long-standing vacancy.

The soft scurrying sounds of unseen creatures echoed from these hidden pockets, adding to the eerie symphony of this abandoned place.

Yet amidst its neglect, there was a peculiar allure to this room. It held an uncanny comfort I hadn't experienced in what felt like lifetimes. It was as if this place, despite its forgotten state, resonated with a part of me that had been missing for far too long.

As I forcefully opened the door labeled "janitorial supplies," the rusty hinges emitted a shrill screech. The small room contained shelves of half-used cleaning products, their labels faded and peeling. The overpowering stench of bleach and disinfectants burned my nose, stinging my eyes.

With determination and the help of some robust cleaning supplies, I began to strip away the layers of grime that had accumulated over years of neglect. The daunting task was intimidating, but I was determined to return this forgotten space to its former glory. My hands gripped a worn mop and a bucket filled with soapy water, ready to scrub and shine until every surface gleamed with renewed life.

“Maggie, we’ve found our sanctuary,” I murmured, my voice echoing through the silence. Her eyes gleamed with trust and excitement, her panting sounding like whispers of encouragement.

After growing tired of mopping and dusting, I resumed my exploration of the other mahogany-paneled rooms. I couldn’t help but imagine the stories that once unfolded within these walls.

The faded photographs on the walls depicted brave officers in uniforms. Their expressions were resolute and determined. Now, their legacy lives on only in these crumbling hallways.

Suddenly, a creaking floorboard broke the silence, snapping me out of my reverie. I turned to find Maggie investigating a half-opened drawer, her tail wagging furiously. Curiosity was her nature, always seeking adventure in odd places.

"Maggie, what have you found?" I asked, kneeling beside her. She nudged the drawer with her nose, revealing a collection of forgotten trinkets. Among them was a worn notebook. I flipped through the pages, finding fragments of investigations and clues scattered across the worn-out paper.

The more I read, the deeper I delved into a web of secrets and hidden motives. Each page seemed to unveil an additional layer of complexity, leaving me intrigued and perplexed. I couldn't help but smile. Perhaps this quaint police station held more intrigue than I expected.

"Maggie, it looks like we've stumbled upon a treasure trove of tales," I said. My voice tinged with excitement. Maggie barked in agreement, her tail swishing back and forth. She eagerly sniffed her way inside the desk drawer.

She was pushing aside crumpled notepads and discarded pens to find something interesting. Her desk diving paid off when Maggie uncovered a dingy tennis ball tucked away in the back corner. She triumphantly seized it and pranced around the office

After some playful time with Maggie's newfound treasure, she leaped onto a dusty chair. Her claws dug into the fabric, leaving behind tracks in the accumulated dust. I couldn't help but smile at her nimble movements, a bright spot of joy in this dreary room.

On the other side of the office stood the police radio. The radio, its face covered in knobs and buttons worn from years of use, sat silently in the corner. It was a dull gray presence that oozed history.

I flicked a few switches but only received bits and pieces of broken static and ghostly crackling as a response. Beside it, Maggie stood alert, her tail thumping against the floorboards as she leaned closer to investigate. Her nose twitched as she sniffed at its edges with curiosity.

I couldn't resist the infectious joy radiating from her. Soon, we found ourselves engaged in a playful fetch game with a forgotten police baton. "Good girl, Maggie!" I exclaimed, laughter bubbling from deep within me. It was a rare moment of fun in this lonely existence, a reminder that life could still bring joy in all its simplicity.

Maggie and I settled into our newfound sanctuary as the hours turned into days. We made the police station our home, finding comfort in its walls. Maggie would often curl up on the red leather worn-out couch, her head resting on my lap, as I recounted tales of the world that once was.

We often ventured into town, hoping to find a living soul. I would call out to the empty streets, my voice swallowed by the vast emptiness. The echoes of our loneliness reverberated back to us, mocking our futile attempts.

Each day, as the sun dipped below the horizon, we returned to the police station, our spirits dampened by the fruitless search. Maggie nuzzled against me, her eyes filled with longing. We were two lost souls, adrift in a sea of desolation.

One evening I took advantage of my occasional perk and powered up the generator. The dull hum of the machine filled the air as I made my way through the dimly lit office. My worn boots scuffed against the age-worn linoleum floor, stirring up puffs of dust that danced in the dim light. The radio console glowed softly in the corner, its buttons and dials illuminated by a soft orange light that cast ghostly shadows across the room.

My fingers delicately traced the edges of each dial and knob, my movements precise and deliberate. I settled into my chair. I tweaked each button, carefully adjusting and fine-tuning until they were just right. Suddenly, a sharp crackle burst through the previously quiet room, its raw energy filling the air with a jolt of electricity.

Taking a deep breath, I braced myself and pushed the microphone button with shaky hands. My voice vibrated off the concrete walls, blending with a sizzle of static in a chaotic crescendo of optimism.

"Hello...anybody there? I need help. Please tell me someone's out there?" Quietness was all that came back at me, impersonating an empty black hole ready to swallow me up.

As my heart seemed to sink into despair, a sudden and unfamiliar voice sliced through the overwhelming stillness. Its words were like a beacon in the pitch-black night, bringing a glimmer of hope I had not felt in what seemed like ages.

"Yes...I can hear you," it whispered.

CHAPTER THIRTEEN

Cryptic Words

A surge of electricity shot through my body, jolting me with anticipation as I brought the radio headset to my ear. The crackling static seemed to amplify the suspense, making the hair on my arms stand on end. And then, like a beacon in the darkness, a faint voice emerged from the chaos.

Soft and ethereal yet filled with an undeniable sense of hope, it spoke: "The truth lies in the shadows, in the places you least expect it." I shivered as I heard the voice speak. I knew there was more to these words than just a simple phrase. It was like a puzzle, and I was determined to solve it.

I jotted down the words I had heard, hoping to decipher their meaning. As I studied them, I felt a strange sense of familiarity. It was as if I had listened to these words in a dream or a long-forgotten memory.

"I don't have much time," the voice continued, its urgency hanging like a palpable weight. "But I wanted to let you know I'm here." Joy surged through my veins like a raging river. I gripped the microphone tighter, feeling its cold metal press against my palms as I hung onto each word. It reignited my sense of purpose.

"Who are you? Where are you?" I asked, my voice trembling with emotion. But before the voice could answer, the connection wavered. Static consumed the airwaves once more.

I yelled until my throat was raw, begging for the voice to return, so I could hear its comforting words a little longer. But no answer came. All I heard was the harshness of silence. I collapsed against the chair, a heavy stone settling on my shoulders again.

The moment she left, I found myself with more questions than answers. But through the disappointment and frustration, a fire ignited within me, fueled by a newfound hope. I would find this mysterious voice, this guardian angel of the airwaves.

I would search every corner of the desolate world and face all dangers. And overcome any obstacle, for that voice had given me something I had long lost: The belief in humanity's staunch spirit.

My mind spun with a whirlwind of emotions: surprise, confusion, perplexity, all tangled together in a chaotic dance. How could this voice have disappeared so abruptly? It was as if someone had pulled the rug out from under me just when I thought I was gaining solid ground.

A knot formed in my stomach as reality sank in. Perhaps this mysterious guardian angel was not what it seemed after all.

Early the following day, I wandered through the city. I searched for any sign, any clue that could lead me to her. But the city remained silent, its streets devoid of life.

With each passing day, my radio remained silent, with no sign of life or communication from her. I worried I might never hear her voice again, let alone locate her. Doubt and despair consumed me, extinguishing the flicker of hope within me. But I was determined not to allow the darkness to consume me completely.

Maggie and I set out with renewed hope of finding this woman daily, but we return empty-handed each evening to the station. Today was no exception; after a meager dinner, I sprawled out on the worn red leather sofa by the front window and heard rain tapping against the glass.

But tonight, the air seemed different. The sound of the rain relentlessly hitting the windows was like a desperate plea for entry. The tension in the room was palpable, weighing down on me like a heavyweight. I could tell Maggie was just as unsettled as I was; she could sense the looming danger outside just as much as I could.

The heavy rain pelted the window as lightning lit up the sky. Despite the loud sound of thunder, all I could hear were my racing thoughts. I huddled in a corner of the room, clinging to what little shelter it offered me from the elements.

As the darkness settled over me, my thoughts swelled and danced like the shadows on the walls. Each flash of lightning illuminated a distinct memory. Each clap of thunder echoed my inner turmoil.

The storm outside mirrored the tempest within me, causing my mind to race and my heart to ache with uncertainty. Was this just a coincidence or a sign from the universe? A challenge to test my strength in the face of chaos? I couldn't help but wonder as I lay there, listening to the tumultuous symphony outside. The storm was relentless while I fought to make sense of my inner storm.

The wind rattled the windows and shook the doors, whipping through the trees and creating menacing howls that echoed into the early morning hours. It sounded like a chorus of ghosts singing in the dark.

With a heavy, exhausted sigh, I collapsed into my sleeping bag. My body felt like it had been through the wringer, drained of energy and consumed by discomfort.

The darkness of night encircled me, but it was no comfort as the heat of a raging fever burned beneath my skin. Unrelenting and impossible to ignore, it prickled and prodded at my senses.

Tremors shook my body, each icy shiver sending shockwaves

through my core. Despite the clammy warmth that radiated from within, my fingertips were cold and shaky.

Minutes seemed like hours as I tossed and turned in my cover of nylon and fluff. But there was no refuge from the relentless fever, even in fitful sleep. Every muscle seemed to convulse in protest, seeking relief that never came. Desperate for coolness, I searched for any patch of fabric that wasn't saturated with moisture, a futile effort.

Sweat dripped down my face and soaked through every layer of clothing until even the interior walls of my sleeping bag clung to me like a second skin. The dampness seeped into every crevice, leaving me feeling suffocated and trapped.

With each shiver came a rustling chorus from the walls, a reminder of my solitary struggle against the night and its haunting symphony outside.

In my delirious state, time seemed to warp and twist, leaving me confused and disoriented. Waves of pain crashed over me, blurring my thoughts until they were just disjointed fragments.

Lost in a hazy realm of uncertainty, I drifted aimlessly without a concept of time or reason. Whispers, barely audible at first, grew louder and turned into a dissonance of agony. The sound echoed through every fiber of my being.

My grip tightened on the blankets as I convulsed in a desperate attempt to escape the madness that threatened to consume me entirely.

It was like being trapped in a never-ending nightmare, each moment stretching on for an eternity. The air was thick with a sense of foreboding and despair, suffocating me as I struggled to find clarity or understanding.

Suddenly, I heard a low static hum from the radio from somewhere in the darkness. My heart stopped for an instant and then thumped against my chest. Could it be her? Was she out there looking for me? A tiny flame of hope flickered in my mind.

Tiredness pressed down on my body like a ton of bricks, but with every ounce of strength, I pushed myself up and stumbled towards the console. My desire to find the source of the voice echoed in my dreams and drove me forward.

And then, amidst the static, I heard a voice say, "Are you there? Are you there?" Joy filled my soul as I struggled to respond.

I yanked on the microphone's cord, bringing the mic down to my level on the floor. The metallic clink of the stand echoed through the room. My fingers curled around the cool metal of the mic as I brought it closer to my lips.

My voice was weak and barely audible, but I whispered, "Yes… yes, I'm here." The voice on the other end sounded relieved.

"I've been trying to reach you for days. I was worried something had happened to you."

I coughed, my throat raw and dry.

"I've been sick… but I'm here now. Please, tell me who you are. Where are you?" There was a pause, as if the voice was considering its response.

"I can't tell you that just yet. It's not safe. But I promise we will meet soon. I have information that could change everything."

My heart raced with anticipation. "What kind of information? What do you know?"

The voice hesitated, and I could sense the weight of the words it was about to speak.

"Not now. I haven't enough time left, but soon."

A surge of hope coursed through my veins. "How can I help? What do you need from me?"

The voice chuckled softly. "Patience, my friend. I will reveal all in due time. But for now, rest and regain your strength. We will find each other soon."

My limbs felt like jelly, and my breath was shallow. I lay back on my bed, staring at the ceiling with heavy eyes as the voice echoed in my mind. A newfound purpose settled in me, and I found a renewed sense of hope.

I felt my eyelids droop as I replayed the soothing words of the unknown voice. But as time passed, my fever raged on, and it filled my mind with terrifying visions that kept me awake. My body trembled as I fought to make it through each day, and then the fever broke, and I was free from its cruel grasp.

I scoured the few remaining shops for supplies I might need and spent my nights poring over maps and creating a plan. Maggie was like a lamp during those dark days. Her kind eyes and steady presence kept me going when all seemed lost.

Once again, we resumed our daily task in search of the mesmerizing voice. We ventured out into the desolate city, peering down alleyways and up into windows as if our lives depended on it. Yet despite that, we heard no sound besides the echoes of our footsteps.

We pushed the boundaries of our journey today, scaling a steep incline to reach the top of a hillside. It was an arduous climb, but the view from the summit was worth it. The city below sprawled out before us in all its splendor.

I approached the edge hesitantly and looked down at the sheer drop below. My heart raced as I balanced carefully on the slick rocks, feeling a twisting fear in my stomach.

It was nearly dusk, and I could feel my hair being tossed back from my face by the gusts of cold air that swept up from the city below. The hazy orange sky streaked with tendrils of dark gray that seemed to warn me of something sinister.

As the sky darkened, a hum of electricity filled my ears, and tiny hairs on my arms raised in anticipation. Maggie and I raced down the hillside and into the city. The wind ripped through the empty streets like wild animals. Tossing trash cans and scattering papers until they were swirling debris clouds. The storm brought with it an ominous energy that made my heart race.

I dashed towards the police station for safety. Rain showered in cold, sharp drops, stinging any exposed skin. I reached the entrance just as lightning struck nearby, illuminating the daunting building ahead in a flicker of blue light.

The aging structure creaked under the force of the wind that rattled its windows. I found safety at my desk, lit by the comforting light emanating from the radio station's console. A feeling of sereneness came over me as white noise surrounded me, flooding me with recollections of the mysterious voice.

I wondered if the voice had found refuge from the raging storm. I hoped that, eventually, the chaos would subside. But as time passed, so did the storm's fury.

I sat upright in my chair, wringing my hands together as my mind wandered. The storm outside had worsened, and I felt a strange anxiety rise inside me, as if it were warning me of what was to come.

I stood up and made my way to the window. A sudden boom of thunder rattled the glass and sent a shockwave through the room. A blinding flash of lightning followed, illuminating the street below. The intense heat from the bolt seared my skin, causing me to stumble backward and collapse onto the floor.

My limbs felt sluggish, and my head spun as the fever took hold of me once again.

I shivered as I shuffled into my sleeping bag, huddling into a tight ball. A searing fever surged through my veins, blurring the world around me and making it difficult to think. The heat boiled up inside me until it drenched me in sweat.

I tossed and turned, my mind a battlefield of terrifying images. I felt trapped in some kind of twisted nightmare, unable to escape. And then, the radio sparked to life. I swear it was like a voice from another world reaching out to me. "Are you there? Are you there?" It said repeatedly.

My heart rate picked up. I knew I had to answer and prove that I was still alive and present. But how? I felt like I was teetering on the edge of a cliff, each passing moment taking me closer to a point of no return.

I tried to speak and make any sound that would show my presence, but nothing came out. My body felt numb and unresponsive, as if frozen in time. Panic set in as I realized how far away I was from help.

The voice on the other end seemed to grow more urgent with

each passing moment. It was a desperate plea for help that left me feeling helpless and alone. Tears blurred my vision as the darkness crept closer and closer.

I strained to hear the distant voice calling out my name, praying for an end to this nightmare. But even that faded as exhaustion took hold.

At that moment, with nothing left but my thoughts, I silently begged for anyone to save me from this madness before it swallowed me whole.

The next day, the next week, I don't know. I opened my eyes to an unfamiliar stillness. Rain pattered against the windowsill, and a chilly breeze blew through the open window. The radio lay silent. It's usual-static now, just a hiss of emptiness. I dragged myself out of bed, feeling my strength return with each step.

I twiddled the dial of the radio, seeking a static-free station to fill my ears with a voice I hadn't heard in days. I sat for hours in silence as the room grew dark. Did I anger or displease the voice so much that it never wanted to return? Yet, despite my pain and loneliness, a faint wisp of hope remained that perhaps the voice would come back one day.

I slowly regained my energy. I shuffled through the deserted streets, leaning heavily against Maggie's comforting presence. We passed over cracks in the pavement and broken glass from shattered storefronts. The ghostly quietness thickened with each step. There were signs of destruction everywhere we looked, but no trace of the mysterious voice.

My hope felt like a flame doused with water, and I wondered if the voice I had heard was nothing more than my desperate dream. Doubt filled my mind until it seemed like the fire had never existed.

But then, one day, sitting on a park bench outside the police station and watching Maggie dragging a stick she found. I heard a familiar crackle from the radio inside. My heart skipped a beat, and I raced inside to retrieve it. Could it be her? Could she have finally found me?

I pressed the button to transmit, my hands trembling with anticipation. And then, amidst the static, I heard a voice say, “I’ve found you. Meet me at the old radio tower on the outskirts of the city. It’s time.”

A wild energy surged through my body, obliterating every shred of doubt lurking deep within me. I felt alive. This was the moment I had yearned for. My heart raced with an icy thrill as I embraced the possibilities that lay before me.

I filled my backpack with provisions and set off towards the distant radio tower, Maggie trotting by my side. With each footstep, the city seemed to get more dilapidated. Buildings were half-collapsed, and vines snaked through rusted chain-link fences. But I didn’t let any of it deter me. I kept pushing forward, driven by the mysterious voice I had heard and the promise of something better that lay beyond it. As we trudged through the ruins, I felt a surge of hope.

At long last, I arrived at the abandoned radio tower. The building towered over the shattered cityscape in a stark, yet comforting way. Despite this despair, the tower told me all would be well again one day.

Inhaling a shaky breath, I mounted the tower ladder, my feet heavy with intimidation. The voice that had pursued me had led me to this place, and soon, I would confront it in person.

I pushed open the door at the top of the tower, and there, standing before me, was the woman whose voice had kept me going all these months.

CHAPTER FOURTEEN

Carpentry For Dummies

The mysterious voice I had been trying to find for weeks was not from a person, but from a computer. Before me stood a massive bank of computers, each bearing the engraved words "A.I.R.S., Artificial Intelligent Response Systems, property of Forest Grove Technical Institute."

I stood frozen in the dimly lit chamber, my breath caught in amazement and terror. The very air around me hummed with the pulsating hum of a thousand processors, each beating like the heartbeat of some digital giant lurking in them. The glowing embers of countless LEDs cast eerie shadows on the walls, dancing as if alive with the ghosts of questions sought and answers given.

For a moment, I doubted whether I was even at the right place until I peered through the grimy window on the opposite side of the room. I felt disappointed as I gazed upon Forest Grove Technical

Institute, its once-impressive buildings now crumbling into decay.

The shattered windows of the school reflected the sunlight, their sharp edges glinting as the overgrown vines clung to the sides of the buildings. The doors hung precariously on their rusted hinges, as if daring anyone to enter its abandoned halls. It was like a foreboding fortress, intimidating and uninviting.

I fought to regulate my breathing, but the rage inside me was almost overwhelming. I grasped for something, anything, to hold on to as my frustration continued to build. My mind felt like it was spinning out of control, and I was teetering on the edge of an endless void. I knew I had to leave this place before it consumed me entirely.

I push through the door, my fingers gripping the metal railing at the top of the tower to steady myself. As I leaned over the railing, the wind roared in my ears, snatching at my clothes and trying to pull me down.

My hair whipped wildly around my face, obscuring my vision as I gazed at the ground far below. A sense of vertigo washed over me, making my head swim and my stomach churn. The distant view of the earth spread out below me, like a patchwork quilt of greens and browns, made me feel insignificant against the vastness of nature.

As I descended towards the hard ground, the metal ladder creaked and groaned beneath my weight. The cool metal pressed against my palms and the soles of my feet, grounding me in the present moment. My initial disappointment slowly dissipated with every rung I left behind.

As I reached the bottom, a dry laugh escaped me as I glanced over at Maggie and muttered, "No one home."

I left the radio tower and started the long walk back home. I felt my heart heavy with disappointment as I thought of the endless wasteland before me. I had been searching for so long but only found my loneliness.

I thought of Maggie and the warm feeling of companionship she had given me. I had been so sure that I would find someone out there, someone to share my life with. I had been so desperate to escape the loneliness of my life, to find a home.

But there was nothing out here. All I found was a bleak, empty wasteland. I was alone, and I was going to stay that way. I shuffled forward, determined to make it back home. I was tired, and I didn't know what else to do. I felt like I had failed and wasted all my time searching.

In the distance, an enormous warehouse loomed above me with its bright yellow sign that read Builder's Lumber Warehouse. My feet kicked up stones as I made my way towards the entrance, passing towering stacks of wood on either side of me. The crunch of gravel beneath my boots echoed in the empty lot, leading me closer to the large metal doors at the end of the pathway.

When I entered the lumber store, my nostrils filled with a pungent mix of sawdust and wood stain. Rows upon rows of shelves lined the walls, overflowing with tools of all shapes and sizes. My gaze traveled from the shiny hammers to the electric drills and everything in between, captivated by the endless possibilities for DIY projects.

I grabbed a cordless drill from the pegboard, my palms tingling with excitement. After months of searching every town, I finally had a collection of books that needed a proper home, a bookshelf. My fingers were practically itching with anticipation as I imagined each shelf coming together like puzzle pieces. With each hole drilled and screw tightened, my project would take shape, a testament to my dedication and determination.

As I walked through the lumber yard, I marveled at the sheer amount of wood surrounding me. The variety of colors and textures was astounding, each piece telling its unique story. I could imagine the trees being carefully harvested and crafted into these slats, ready to be used for various projects.

As I made my way towards the back of the yard, a stack of rough, unfinished logs caught my attention. They stood tall and proud, their bark still intact. I couldn't help but wonder what they would become in the hands of a skilled carpenter.

Would they become a beautiful dining table or perhaps a sturdy bookshelf? The possibilities seemed endless, and I found myself lost in thought, imagining how I could transform these simple logs into something new.

A brilliant idea struck me like a bolt of lightning. Why not build that bookshelf while I'm at it and remodel the old police station? With newfound conviction, I marched back into the store and handpicked all the tools and supplies.

With each item I added, my bag felt heavier, but I knew they were essential for bringing my vision to life. As I returned to the police station, excitement bubbled inside me like a pot on the stove. I couldn't wait to get started on this rousing project.

Despite my lack of experience, I eagerly donned a dusty carpenter's apron from the Builder's store and secured it around my waist. A trusty tape measure swung from my belt as I gathered the materials for my first construction endeavor.

With grit in my heart and tools, I meticulously measured and marked each piece, my hands shaking with anticipation and nerves. Little did I know that this simple task would turn into an all-day adventure, testing my skills and patience to the limit.

Maggie watched me from the doorway. She noticed that my clumsy attempts at completing the task resulted in more mistakes than successes.

"Don't worry, Maggie," I said, scratching behind her ears. "We'll figure this out together."

My fingers traced the familiar pages of my well-worn carpenter's handbook, filled with my scribbled notes and precise measurements. I chuckled at the title, "Carpentry for Dummies," knowing it perfectly fits me.

My hands trembled as I attempted to align the edges of the wooden bookshelf, surrounded by an intimidating array of tools. A hammer, saws, and measuring tapes lay scattered around me, a testament to my resolve to get this project right.

Yet, despite all of my preparation and equipment, the wood seemed to have a mind of its own, resisting my attempts at shaping it into a functional piece of furniture. I checked and rechecked my measurements, but the project continued to go badly.

I stepped back, wiping the fine sawdust off my calloused hands and onto my dirty jeans. Frustration boiled in my chest, ready to burst out at any moment. Cursing under my breath, I surveyed my latest project.

The bookshelf's wonky edges and uneven cuts were a glaring reminder of my lack of skill as a woodworker. I still had a long way to go before creating anything remotely impressive with this stubborn material. If I wanted to produce something more than mediocre, I needed much more practice and experience.

Maggie bound around the workshop, picking up scrap pieces of wood to play with as I sifted through heaps of wood and scattered tools. To redeem myself after a disastrous first attempt, I handpicked each piece for my new project, a storage table. I scrutinized the quality and condition of each piece, ensuring that they were sturdy and free from any defects.

With Maggie's playful energy keeping me company, I felt inspired to create a beautiful, functional piece of furniture that showcases my improved woodworking skills.

With sawdust clinging to my work gloves, I proudly surveyed the finished product. It was almost perfect, except for a tiny mishap. I noticed that I had attached two of the legs backward! Amidst Maggie's barking and wagging tail, I couldn't help but laugh at my silly mistake.

My hands were sore from hours of work, and I felt like I was making still more mistakes. I had made so many, but I was determined to get it right this time.

I had spent days constructing, sanding, and staining the wood, and finally, my storage table was complete. The smell of sawdust filled the air with pride as I looked around the room. I had done it, and I was ready for the next challenge.

The table creaked as it held the weight of two cases of bottled water, two 25-pound bags of dog food, and a Labrador retriever, who seemed to enjoy the attention of being the center of the display.

Her tail wagged as she pawed at the items, creating a cacophony of clinks and clangs that echoed through the room. The table stood steadfast as the items continued to be piled on top, its sturdy surface not showing any signs of strain. Now, onto my next project.

The screwdriver slipped from my fingers as I cursed, watching the tiny screws for my living room chair bounce on the floor. The wet sensation of a canine nose nudging my arm jolted my attention. Maggie was rigid, her eyes darting to the door with intense focus. Every muscle in her body seemed on high alert, waiting for something to come through.

I spun around, coming face to face with a tiny squirrel. Its tail quivered as it gazed at us with an expression of bewilderment. Maggie barked and dashed around the room, leaping over furniture frantically to capture the fuzzy critter. The madcap chaos of the scene brought a wry smile to my lips despite my desolation.

Maggie darted across the room, her tongue lolling and tail wagging wildly as she chased the squirrel from one corner to the next. I couldn't help but chuckle as I watched her until she finally scared the intruder away.

Over the next few days, I devoted myself to perfecting my projects, each day bringing improvement and growth. At last, one morning, I carefully hammered in the final nail, the satisfying sound echoing through the room.

My hands were sore, and my back ached from weeks of hard work. But it was all worth it to see the wonky bookshelf stand tall and strong, no longer sagging under the weight of books. I transformed my old, wobbly storage table into a sturdy piece of furniture.

Each item held its story, a testament to my tenacity and passion for this project. It was not just a physical transformation, but a personal one as well. My hard work and perseverance had paid off, and I felt a sense of pride and accomplishment.

Sitting on a log outside the newly remodeled police station, I couldn't believe how much it had transformed from a dilapidated shell into a quirky, one-of-a-kind shelter. It may not have been a masterpiece, but it was mine.

Just as I was about to revel in my accomplishment, a voice broke through the silence.

"Hey there." it said, sending a shiver down my spine.

CHAPTER FIFTEEN

Mystery Woman-

I whirled around, my pulse pounding in my ears. A young woman, thin and disheveled, stood behind me. We were both in tattered clothes, and her hair was streaked with mud as if she had been crawling through it. Our despair was palpable, like two souls connected in a moment of shared suffering.

The air between us was heavy, like a tangible force. Her eyes held the same hopelessness as mine, and I suddenly felt like we were two sides of the same coin.

My voice trembled barely more than a whisper as I asked, "Are you okay?"

She nodded, her face pale and drawn, her eyes reflecting the weight of her struggles. "I'm as okay as I can be. Mind if I join you?" she asked softly, gesturing towards the log beside me.

I nodded, unable to find words to express my gratitude for her company. She settled down next to me, folding her legs beneath her with ease.

We sat there momentarily, our eyes locked in a silent conversation, the tension and unspoken emotions between us palpable.

My hands shook as I nervously ran my fingers through my tangled hair, trying to smooth it down.

"Uh, hi," I stammered, my voice cracking with embarrassment. The dirt and sweat on my brow were evidence of days without proper hygiene. "I'm Collin."

As I extended my arm towards her, a rush of warmth coated my skin when our hands connected. Her touch was comforting and inviting, the first human contact I had experienced in years. A genuine smile spread across her face, causing the corners of her eyes to crease with joy.

"Collin, huh?" The woman echoed my name. "Nice to meet you. I'm Kathleen." Her smile radiated warmth, instantly putting me at ease in her presence.

As I looked at her, a sense of relief flooded through me. The weight of isolation and loneliness began to lift as we stood together, the old police station looming behind us. It felt odd to have someone else beside me after years of solitude. My heart pounded with a mixture of bewilderment and excitement.

“How did you find me?” I couldn’t help but ask, amazed that someone did.

“I heard hammering and knew someone must be here,” she said.

Suddenly, laughter bubbled up from Kathleen’s throat, breaking the heavy silence like a burst of sunlight piercing through storm clouds.

“I can’t believe it; after all this time, I’d finally stumble upon another person by following the sound of hammering,” she chuckled, her eyes sparkling with amusement.

I found myself laughing too. The sound felt strange and foreign after years of solitary silence. “

Kathleen’s eyes widened as she looked at Maggie beside me. “Well, well, what do we have here?” she said, her voice filled with surprise. “Another survivor?”

Maggie’s tail wagged eagerly as she greeted Kathleen with a happy lick. Kathleen’s hand reached down, her fingers brushing through Maggie’s fur as she patted her head. I couldn’t help but smile at the sight of them, a connection between them I hadn’t seen in a while.

“I still can’t wrap my head around it,” I said, running a hand through my hair. “I was convinced I was the only one left on this desolate planet until Maggie unexpectedly showed up for dinner one night."

“Well, it looks like fate had different plans for you, didn’t it?” She laughed, the sound filling the air with life and warmth.

I nodded, feeling a weight lift from my shoulders at her laughter. It was a sound I didn’t think I would ever hear again.

“And now, fate has brought us together,” Kathleen said, a hint of hope shining in her eyes.

Her words rang true in my heart as we stood beneath the shelter of the old police station, the building creaking with the weight of time. It was as if the universe had conspired to bring us together in this unlikely place under these impossible circumstances.

Kathleen glanced at the decaying wall I had been working on. “What exactly are you doing?”

"I'm just trying to fix up this abandoned police station. I figured it could make for a decent shelter, you know?”

“Well, it won’t be a luxurious five-star hotel,” Kathleen said with a smirk.

“More like a one-star prison,” I joked in response.

She nodded. “As for me, I’ve been staying in a supermarket.

It's not the most comfortable place, but it gets the job done."

As I welcomed Kathleen into the old police station, I felt joy in seeing another human being after years of isolation. She blinked in the dim light of the flickering candle, her eyes wide with wonder as she took in the peeling walls and faded posters.

"Wow, this place is something else," Kathleen said, a hint of laughter in her voice as she settled onto one of the rigid and tattered chairs. "I can't believe this is where you've been living all this time."

I chuckled, the sound echoing off the walls. "Yeah, it's not exactly the Ritz, but it's home."

I handed her a cup of hot coffee, savoring the rare and precious find. The aroma filled the air, mingling with the scent of dust and neglect that seemed to cling to everything in the station.

Kathleen took a sip, closing her eyes in bliss. "This is amazing. I don't remember the last time I had a cup of coffee."

I nodded, watching as she wrapped her hands around the mug, a small smile tugging at her lips. For a moment, the weight of the world seemed to lift from my shoulders as we sat in companionable silence, the only sound filling the room being the soft hum of the flickering candle.

"So, how did you find this place?"

I leaned back against the old police desk I used as a dining table, running a hand through my unruly hair.

“It was pure chance, to be honest. I stumbled upon it while scavenging for supplies from one town to another. And strangely enough, this place felt like home to me.”

“Home? A police station felt like home, what are you a criminal on the run?” She laughed but I think maybe she had some doubts about the stranger sitting next to her.

“No, no!!” I said. “Sorry I worded that poorly, I only meant the town felt like home.”

My gaze fixed on the floor, my cheeks burning with embarrassment and shame at my foolish words. I could only imagine what she must have thought of me. Then suddenly, a burst of laughter erupted from her lips, shattering the tense and awkward silence that had fallen between us.

"I'm glad to know that," she said through giggles, "I was beginning to wonder if Maggie was the jailer."

Our laughter filled the once-quiet room, echoing off the walls as I nervously fiddled with my hands. It was clear that I hadn't engaged in a conversation with anyone in quite some time, but her infectious joy and warmth made it easy for me to let go of my own inhibitions and join in the merriment.

Kathleen's eyes widened, an incredulous smile lighting up her face. "I never thought I'd run into another living soul. It's like a miracle."

I nodded. "You're telling me. I had almost given up hope of finding anyone else out here."

We shared tales and jokes, basking in each other's presence and comfort.

Suddenly, she sat up straight in her chair, her hand shooting up with a spark of excitement. It was as if she was back in grade school, eager to share the answer.

"I'll never forget the time I was stuck in a dark, dingy basement with nothing but a mop to defend myself against a horde of scurrying rats," She hugged her arms tightly to her body, pressing her knees together and bouncing her feet up and down in a fidgety rhythm. A look of revulsion flashed across her face as she scrunched up her nose and exclaimed with disgust, "Ugh."

Her sparkling hazel eyes met mine, and a smile slowly spread across her face. As she let out a small giggle, it quickly escalated into a full-blown snort. The sound echoed through the room, causing her to blush and cover her face with her hands in embarrassment.

But as I couldn't contain my own laughter, she relaxed and let out one final snort before composing herself. Her cheeks were flushed pink with mirth, and her eyes sparkled with joy as we shared a moment of pure hilarity together.

"That must have been one heck of a battle," I chuckled. I leaned in closer, speaking in a hushed tone. "One time, I had to use an old tire as a makeshift toilet. Desperate times call for creative solutions, don't you think?"

Kathleen chuckled and shook her head, impressed by my resourcefulness. She expressed relief that she never had to resort to such tactics.

I savored the warmth of her laughter amidst the coldness of our surroundings. The flickering candle on the makeshift table cast dancing shadows on the walls, adding a touch of whimsy to our conversation.

Memories were all we had now, pieces of a world that crumbled around us. But as Kathleen shared her story, it felt like those fragments were coming alive again, breathing new life into our lonely existence. Her resilience and humor ignited a spark, reminding me that joy still existed.

I watched tears stream down her cheeks as she doubled over in uncontrollable mirth. Her laughter was like a breath of fresh air, filling me with joy and breaking through the numbness that had settled over me for so long.

Maggie's tail wagged furiously as she sprinted in happy circles around us, her pink tongue lolling out of her mouth. Her soft brown eyes were bright with excitement, and her goofy grin was infectious.

As the laughter subsided, a heavy silence filled the room. Kathleen's face changed from lighthearted to serious as she asked me, "How did you manage to endure all this time? The burden of loneliness must have been overwhelming. I know it was for me." Her voice quivered with empathy.

As I look down at the cracked floor, a symbol of all that has gone wrong in my life, I let out a heavy sigh.

"Loneliness was my constant companion, too. It was like a shadow that never left my side. Every morning, I struggled to find the motivation to get out of bed. Without Maggie, I may have succumbed to my darker thoughts."

Kathleen's eyes glisten with unshed tears, a deep well of sorrow bubbling beneath the surface. "I won't sugarcoat it, Collin," she said, trembling. "It was excruciating. But I clung to books, paintings, and anything that I could find that would offer even the briefest refuge from this brutal reality. With you and Maggie beside me, I finally feel like I can release all the tension and have more faith in something."

Her words were a thunderous battle cry, igniting a fierce sense of determination within me. We stood tall, the last remnants of humanity in a world ravaged by chaos and destruction. We made a promise that day that we would refuse to succumb to despair any longer. We would unite against whatever hardships lay ahead on this desolate battlefield.

Outside, a gust of wind swept through the streets, almost like it carried hope on its invisible wings. At that moment, I couldn't help but feel optimistic as I thought about our new friendship and how it would keep us grounded amidst the turmoil and desolation surrounding us.

"Kathleen, I'm glad you found your way here," I said with a smile tugging at my lips.

She returned the smile and extended a hand toward me. "Likewise, Collin. Let's do this, shall we?"

Maybe if we had been able to glimpse into the future, our confidence would not have been so unshakeable.

CHAPTER SIXTEEN
Despair in the Night

My eyes fluttered open to the camper stove's gentle hiss and the flickering flame's dim glow. The scent of coffee drifted through the air, mingling with the musty smell of the police station.

Kathleen sat hunched over the stove, her small frame barely visible in the shadows as she carefully heated our morning brew. Her auburn hair was in a ponytail, and her wrinkled shirt showed wear from her travels.

Our plan for the day comprised a hasty breakfast of cold rice and coffee before exploring a five-mile radius of our station. The cool morning air made for a pleasant walk as Maggie searched for her latest treasure. After about two hours of searching, we stumbled upon the ruins of a strip mall with a few stores that were not wholly destroyed.

A colossal warehouse store sat at the mall's heart. It used to be a one-stop shop, selling everything from small trinkets like chewing gum to large household appliances. Luckily, the devastation only demolished half its structure, making it a unique find in this desolated world.

Regrettably, the area containing non-perishable items and canned goods had sustained severe damage. Despite this, there were boxes of popcorn that withstood the destruction. After all, you can't just sit and witness the world's end without a bowl of freshly popped popcorn.

Despite the wreckage surrounding us, the electronics and clothing sections of the store remained surprisingly untouched. Kathleen wasted no time sifting through the racks of clothing, her deft fingers caressing fabrics and colors as she selected sturdy jeans, warm shirts, cozy socks, and even camouflage overalls.

I couldn't help but raise an eyebrow and ask her why she needed such an item in a world where most forms of life had been decimated. She flashed me a mischievous grin before coyly replying that one could never be too prepared. Then she turned and continued shopping.

Kathleen, always the optimist, suggested we gather as many comforts as possible, which could run on batteries like a CD player or portable DVD player. We even found some camping supplies and a 40-watt solar generator to help make our lives a little easier.

Amid the heavy burden of our reality, we craved a sense of normality, even if it was just temporary. It was surprising how much a few songs and movies playing in the old police station could make a difference.

So, each night, we would heat our precious popcorn over the camper stove and immerse ourselves in the glow of a movie playing on a battery-powered portable DVD player. It was our fleeting escape, a stolen respite from the relentless demands of survival.

But as the days stretched on, the comfort we found in those movies felt like a cruel taunt. The characters on screen lived everyday lives, free from the shackles of this suffocating reality. It became unbearable to witness their laughter and love, tormented by a world that was forever out of reach.

"We should spend a night under the stars," Kathleen's voice broke through my reverie. "Just us, the sky, and the silence."

I nodded in silent agreement. And so, as the stars emerged in the ink-black sky, we gathered blankets and ventured outside, leaving the safety of the police station behind. The night air was cool, carrying whispers of a world long gone but not forgotten.

A bittersweet sense of freedom washed over us as we lay under the vast expanse of the heavens, mingling with the remnants of hope that refused to be snuffed out.

As the chilly evening air nipped at our skin, Kathleen and Maggie huddled close together for warmth, their breaths visible in the fading light. I let out a tired sigh and leaned against a pile of rubble, grateful for the brief respite from our harsh reality.

The flickering flames provided some comfort in the darkness, but they couldn't erase the fear and unease on our faces. These past weeks had been tough on us; supplies were dwindling, and we were exhausted and needed a break.

As I turned to face Kathleen, the warm fire illuminated her long, wavy hair that fell in cascading layers down her back. She had a distant look in her eyes, and it seemed she carried a heavy burden on her shoulders. The flickering light cast shadows across her face, adding to her troubled expression.

I reached out and put my hand on hers, trying to comfort her. She smiled sadly and squeezed my hand tightly, as if I was the only thing keeping her from crumbling. We sat silently, watching the flames dance around us as the night crept closer.

I could feel the despair in the night. Even the stars seemed dimmer, as if they were mourning the loss of so many lives. I wanted to tell Kathleen everything would be okay, but I knew better. Nothing would ever be the same again.

"Kathleen," I began cautiously, my voice breaking the silence like a distant echo. "What was it like before... all of this?"

I could see the glimmer of tears in Kathleen's eyes as she looked at me, her lips trembling. She fidgeted with the frayed cuffs of her leather jacket, trying to hold back the emotions threatening to overwhelm her. Her voice caught as she spoke, and I could tell memories were resurfacing from a place deep within her.

"Oh, Collin," she finally spoke, her voice tinged with melancholy. "You want to know about my life before all this?"

I nodded, urging her to continue. "Yeah, I'm curious."

"I grew up on a dairy farm, you know. Waking up at the crack of dawn was a daily ritual. My brothers and I would stumble out of bed, bleary-eyed and half-asleep, to milk and feed the cows. It wasn't a simple life, but it was ours."

I leaned forward, entranced by her words. "What was it like?"

Her voice softened with fondness, and she smiled as she spoke. "I remember those days on the farm," she said. "While the boys were out milking the cows, my mother and I would be in the kitchen. The smell of sizzling bacon filled the air as we cracked two dozen eggs into a skillet. And when it was all done, we'd sit down to a stack of fluffy hotcakes piled high like a mountain."

As she described the savory dishes vividly, my stomach rumbled loudly, giving away my hunger. "That sounds like a feast for a band of warriors," I exclaimed.

She smiled, her eyes twinkling as she nodded. "That's it, that's exactly what it was. The kitchen was the heart of our home - a place of comfort, warmth, and sustenance."

"Our farm had been in our family for generations," Kathleen continued, her eyes clouded with sadness.

"But my brothers grew tired of that life. They dreamed of escape, a life without cows and manure. In their eyes, this farm was a burden. They even hoped our father would die soon so they could inherit and abandon the farm."

"My father, however, had no plans of letting go of our farm. Even after his passing, he envisioned our family continuing the tradition of working the land. He held onto this dream for as long as he could, and it was only when his health had deteriorated my brothers got their chance."

A gasp escaped me, unable to fathom such cruelty. "What happened next?"

I expected her to go on about her brothers, but the story veered differently. She surprised me by launching into vivid descriptions of her childhood. She reminisced about the smell of freshly plowed fields, the prickly feeling of hay under her bare feet, and the taste of sun-warmed tomatoes plucked straight from the vine.

Her face lit up as she spoke, and these memories brought her more happiness than any story about her brothers ever could. It was a life that may have seemed mundane to her brothers, but it was a life of joy and beauty to Kathleen.

The fire crackled and popped as we sat silently, our eyes fixed on the dancing flames. Kathleen's posture was tense, her shoulders hunched and her fingers nervously playing with the zipper of her jacket.

She took a deep breath and turned to me, her eyes pleading for understanding. I could see the struggle within her as she searched for the right words to continue her story. Eventually, she found the courage to speak, and her voice trembled as she shared more about her past.

"The day our father died, my brothers swarmed in like vultures to pick apart the carcass of our family's wealth. They left my mother and me alone, abandoning us to bear the burden of running the farm. But we were no match for their greed and cunning."

"Slowly, piece by piece, they took away everything from us until all that was left was a barren wasteland with no trace of our legacy. My mother, broken and defeated, sold what little remained to survive. The pain and betrayal still burns within me, a constant reminder of their ruthless betrayal."

Her words carried a heavy weight, the sorrow of her lost childhood reverberating through the crumbling remains around us. But then, as if revealing a hidden vulnerability, Kathleen offered something more.

"That's when I went to college. I wanted to change my life, to escape memories and create something different."

"And you did?"

Her eyes sparkled. “Yes, I did. I pursued my dream of becoming a nurse and worked my way up to the surgical ICU. It was challenging, but rewarding. I was there for people when they needed it the most.”

I couldn’t help but smile at her resilience, the quiet warrior with a past intertwined with mine. We were bound by this shared experience, like two lighthouses standing resolutely amid chaos.

As the flames danced before us, Kathleen and I sat in contemplative silence, the weight of our shared past heavy upon our hearts. Together, we learned that survival was not just physical endurance but also finding comfort in each other’s company. In those moments, we found strength in opening up and empathizing with one another, knowing that actual survival meant having someone to share the journey with.

Her stories captivated me, and I was eager to hear more. “Kathleen, can you share where you were when the explosion happened?” She hesitated, fiddling with a strand of hair, before finally meeting my gaze.

Her deep green eyes widened with terror, sparkling like emeralds in the fire’s light. The flickering flames cast a macabre glow on her pale skin, exaggerating every wrinkle and crease of worry etched on her face.

Her petite hands trembled violently, almost crushing the fabric of her jacket as she desperately clung to it. After what felt like an eternity, she finally spoke, her voice trembling with fear and desperation.

"I was at the hospital. In the basement, to be exact."

My eyebrows scrunched together as I leaned in closer, eager for an explanation. "What on earth were you doing down in the basement?" I asked, unable to hide my intrigue.

She curled her arms around herself, hugging her chest as if trying to hold herself together. Her chin trembled, betraying the emotion in her voice when she spoke.

"I was looking for some old medical records for a patient," she said. "They weren't in the computer system yet, so I thought they might still be in the archive records in the basement, you know? Just in case." Her gaze shifted between me and the ground.

I nodded, trying to understand her actions. "What happened when you were down there?"

Kathleen gasped sharply, and a solitary teardrop rolled down her cheek. "At first, I thought it was an earthquake. The ground trembled beneath my feet as I raced up the stairs, my mind racing with fear and uncertainty about what I would find."

Her voice trembled as she recounted the events, and her hands shook. I could almost see her tiptoeing through the dimly lit hospital hallway, her footsteps echoing off the sterile walls.

"When I reached the first floor, the sight before me was... indescribable. Lifeless bodies, scattered everywhere."

Chill-like icy fingers gripped my heart as I imagined the horror she must have witnessed. A pristine hospital, a beacon of healing and health, now transformed into a haunting cemetery. A place where life should thrive was now consumed by death.

"What did you do?"

"I couldn't stand there," Kathleen said, her voice filled with anguish. "I searched room after room, hoping to find anyone still clinging to life. But all I found was death."

My mind reeled, a thousand questions buzzing like bees in my head. I felt the tightness in my throat and a sickening knot in my stomach as Kathleen's words sunk in. Her voice was heavy with sadness, a deep sorrow for all that she had seen. But something else lay beneath her words, something she hadn't dared to mention yet. I had to know what it was.

"And then?"

Kathleen's lips quivered as she exhaled, her last breath of courage before the tears fell. Her eyes filled with regret and remorse as they met mine, and I felt my heart break for her.

"I saw her... a nurse, barely clinging to life. The explosion shredded the nurse's lab coat and soaked it in blood. The desperation in her eyes was immeasurable. I rushed to her side and held her hand as she gasped her final breath."

Kathleen's sorrow was so intense it felt like a physical presence stifling us both. She had been through so much pain and sadness. To think she thought she was possibly the last person left after the disastrous apocalypse. And in that moment, I grasped the gravity of her ordeal and how heavy the load she carried was.

Suddenly, my body convulsed, and an icy chill shot through my veins. Goosebumps erupted all over my skin as a wave of nausea crashed over me. My breaths came in ragged gasps, and my heart pounded wildly. Beads of sweat formed on my forehead, and I struggled to keep my balance as dizziness threatened to pull me under.

"Kathleen... I don't feel so good," I stammered.

As Kathleen rushed towards me, I could sense her fear in the air. I felt my legs buckle beneath me, and my vision blurred. The world around me spun and darkened.

As my vision blurred, a suffocating void seemed to engulf me, drowning out all other sensations. My body went rigid, and I couldn't even scream. Kathleen's face appeared, her features twisted with worry as she reached to grab my hand. Her grip was desperate, like a lifeline in the darkness.

Her voice sounded far away and muffled, like I heard it through a tunnel. My limbs felt heavy and uncooperative, as if invisible chains weighed them down. I strained to understand her words, but they seemed garbled and unfamiliar. Panic rose in my throat as I struggled to break free from the fog that held me captive.

Then my eyes closed, and I was alone in the darkness. I felt disconnected from my body, like a puppet controlled by strings I couldn't see. I could feel myself falling, but I could not slow it down. I was desperate to break free, but my attempts were futile.

I wandered in the shadows for an eternity, my hope dwindling with each passing moment. But suddenly, a small glimmer of light appeared in the distance, drawing me closer and closer until I could make out the silhouette of a woman. Her hair glowed in the light, but her face remained shrouded as she beckoned me towards her with open arms.

CHAPTER SEVENTEEN

Grateful for Kathleen

Have you ever thought about the person who risks their own life to save someone else's? They are the ones who fearlessly charge into blazing buildings or dive into freezing waters to save a stranger. Who are these noble heroes, and why aren't we all capable of such extraordinary acts? And do our lives truly merit their valiant deeds?

I groaned as my eyelids slowly lifted, revealing a dimly lit concrete floor beneath me. The cold seeped through my clothes and into my bones. My head throbbed with pain, and I couldn't remember how I got here. Confusion swirled in my mind, making it hard to focus or make sense of my surroundings.

My muscles quivered as if I had plunged into an arctic pool. My skin prickled with goosebumps, and my teeth chattered together desperately to generate warmth. A throbbing heat radiated throughout my body. It was as if a feverish inferno had engulfed me, its blazing hold tightening with each passing moment.

I desperately sought relief from suffering, but all that met my vision was darkness and the fever that had taken over my body. The looming threat of death hovered over me like a dark cloud, casting a shadow over the long, harrowing night ahead. It was as if I was trapped in an inferno, desperately seeking any relief from the relentless flames.

In and out of consciousness, I heard a faint voice calling me from the far corner of the room. Slowly, my heavy eyelids lifted, and I saw a figure standing there. Through the haze in my mind, I struggled to recognize who it was.

The vague shape spoke words of comfort and reassurance directly to me. "Don't worry, just rest." I felt relief wash over me at their soothing tone, but I couldn't find my voice to respond. Instead, I weakly nodded as the figure kindly draped a warm blanket over my trembling body.

As I slowly regained consciousness, I recognized the figure above me as Kathleen, her kind face and gentle touch soothing me. My fever had clouded my mind, but now I remembered she had been watching over me during my illness. Gratitude washed over me as I gazed up at her familiar face.

Her eyes darted around my flushed face, taking in the beads of sweat and how I was shivering despite the thick blankets covering me. "Collin," she whispered, "your temperature is through the roof. The symptoms are all there. It has to be malaria." Her hand rested gently on my forehead as she spoke.

The worst likely outcomes consumed my thoughts, causing my entire body to shake uncontrollably. The room seemed to spin around me, intensifying my panic with each passing moment. All I could do was listen in terror as Kathleen spoke.

"You need Coartem." Her voice was steady but determined. "It's the only medication that might save you. There's a chance it could be available at the military hospital if it still stands."

I looked into her eyes, filled with desperation. I knew I couldn't let her put her life at risk. "You can't go, Kathleen. It's too risky and too far for you to travel alone."

I reached out to touch her hand. "Just give me a day or two, and I'll be fine." Her green eyes softened, and her lips turned down sorrowfully.

"Collin, I need to go. You need this medication." She tried to sound confident, but I could sense her fear. "I don't want to leave you alone, but there's no other choice."

She leaned in, her breath warm against my ear, as she whispered urgently, "I have to go. This is a matter of life and death." Her lips brushed softly against my forehead in a fleeting kiss before she pulled away. The gravity of her words hung in the air, causing my heart to race with fear and concern.

"I promise I'll be back as soon as I can. You just rest and try to stay hydrated. I'll leave some food and water for you before I go."

Kathleen's voice trembled when she spoke those dreaded words: malaria. It was as if each syllable carried an unbearable weight that threatened to crush us both. My hands shook uncontrollably as I tried to process what she had just revealed.

Malaria was a disease that could steal away everything we had fought so hard for. Desperation welled inside me like a tidal wave, threatening to drown out any semblance of hope or strength.

The room fell silent, engulfed in a suffocating atmosphere of despair. Time seemed to stand still as we both absorbed the gravity of the situation.

My hands clenched into fists at my sides, trembling with frustration and powerlessness.

"I can't stop you," I said. "But please, promise me you'll be careful. I can't bear the thought of losing you."

She turned to face me, a slight smile playing on her lips. However, as I gazed into her eyes, I could detect a hint of uncertainty lurking beneath the surface. I had full faith in her skills and capabilities, but I also understood the immense burden that would soon rest on her shoulders. We were both aware of the risks she would encounter, and a sense of worry settled in my gut. Her courage and determination humbled me.

"I guarantee you, I won't abandon you." She kissed me on the forehead and stepped away.

Kathleen kneeled on the floor of her makeshift shelter, sorting through cans and jars for any remaining food. She pulled out a map, worn and creased from constant use, and traced her finger along the route to the military hospital.

With efficient movements, she carefully packed a sturdy backpack with essential items for survival. Cans of beans clinked against each other as she placed them next to water bottles and a compact first aid kit. As she tucked a sharp knife into a side pocket, it gleamed in the sunlight.

Her determined gaze met mine as she stood up, filled with determination and courage. She effortlessly swung the pack over her shoulder. With a confident stride, she set off on her journey. As she disappeared, the crunch of shattered glass and scattered debris echoed beneath her boots.

It's hard to describe the emotions I experienced at that moment. Someone who hardly knew me would risk her life for mine. I couldn't help but question whether I deserved such a selfless act of kindness.

As she faded into the barren wasteland of the outside world, the once familiar sounds and sights dissipated, leaving behind a deafening silence and all-consuming darkness. My old friend, nothingness, crept back in with its suffocating grip.

I was alone again, with only my thoughts for company. The unsettling quiet in the empty police station intensified the loneliness. I fought the urge to give in to my fever, but the darkness wrapped its cold arms around me and drew me into its mysterious depths as I drifted in and out of consciousness.

CHAPTER EIGHTEEN

Feverish Past Confrontation

Do we ever truly escape from the weight of our past? It hovers over us like a dark cloud, ready to unleash a storm of regret and doubt at any moment. No matter how hard I tried to live in the present, my mind always returned to what had already happened.

Today, my fever persisted, a relentless blaze coursing through my body, reigniting my past demons. Each thought became a battlefield where memories and emotions clashed in a never-ending war, an internal turmoil that mirrored my physical illness.

Lying in bed, beads of sweat formed on my forehead. Lines between reality and recollections blurred. The fever unlocked the chambers of my mind, releasing a flood of vivid images and haunting emotions I thought I had buried deep within.

The room felt saturated with the weight of the past, and the air became charged with unresolved sentiments. Each memory was a sharp blade, slicing through my consciousness, leaving wounds that throbbed with pain and regret. In the fevered haze, faces and voices from my past emerged like ghosts, haunting my mind.

The battle within me intensified as the fever persisted, a relentless force that seemed determined to unearth and confront the shadows I had long tried to suppress. Every rise and fall of my chest echoed the tumultuous clashes within. The pulsating sensation that had started as a physical response now mirrored the emotional upheaval.

I closed my eyes, hoping for peace, but the fevered dreams that ensued were like a reel of beautiful and agonizing moments playing out before me. As the fever continued its relentless assault, it became clear that this was not just a battle against a physical ailment; it was a reckoning with the unresolved fragments of my past, a confrontation that demanded acknowledgment and acceptance.

My frail body, a canvas splattered with the shades of both physical and emotional torment, lay drenched in sweat. As I surrendered to the comfort of slumber, a world of terrifying visions emerged in my dreams. Despite my best efforts to push them away, the haunting recollections of the Afghanistan War refused to leave an ever-present ghost that clung to my subconscious.

Each image was as vivid as yesterday. The faces I saw there tormented my dreams, suffering in ways I could not bear to think about. While I wanted nothing more than to forget, I still felt a heavy responsibility for my actions.

In my mind, I reached out to anyone for consolation, but my grasp found only empty air. I opened my eyes to see that I was alone. I had always been alone. It felt like an eternity since Kathleen had left to find Coartem, the medication I desperately needed. I prayed she would be alright out there, battling the dangers that roamed the decrepit towns.

Maggie curled up by my side, providing comfort. She may not understand what plagues me, but her unwavering loyalty eases my troubled mind, even if just a little.

"Why? Why did it have to be this way?" I asked the empty room. "So much suffering and loss, all for what?"

No one answered my desperate call as the wind blew my words into oblivion. A cacophony of moments flashed through my mind, weighing me down with emotions I couldn't shake. I hugged my sleeping bag closer to my body in a futile attempt at comfort. Overwhelmed by sadness and regret, I tried to find the courage to stand, but it was in vain.

I shut my eyes and drifted deeper into my dreams. Soon, the murkiness returned. It wrapped itself around me like a suffocating shroud. My mind was a whirlwind of never-ending thoughts, trapping me in their midst.

"Is this the moment I finally face my inner truths?" I whispered into the silence, barely able to hear my voice.

I heard a guttural growl, and my chest tightened as I strained to see the figure looming out of the darkness. Closer it slunk until I felt its rancid breath on my neck and saw myself in its eyes. Or what used to be me. The demon's eyes bore into mine with intense malice, and its lips curled up in an unholy grin of contempt.

The image answered my query with a single syllable. "Yes."

I knew what to do, but facing my true self scared me. Yet, I knew I had to face it if I wanted to be saved.

"You cannot escape me," it hissed, its sound dripping with venom. "I am your deepest fears and darkest desires."

I felt the crushing force of its words encompass me. Confusion was rampant and pulled me back to the sands of Afghanistan. Something suddenly filled my mind with a vivid recollection of the atrocious experiences that I had endured, leaving me utterly overwhelmed.

I felt the sweat pouring down my back and my pulse pounding as recollections of the battle reverberated. I licked my lips, tasting a metallic tang of blood.

The mud squelched beneath my boots, heavy with moisture and despair. Explosions thundered in the distance, a constant reminder of the horror that surrounded me. I could hear bullets whizzing past my head and smell acrid smoke rising from burning fires.

I marched forward, my grip tightened on my weapon with each step. I heard a cry that sent chills through me. Turning around, I saw a soldier lying in front of me in a pool of blood. His eyes were glazed over, pain etched into his face. As he stared at the sky, I silently prayed before turning away. I had left him behind as I continued with my mission.

I heard the ear-piercing screech of bullets and cries of agony. The stench of death filled my nostrils, making me nauseous. Panic coursed through my veins as I frantically wished for this nightmare to end.

I watched myself as I raised my bloodied rifle, my trembling hands trying to steady my aim. Across the field, shadows danced amidst the smoke, and silhouettes of enemy soldiers lurked behind the trees. I squeezed the trigger, and with a deafening crack, I sent a bullet flying towards my target. With grim satisfaction, I watched my enemy fall to the ground.

Once more, I aimed and squeezed the trigger, sending a single bullet flying. It hit its mark with lethal precision. The sound was like a sinister song reverberating in my ears. As I watched another enemy soldier perish, a wave of conflicting emotions washed over me.

Amidst the thick, gray smoke, figures emerged, their eyes locked onto mine with fierce determination. I gripped my weapon tighter, muscles tensed and ready to fight. Each pull of the trigger sent sharp bursts of sound echoing through the air as bullets flew towards my enemies like whispers of death.

One by one, they fell to the ground, some clasping at their wounds while others collapsed in pools of blood. But for every enemy I took down, ten more seemed to rise from the haze, their guns aimed at me. The battle raged on, a never-ending cycle of destruction and death.

My eyes widened as the chaos and destruction of the battle surrounded me. The sound of gunfire filled my ears, numbing my senses to its intensity. One by one, an endless barrage of bullets was killing my Boot Camp buddies and tearing apart their bodies.

My heart bled for them, a relentless fire burning in my chest as I vowed to protect them at all costs. Their sacrifices would not be in vain.

"I won't let them down!" I thought to myself.

With all the strength I had left, I rushed forward into the fray, bullets flying past me like menacing whispers. My heart thudded against my ribcage like a war drum, every beat urging me on as I leaped over fallen comrades and navigated around craters in the earth.

"Collin, do you think this is the right thing to do? Do you think you can save a life by taking a life?"

My eyes darted around the battlefield, trying to ignore the voice coming from all directions. Despite my hesitation, I knew I had no choice. With heavy steps, I made my way toward the figure, who stood in the middle of the fray with an unsettling smile on its face. Deep down, I wanted to turn away but knew I couldn't.

“I don’t know,” my voice choked with exhaustion and despair.

A twisted smile crept across its face. “And what if you fail? What if you cannot save a single life?”

My confidence shattered, leaving me feeling unsure. I couldn’t justify any admiration for my actions, and it overcame my psyche with doubt. But I gathered my courage and reminded myself that despite the mistakes I had made along the way, my intentions were still genuine.

I looked into the figures’ eyes and answered. “Then I’ll die trying.”

The figure laughed, the sound melding with the noise of war. “So be it.”

The mysterious figure disappeared in a blink, and with it, the nightmare. An unsettling stillness surrounded me, broken only by the thumping of my heart. Sorrow filled every inch of my being as I mustered the courage to open my eyes and face the harsh truth.

Trapped in a never-ending nightmare, I am constantly fighting against an unyielding force that refuses to let me go. Will I ever find freedom from this torment? The memories of my past continue to haunt me every day, a constant reminder of the horrors of war.

No matter how hard I try to escape this relentless nightmare, it holds onto me tightly, unwilling to let go. What else can I do in this ongoing battle? How much longer must I carry the weight of suffering on my shoulders?

I felt each life's loss, their cries of pain and anguish reverberating through my being. I was a vessel of destruction, caught in an everlasting hurricane of suffering. Although I wanted to end it, I couldn't. I was forever cursed to bear my sins, knowing that I would never atone for them.

The idea of taking a life in the name of a just cause seemed noble, but the weight of its consequences was suffocating. The guilt and anguish that came with it would burden my conscience forever.

It made me question the actual cost of war and the unimaginable suffering it brings. It also forced me to contemplate the value of life and the conflicting emotions that come with it when faced with such tough decisions.

I whispered to myself, "It's over now." I tried to convince myself that it was time to move on. But deep down, I knew that no matter where or what I did, the past would never let me go. With one last scream, the nightmare that had held me captive for so long finally released its grip. As my vision cleared, the old police station came into focus.

Dust particles floated through light beams that shone through broken windows and danced in my vision like tiny fireflies. With each breath I took, the musty scent of mildew filled my nostrils and reminded me of where I was.

The hours seemed to stretch on endlessly as I sat in the musty room of that old police station. My clothes and skin were slick with sweat. My legs and arms felt like lead weights. I did not know how long I'd been there, stuck in this place where time seemed to stand still. All I could do was sit and wait, praying for the end of my torment.

Maggie whined softly, mirroring my impatience. I stroked her gentle head, feeling warmth amidst the cold despair.

Then, a glimmer of hope appeared when all seemed lost. The reverberating clatter of feet echoed through the desolate hallway. My heart raced, filling me with relief for the first time in an eternity.

Kathleen burst through the door, waving a medication bottle. "I found it!" she exclaimed. "We'll get you feeling better soon, I'm sure."

I looked at my friend, overwhelmed with gratitude. "You do not know how much this means to me. I can never thank you enough for this."

She gently touched my forehead, brushing away the damp hair clinging to my skin. "You don't need to say a thing," she whispered. "Just focus on getting better."

Her hand paused on the lid of the medication bottle before twisting it open to remove a single white pill.

I took the Coartem medication and prayed for a speedy

recovery. Kathleen assured me she would remain by my side until the fever breaks, providing the comfort and support that only she can. I took a deep breath and drifted off to sleep.

But once more, the hallucinations danced before my eyes like phantoms. Reality and my imagination mixed, making it difficult to tell what was real and what wasn't.

In my delirium, I walked through a desolate wasteland, the remnants of a world ravaged by some unknown catastrophe. Charred buildings loomed on the horizon. Their skeletal remains were a stark reminder of the lives that once thrived within.

A loud, authoritative voice echoed through the air, almost as if coming from an unseen source. It said, "Arise and face your greatest test." As I approached the tall judge's desk, a brilliant light emanated from it, so bright that I could not distinguish who was sitting behind it.

I stumbled forward, exhausted and overwhelmed by multiple voices from an unknown source. As I got closer, my heart raced at seeing a gigantic amphitheater carved out of rocks. Its walls were tall and intimidating, like silent sentinels guarding the stage below. I squinted through the bright lights to make out a figure stepping out of the shadows with slow, deliberate steps.

"Welcome, my dear Collin, to the trial of your own making," the figure announced. Its voice carried a chilling echo that sent chills through my body. "Here's your chance for the freedom you request. Pass this test, and you shall find peace. Fail, and you shall remain lost in purgatory forever."

The trial began. As I walked, the memories of my life unfolded before me, blurred by the surreal dream-like state. My true love, Michelle, appeared before me with a longing and sorrowful gaze. "Do you still love me?" Her voice asked almost painfully.

"I never stopped," I stammered, my heart torn between joy and pain. "But you're gone, lost to me forever."

She smiled, a hauntingly beautiful expression tinged with sadness. "Then prove your love, prove that you are worthy. Sacrifice everything to save what's left of this world, including yourself."

I reached out to touch her, yearning for her warmth. But as my fingers grazed her ethereal form, she vanished, leaving me in a void of emptiness.

The trials grew increasingly perilous, obstacles born from my memories and regrets. I battled my inner demons, facing my darkest parts head-on. Fear, doubt, and despair threatened to consume me, but I summoned every ounce of strength within.

The hallucinations filled my mind with fear and anguish as grotesque demon forms manifested during my delusions. I felt self-hatred and could not let go of my past mistakes and failures.

I stood there, completely overwhelmed by the memories that washed over me. A ray of light suddenly cut through the darkness, and I gasped as it revealed the figure before me. It was tall and thin, with a long white robe that seemed to flutter in a non-existent breeze.

Its face remained hidden in the shadows, making it almost impossible to distinguish its features. I turned away as the strange being's laughter filled the surrounding air.

"Here, you must choose between death or a fate worse than death," it said in a deep voice. "Continue your test or accept your mortality and wander forevermore."

As I closed my eyes, darkness engulfed me like a suffocating shroud. It tightened its grip around my trembling body. This dream, this ethereal realm, was not a sanctuary but a treacherous labyrinth where my demons lurked in every shadowy corner.

When I opened my eyes again, I stood on the edge of a shimmering swimming pool. The familiar scent of chlorine filled the air. The sound of splashing water and children's laughter echoed around me. While the scene was vibrant, I noticed a tiny figure bobbing up and down in the sparkling blue water in the distance.

"Papa," a gentle voice called out, piercing through the darkness like a ray of light. It was my son, his innocent laughter echoing in my ears. His small face lit up with excitement as he swam towards me, his arms slicing through the water with determination.

"Remember when I was little? The time you taught me how to swim?" he asked.

The corners of my mouth curled into a tender smile as memories flooded my mind. A vivid scene unfolded before me. Our laughter mingled with the wind as I held his tiny hand, guiding him on his first independent journey into the deep end.

With each stroke, my heart soared with pride. His triumphant cheers filled the air, igniting a fire within me. In this dream, my son swam effortlessly to where I stood, a glimmer of accomplishment shining in his eyes.

"I did it, Papa!" he exclaimed. It filled his voice with joy and triumph. I knelt, wrapping my arms around his small, waterlogged body, unable to contain my pride.

"You did," I murmured, my voice thick with emotion. "You conquered your fears. I knew you would." And in that moment, as I held my son close, the world's weight lifted from my shoulders. And then, abruptly, the dream dissolved into darkness.

After a few moments, I heard my daughter's voice echoing through my mind. We stood among a lively crowd at the Girl Scout Father-Daughter square dance. The air buzzed with anticipation, knowing this would be a night we would remember forever.

"Papa," she whispered, "do you remember how we danced together at my Girl Scout father-daughter dance? We did our first square dance. You were so proud of me."

My daughter smiled, her eyes sparkling with excitement. I

couldn't help but mirror her joy, my heart swelling with pride at sharing this moment with her.

Together, hand in hand, we dove into the whirlwind of instructions. Left and right, do-si-do, allemande left, and promenade. We moved with hesitant grace, with each step intricately woven into the intricate dance. A symphony of giggles and laughter filled the air as we fumbled through the steps.

But despite our rookie status, every misstep strengthened our resolve. We pressed on, fueled by determination, our faces alight with growing confidence.

Those moments defined us, the trials that shaped our bond. And as the music swelled and the crowd cheered, my daughter glanced up at me, her eyes brimming with an intoxicating mix of triumph and love.

In that dream-filled moment, a surge of warmth coursed through my veins as memories of her radiant smile flooded my consciousness. The pride and joy I felt at that moment swelled within me like an orchestra building to an overwhelming climax.

And just as the dance concluded, my heart pounded with exhilaration. I knew this was not just a celebration of a dance mastered. Instead, it was a testament to the bond forged.

My daughter's gaze locked with mine, and emotion rushed through me. In that instant, I realized the depths of our bond and the trials we had conquered together. As long as we stood united, there was no obstacle too great, no challenge too daunting for us to overcome. Our journey had brought us to this defining moment, and without hesitation, we faced it hand in hand, ready to conquer whatever lay ahead.

With a twinkle in her eye, she gently squeezed my hand and whispered, "We did it, Papa."

"We love you, Papa!" The children's voices resonated in complete harmony and faded into the darkness.

Their laughter echoed through my very soul, filling me with an overwhelming sense of gratitude and love. Tears welled up in my eyes, threatening to spill over as I realized just how precious and irreplaceable these moments were with them.

From the depths of my soul, I knew their love would be my salvation. I opened my eyes with renewed purpose, ready to face my demons head-on.

"I'm done running," I declared, my voice unwavering. Darkness will no longer control me.

In a burst of light, I embraced determination fueled by my children's love. As I advanced, the demons trembled in fear, their malevolent energy cowering before my radiant warmth.

The battle was fierce, the clash of my newfound strength against their relentless darkness. Yet, I pressed on, my will unwavering.

With each strike, I shed the shackles of my past, forging a path towards redemption.

And then, in a final, triumphant crescendo, I emerged victorious. Love overcame the demons, which vanished into nothingness.

With one final push, my world shattered, collapsing into a swirling vortex of emotions and memories. And in that moment, I awoke from my fever-induced nightmare, my body drenched in sweat and trembling with exhaustion.

As my temperature subsided, I realized how lucky I was to survive. To have someone like Kathleen, who never gave up on me, who braved the dangers of this deranged world to relieve my suffering.

I owe her my life and will never forget her courage and selflessness. I will forever be grateful for the kindness she showed me and for her unwavering devotion to helping me.

My mind felt like an overloaded computer, trying to process the immense weight of my experiences. I was grateful for so much, yet some memories will always be wrong, like the endless horrors of war.

The images of war and emotions of what I endured will haunt me forever - the overwhelming fear, excruciating pain, and sheer desperation to survive. But amidst the darkness, glimmers of light refused to be snuffed out.

I held onto the unwavering resilience of those I helped and their steadfast refusal to give up despite facing unimaginable challenges. This will be the legacy that propels me forward, pushing me through a world still torn apart by conflict.

But there's the other beautiful side, the memories of my lovely children. Without them, I have no reason to fight. I keep them close to my heart, the moments we shared, the good times we had together.

I remember all the laughter, love, smiles, and joy they brought into my life. Even now, in the darkest of times, I can find a glimmer of light in the memories of my children.

They gave me the strength to keep going, never to give up, and to keep fighting, no matter how hard the battle may be. With them in my heart, I know I can make it through, no matter how tough it may seem.

And so, I released the pain of my past and embraced a future full of new possibilities. My family was my rock, providing me stability during all the turmoil. They never stopped encouraging me to keep fighting, and eventually, I found the courage to break free from my distress. To them, I owe everything. They are my reason for living.

CHAPTER NINETEEN

Leap Into The Unknown

Some days just feel like magic, you know? It's like the universe is winking at you, whispering that everything will fall into place. Today was one of those days for me. An overwhelming sense of hope and positivity filled me, as if the universe was guiding me towards success despite any obstacles in my path.

I had complete confidence that no matter what difficulties arose, I had the courage and resilience to overcome them and emerge even more invigorated and fearless.

Underneath my boots, the crisp symphony of twigs and dry leaves echoed through the thicket, a harmonious crunch that marked my cautious progress. Each step was a dance, avoiding the treacherous embrace of sharp stones and the labyrinth of tangled roots.

The late winter sun played hide-and-seek, casting a dappled

masterpiece of light onto the mossy carpet beneath the twisted limbs of timeless trees.

Kathleen, a silent companion in this woodland ballet, walked a few strides ahead. Her head swiveled left and right, a painter's brush capturing every nuance of the tranquil forest. Her keen, searching eyes were on a mission, scouring the shadows for any hint of movement or sign of life.

The desolate expanse seemed to stretch on for eternity. Its unforgiving terrain constantly reminded us of the struggle for survival that defined our existence. Each weary step was a battle won, and our tattered clothes and weary faces told tales of the hardships endured along the way.

The hours they seemed to slip away like sand through our fingers, each second a frantic race against time itself. We were teetering on the edge of survival, grasping the tiniest scraps that could piece together another day of life.

Our existence hung in the balance, fragile and uncertain like a spiderweb in a storm. Time seemed to slip away, and we struggled against it like sinking into quicksand.

How much longer could we endure in this harsh reality? How many more moments could we hold on before it all fell apart?

"Hurry, Collin." Kathleen's voice tinged with excitement. "We don't have much time."

I nodded, trying to catch my breath after scaling the steep incline. Sweat dripped down my face, and my heart was throbbing.

Maggie darted up the rich, brown trail, her short legs pumping with energy. Her wet nose twitched as she investigated a clump of fallen branches and moss-covered rocks. She scraped aside some damp leaves to reveal the rotting log underneath, sending clouds of earthy spores into the air. Her tail wagged with excitement as she went from one smell to another.

As we trekked through the desolate terrain, each step brought back memories of all we had lost. Each turn of the path showed us an unfamiliar landscape that filled us with gloom. We were uncertain about what lay ahead, and the unknown weighed on our mind. Every movement sent a wave of paranoia through us.

Lost in the labyrinth of my thoughts, a sudden betrayal beneath my feet shattered the fragile serenity. The ground, once steadfast, surrendered to an opening, plunging me into an deep pit. Panic surged as my limbs thrashed in futile defiance, plummeting through the chilling void like a discarded soda can.

"Collin! Are you alright?" Kathleen's voice echoed through the obscureness.

"Just a few bumps and bruises," I replied, trying to sound nonchalant even though my back protested each move I made. "But hey, look where we ended up!"

Kathleen swung her legs over the opening and jumped into the dark tunnel before I could stop her. Our flashlights illuminated the walls, revealing more enormous cobwebs than you would expect, even in a haunted house. The air was pungent with must, adding to the heavy sense of mystery that encased us as we looked around in wonder.

A mysterious allure called to us, beckoning us further into the depths of the hidden passage. With a wary glance at me, Kathleen said, "Well, we've come this far. Might as well see where it leads."

Geez, this woman must have a PhD in courage. She marched forward with her flashlight as if on a quest to find the Holy Grail. Meanwhile, I trailed behind, torn between my curiosity and anxiety. It felt like I was being invited to my funeral. It was not quite the thrilling scavenger hunt for supplies I had expected.

The further we walked, the darker the tunnel became. The lack of light wasn't a problem, though, as the beam from Kathleen's flashlight easily cut through the veil of darkness.

As we made our way through the underground passage, we felt as if time had frozen in mid-air. Eventually, we came upon a thick steel door that loomed before us. Expecting it to be secured, I tugged on the handle with all my might, and to my surprise, it opened with ease.

We stepped into the chamber, and our eyes widened in amazement. It felt like we had stumbled upon a secret treasure trove that someone had hidden away for centuries.

Someone meticulously organized and stocked the room with every provision one could imagine. There were canned foods, bottled water, and medical supplies. It was a sanctuary amidst the desolation outside.

One essential item that had been eluding us was winter clothing. However, luck seemed to be on our side in this bunker as we stumbled upon boxes of sturdy jeans, durable jackets, and warm winter coats of excellent quality. To top it off, some hats and hoodies completed our outdoor attire perfectly.

Yet, amidst the bounty, ten bricks of gold gleamed, their shimmering surfaces capturing our attention. We exchanged glances, stunned by the discovery.

Who were these preppers, Bonnie and Clyde? Why did they believe that gold would be more valuable than provisions in a disaster?

"Well, well, well," I said, a mischievous smile tugging at my lips. "Looks like we've struck gold, literally."

Kathleen chuckled, a playful spark in her eyes. "Don't get any hopeful ideas. Those bricks of gold won't buy you a lifetime supply of pizza."

I pretended disappointment, clutching my heart. "My dreams of a pizza-filled apocalypse shattered! What a cruel world we live in!" We both laughed, our voices echoing through the chamber.

"But seriously," Kathleen's voice turned sober. "We should consider what we take from here. It might be our only chance to find such well-stocked supplies."

I nodded in agreement, the weight of responsibility settling upon our shoulders. Survival came first, even in the face of tempting treasures. We examined the supplies, taking inventory of what we needed and could carry.

We worked diligently, our movements slow as we lugged the supplies from the chamber to the surface. The labor was tiring, yet we could see a gleam of anticipation in Maggie's eyes. Her tail wagged with excitement as she ran between stacks of supplies, her tongue lolling out contentedly. We felt a rising optimism that perhaps this work meant something more. Maybe it was leading us towards a brighter future.

"Alright, Maggie," I said, patting her head. "You're in charge of guarding the gold. Bark if anyone gets too close, and remember, no chewing on the shiny bricks!"

The dog let out a playful yip as if to say, "You got it, boss."

As we continued to sort through the supplies, a thought struck me. "Hey, Kathleen, what if there are more hidden chambers like this? More treasures waiting to be found?"

Kathleen raised an eyebrow, a glimmer of excitement in her eyes. “You really want to go on a treasure hunt? That’s bold.”

I grinned, my adventurous spirit refusing to be contained. “Bold and slightly crazy, my friend. But who knows what other wonders we might stumble upon?”

Kathleen chuckled, shaking her head in amusement. “Well, if you’re up for it, count me in. Just promise me we’ll have more pizza party breaks along the way.”

“Deal,” I said, extending my hand toward her. We shook on it, sealing our pact to explore the unknown together.

We secured our backpacks and lifted them onto our shoulders, preparing to make our last journey out of the chamber. As we moved through the musty tunnel, excitement hung thick.

“So, Collin,” Kathleen began as we walked, her voice filled with curiosity. “Do you think we’ll find more gold, or maybe stumble upon a hidden society of survivors with their pizza delivery service?”

I chuckled, the image of a secret pizza society tickling my imagination. “Who knows? The only way to find out is to keep exploring. But let’s hope they have extra cheese options.”

As we joked and teased, the sound of our laughter bounced off the wet walls of the tunnel. Abruptly, a blood-curdling screech shattered the air, creating a discordant symphony in the oppressive darkness.

Time hung suspended as our laughter transformed into a collective gasp.

In a split second, the cheerful mood transformed into extreme fear. We stood frozen, our eyes darting frantically, seeking refuge in the narrow confines of the tunnel. The ominous resonance of an unseen threat lurking in the shadows replaced the echoes of our voices.

The once-friendly tunnel felt like a precarious sanctuary as we huddled together, each heartbeat amplifying the tangible tension in the air.

As Kathleen gripped her flashlight tighter, she whispered, “What was that?”. My ears were straining to hear. A second whoop followed. The flailing sounded like thunder in the night, making it hard to pinpoint the exact location.

“Are we not alone here?” I asked, my voice a whisper. Kathleen’s eyes widened.

“Collin, do you think others might know about this place?”

I nodded, my fear mingling with a surge of adrenaline. “It’s possible. There’s only one way to find out.”

We crept forward, our breath echoing in the darkness. We clutched our flashlights, and with each step, the beam of light bouncing off the walls grew brighter until we turned the corner. In the center of the flashlight beams was an eerie silhouette of a figure on the cold concrete ground.

My chest tightened as I grasped Kathleen's icy, shaking hands. A devilish screech echoed through the hall and reverberated off the cold stone walls. Followed by a booming sound of immense wings beating against the air. Fear rose from my toes to my throat like a flood.

I glanced up just in time to see a hulking creature descending on us with its red eyes ablaze. I grabbed Kathleen and yanked her closer to me as we dove out of the way. Fear propelled our legs into an uncalculated sprint away from the menacing figure.

As the frightening creature flew past us, I could make out its enormous bat-like wingspan stretching as wide as my arm. Its shadowy figure made my skin crawl, and as it advanced closer, its razor-sharp teeth bared menacingly. We covered our heads, feeling the gust of wind as it swept past us just inches away.

Its leathery wings whooshed with each air thrust as it circled again for another attack.

"Collin, hold on!" Kathleen shouted, her voice infused with firmness.

With the bat swinging wildly and pounding the air with a deafening thud, I saw a spark in her eyes that mirrored my own. She clenched her fists and narrowed her gaze as if to say, 'No more running; we're going to fight this.' We weren't just fleeing for our lives anymore; we were standing our ground.

I took a deep breath and, within seconds, let out a guttural roar that resonated through the tunnel. Mustering all of my strength, I lunged towards the unseen enemy. My arm jerked forward as Kathleen's courage drove her to join my crusade against the bat.

Our hands desperately swung through the air, trying to scare the creature away. Its wings provided a constant flurry of noise that resounded off the tunnel walls.

Finally, after what felt like an eternity, the tunnel ahead flooded with a dim light, and the bat retreated, screeching out the opening.

The moon cast a lovely collage of light and darkness around our spoils, as we stepped out of the hidden entrance. The venture here had etched its mark on us, evident in the weariness on our faces and the grit under our fingernails.

As we huddled together, our breaths mingled in the crisp night air, charged with an unspoken excitement that crackled like sparks around us. But unknown to us at the time, our struggles were only beginning.

CHAPTER TWENTY

Fallen Happiness

Like a tired old man, the daylight figured it was time to call it a day, bidding its golden farewell across the sky. Shadows stretched like lazy cats through the trees. And there I was, my fingers numb, but I was determined to build a shelter for us before dark.

As the evening breeze whispered through the leaves, I could feel a sense of urgency creeping up on me. The fading light urged me to work faster, knowing that darkness would soon wrap everything in its dark embrace.

Exhausted from the never-ending hours of foraging, I mustered up the last remnants of my energy to hoist and carefully place several hefty stones, constructing a solid base for our makeshift sanctuary. The weight of each stone pressed against my weary arms, but this structure would provide us with safety and shelter in this unforgiving landscape.

The thick, woody scent of pine mingled intimately with the damp earth, creating a heady symphony that seemed to cling to every inch of my skin. The salty proof of my labor drenched my body, providing evidence of the hard day's work. As the cool evening breeze brushed against my face, it felt like a long-awaited treat from the day's toils.

"We should have enough supplies for a few days," I muttered. I could feel my muscles aching as I surveyed my handwork. Despite my scratched and dirty hands from the work, I persisted until I started a small fire.

Once it was burning, I leaned against an old log in front of the crackling flames, finally able to rest after a long day's work.

"Ah, Kathleen, you wouldn't believe how happy I used to be," I said. Kathleen glanced up from where she was preparing dinner, her eyes kind and attentive.

"Happy? Really?" She arched an eyebrow.

"Oh, there were plenty of good times. When the world wasn't a charred mess, people had dreams and aspirations. I had a family, a job, hobbies... just an ordinary life, you know?"

Kathleen continued her chopping of celery and bell peppers, moving her wrist in a fast-slicing motion. The knife whistled through the air as it cut through the vegetables. She smiled and looked at me with amusement twinkling in her gaze.

"Come on, Collin, tell me about your life before all this. Give me something to remember."

"Well, I used to love going to Disney World with my wife and kids. Every year, it was a tradition to make a trip to Disney. We'd go out early in the morning and wouldn't return until late at night."

"My son and daughter squealed with delight as they scrambled onto the carousel's multicolored horses. The music blared, and the contraption spun endlessly, making them dizzy with glee."

"Then it was off to the teacups, giggling and shrieking excitedly. Later, we rode the boats to It's a Small World, and its catchy tune stayed with us for the rest of the day. And they always insisted on going through the haunted house, holding onto the safety bar with all their might just in case a ghost got loose."

"The sweet cinnamon smell of freshly fried churros wafted through the air as we walked down Main Street, hand in hand. Colorful gift shops with vibrant displays caught our attention, and we couldn't resist stepping inside. We ended up leaving with bags full of souvenirs as we continued to explore every corner of the park."

"You're making my mouth water for a freshly made churro right now," Kathleen said.

"Yes, and I could go for some warm buttered popcorn."

“What else did you guys do?”

“Well, on some evenings, too exhausted to watch the fireworks from the park, we snuggled up in our hotel room, our eyes fixated from our balcony as the spectacular bursts of light and sound illuminated the sky. Our room had an excellent view of the dazzling fireworks display over the park.”

“After the show, we jumped onto our beds and reminisced about our day. We laughed until our sides hurt and even playfully bickered about whether Space Mountain or Splash Mountain was the better ride.”

A soft, deep chuckle started in my belly and slowly rose to my throat. I could feel the tension from our arduous circumstances ebbing away as we relaxed into a calm sensation.

The smell of grilled food hung in the air, mingling with the chilled breeze that blew through the night. We regaled each other with anecdotes that had us smiling and shaking our heads.

We laid on our blankets, and Maggie settled in at our feet. The sky was a canvas of stars, their twinkling light reflecting off the leaves like a million tiny diamonds. We whispered, Kathleen’s voice soothing and comforting, as we shared stories from our days.

“Collin, what did you do before this happened?”

Kathleen’s query brought me back to my layoff from Amtrak. I shifted my gaze towards her and told her about the fateful day they let me go. My manager called me into his office and placed a pink slip on the desk between us. He said, "Ridership is down. We're letting you go."

"It had been eleven long years of blood, sweat, and tears. I had given my all to this job, sacrificing time with family and friends to climb the ranks at Amtrak. It was my passion, my purpose in life."

"But now, as I stood in front of my boss's desk, facing the harsh reality that it was all being taken away from me, I couldn't help but feel a mix of anger and betrayal. How could they not see how much this job meant to me? To them, it was just another casualty in their quest for profit."

I grabbed a burning twig from the fire, holding it gingerly. The dancing flames before me held a hypnotic power, but instead of feeling the usual warmth and comfort, an unsettling feeling consumed me in the pit of my stomach.

The crackling embers were a stark reminder of how fleeting life can be, how easily moments and memories can slip away without warning.

"Kathleen, it was like a punch to the gut," I continued. "Years of hard work and dedication felt like they had evaporated instantly, leaving a hollow feeling in its place."

"So, what did you do?"

“I applied to job after job, never connecting with the right opportunity. Everywhere I looked, openings were scarce. It seemed like there was no room for someone like me in a modern economy. With each fruitless search, my debt accumulated, and it felt like the world’s weight pressed down on my shoulders.”

“It must have been tough for you.”

“It was. So, I traveled to West Virginia and found one business still hiring...the coal company. So, I got a job digging coal. It was filthy. It was hard and nasty work. But it was a paycheck.”

“I can only imagine how tough that must have been for you. I am truly sorry for bringing up these painful memories. I had no idea. Let’s try to set aside those thoughts and instead focus on the happy moments like Disney World from now on.”

“We can always try.” As I drifted off to sleep, my mind couldn’t help but wrestle with the uncertainty of our future. Would things get better or worse? Would we be able to make it through another day, or would the ever-changing tides of fate sweep us away?

Despite my hopes, doubt always lingered in the back of my mind. But for now, all I could do was let sleep embrace me and leave tomorrow’s worries for tomorrow.

Silence filled the night, and our breathing synchronized, echoing the harmony we had found in each other’s company. We sowed a seed of confidence amid the devastation, vowing new warmth and light in the bleak scenery.

The stars glimmered in the night sky, giving us a feeling of invincibility. Yet, hidden in the darkness, an ominous force threatened to take our newfound joy away.

Maggie's frantic barking shattered the peaceful sounds of the forest. I shot up from my slumber. My jaw dropped as orange-red flames rose, casting an eerie glow on the surrounding trees. The heat prickled on my skin as fear bubbled within me, squeezing the breath out of my lungs. It was like a living nightmare. The fire seemed to grow hungrier by the second, devouring everything in its path.

"We have to find a safe distance from the fire." My voice was faint amidst the chaos and the roar of the crackling flames.

Kathleen's eyes widened with terror as she scanned our surroundings, searching for an escape route. "I can't even see through the smoke!" Her voice was hoarse.

Maggie whimpered as she pressed herself against Kathleen's leg. I could see the fear in her eyes as she sensed the danger surrounding us. I had to protect them both, no matter what. Firewalls blocked our path wherever we turned.

The forest echoed with the violence of the raging inferno as it marched forward, the crackling flames casting a terrifying glow on the night sky. Embers danced in the air like malevolent fireflies, frighteningly displaying the danger closing in. The oppressive heat bore down upon us, searing through our clothes and into our very bones.

Each gasp of air felt like a battle as the thick smoke filled our lungs and choked our every breath. Fear took hold of us, its grip growing tighter as we confronted the harsh truth of our situation. The tranquil wilderness had transformed into a merciless foe, with the raging fire turning the peaceful darkness into a fiery oven.

"Collin, what do we do? The fire will turn us into ashes!"

"We can make it. All we need is a thin break in the flames. Just keep looking."

My fingers clamped tightly around Kathleen's hand as I yanked her forward through the smoke and ash. As we ran unthinkingly through the maze of fiery trees, the desperate urgency of the moment heightened our senses.

The shadows danced and twisted around us, transforming the forest into a nightmarish labyrinth. The trees cried out in agony, their crackling and groaning echoing our growing despair.

With Maggie close behind, Kathleen and I sprinted through the inferno, our skin tingling from the heat. Embers whirled around us like a blizzard of red-hot sparks, stinging every exposed inch of our bodies.

Panic and desperation fueled our frantic escape, propelling us through the blistering landscape. The ground shook violently beneath us as the raging flames closed in, threatening to consume us whole.

The thick, fiery ashes on the ground seemed to reach up and grab at our feet as we ran, making it feel like we were sinking deeper and deeper into their grasp. My feet were burning as I ran. Sweat poured down my face, and I could feel blisters beginning to form. The heat seemed to intensify with every step, but the promise of safety spurred us on.

The smoke billowed around us like an ever-increasing gray fog, its hot clouds searing our eyes and skin with each passing minute. We had to crawl and squirm through the murky haze, not knowing what was ahead but driven by a single hope. We scrambled over burning rubble and smoldering ashes with every ounce of strength.

"There!" I pointed towards a lake ahead. "We have to make it to the water!"

The coolness of the lake surrounded us, providing a break from the unrelenting blaze. Submerged beneath the water, our bodies calmed like a soothing balm. We stayed immersed for what felt like hours, savoring the sanctuary the open water provided.

The scorching heat seared our skin, turning it a bright red. I looked into Kathleen's eyes and thanked God we had made it out alive. The fire passed over us, but a long road was still ahead.

I couldn't help but laugh as I watched Maggie frolicking in the water, her tongue lolling out of her mouth in pure bliss. She seemed to have no worries or concerns, as if she were relaxing on a leisurely beach swim instead of fleeing danger.

"We can't stay out here," I said, my voice raspy from the smoke. "Let's find shelter and regroup. We can't afford to let our guard down."

Kathleen's teeth clicked together as she nodded, her voice trembling with fear in the chilly night air. "I can't recall a time when I was this frightened," she admitted, trying to steady her shivering body.

Maggie's fur got soaked from the lake as she kept pace beside us. The three of us slogged up a steep slope, scanning the early morning sky for any signs of shelter. In the distance, we spotted a dark archway emerging, marking the entrance to a cave.

A sudden temperature drop surrounded us as we entered the cave's darkness. The slick walls oozed with moisture, causing our clothes to stick to our skin. The darkness seemed to calm our nerves as we ventured deeper into the cave, feeling somewhat safe from the outside world.

Our legs trembled beneath us, barely able to carry ourselves another step. We collapsed onto the parched earth with relieved exhaustion and closed our eyes as we fell into a deep slumber. The soft chirps of birds were the first sounds to pierce through the silence before dawn's colors brightened the sky. We roused ourselves from our fitful rest with renewed energy, ready for a new day.

We stood in a huddle, our faces painted with exhaustion. I coughed and rubbed the sleep from my eyes, still groggy from last night's ordeal.

"I think we should head back to the police station."

Kathleen nodded, her joints cracking as she stretched. "Do you think we'll ever find others?"

I sighed. My voice was heavy with resignation. "I don't know. It's been months, hell, years since we've seen any signs of life. We might be the last ones left."

I let out a sharp whistle, calling Maggie to my side, and the three of us began the long walk home together. The sun had already clocked out for the day, leaving long shadows on the pavement as we neared the police station. As evening descended, a soft light draped over everything, painting the sky in delicate pastel colors as daylight gave way to darkness.

Stepping into the police station, the atmosphere changed from the dimness of the outside world to the aged hallways inside. The door's hinges creaked as it swung open, revealing a weary interior where the remnants of previous interrogations and hurried footsteps still lingered like fading echoes.

The well-worn floorboards protested under our feet, bearing the weight of many investigations over the years; each step was a reminder of the history embedded in the very bones of the building.

I looked around at the strange place we now called home. Old furniture and remnants of a past era scattered about, giving off a sense of weariness. But despite its tired appearance, there was an unexplainable feeling of belonging in this place, a sense of shared memories, and the potential for a fresh start.

The police station was where it all began for Kathleen and me, in a room filled with forgotten evidence and memories. And in the peacefulness of this unusual place, a feeling of rebirth hung in the air. It seemed as though the walls held the ability to offer us a second chance, a way to rewrite our story.

I looked over and noticed Kathleen staring at me. Her gaze lingered on me for what felt like an eternity before her lips slowly curved into a faint smile. "We made it. Against all odds, we survived."

I nodded, gratitude welling up within me. "We'll keep searching. We won't give up hope. There must be someone out there, just like us, fighting to survive."

CHAPTER TWENTY-ONE

Family Joy

Having narrowly escaped the clutches of the raging wildfire, Kathleen and I sought a peaceful night under the enormous canvas of the night sky. We spread a woolen blanket on the damp grass behind the police station, feeling the dewdrops seep into our jeans with every wince.

As we settled into our impromptu camp, the distant crackling of the fire lingered in our ears. The distant horizon, still aglow with the remnants of the inferno, cast a gentle light on our surroundings. Our tired bodies sank into the blanket's softness, offering a fleeting escape from the destruction that consumed our lives.

Kathleen tilted her head back, tracing the constellations above with her eyes. "Look at those stars," she whispered, her voice barely audible in the night breeze. "They've always shone brightly, even during the darkest times."

The celestial display overhead seized my gaze, and I instinctively followed hers. Millions of tiny pinpricks adorned the night sky, each whispering a hidden secret longing to be revealed. The immensity of the spectacle washed over me, evoking a profound sense of insignificance, yet in that vastness, I felt inexplicably tethered to something beyond myself, something stirring and profound.

As I stared into the sky, ready to share my reflections, a low rumble reminiscent of distant thunder abruptly interrupted my thoughts. A chuckle escaped me as I recognized the familiar sound of my growling stomach. “Well, moments like these remind me that I need some food,” I added with a light-hearted laugh.

Kathleen flashed a mischievous smile. “Seems like you’re always hungry,” she teased. “I’ll warm up some soup while you brew us some coffee. And remember, Maggie, keep watch.”

With a mischievous glint in my eye, I nodded and let out a playful laugh. “It looks like I’ll be playing the barista role,” I joked, attempting to maintain a serious demeanor amid the serenity of the night.

Kathleen disappeared into the police station, and I went to a small storage shelter nearby. The cool night air nipped at my skin, prompting me to pull my jacket tighter as I eagerly sought refuge from the chilly night.

Maggie nudged my leg with her snout and let out a contented

sigh. I smiled down at her before opening my footlocker and pulling out a beaten-up pack of coffee beans, a treasure we had stumbled upon during one of our scavenger hunts, now one of our most treasured possessions.

The freshly ground coffee beans aroma filled the air as I reached for the battered metal kettle. As I poured water into the pot, my mind wandered back to when a simple cup of coffee was quickly within reach.

Meanwhile, Kathleen's knife hit the cutting board with a rhythmic tap, tap, tap as she sliced through carrots and onions, their juices bursting in tiny explosions of sound. I scooped the coffee beans into the grinder and turned the handle.

Maggie sat upright with her brown eyes fixed on Kathleen as she expertly moved the veggies around in the cast-iron skillet. While Kathleen was engrossed in cooking, I was busy boiling water and pouring it over the freshly ground beans. The comforting hum of brewing coffee and the sizzling melody of the meal taking shape filled the air.

As the food cooked, we sat in peaceful silence, our senses captivated by the bubbling oil and wisps of steam rising from each sizzling piece of food.

After dinner, Kathleen wrapped herself in a blanket, creating a cocoon of warmth against the night's chill. In that peaceful moment, Kathleen caught me off guard with a question I wasn't exactly prepared for, and maybe, deep down, I wasn't ready to answer.

"Tell me about your wife."

Her inquiry hit me like a wave, drowning me in a sea of grief. The ache of her absence was a heavy burden, one I usually tried to push away. My voice wavered as I reluctantly let the words escape.

"My wife passed away from cancer some time ago."

Kathleen's expression softened with empathy, and her eyes reflected understanding. She spoke softly, "I'm sorry for bringing it up. Forget I even asked."

But I shook my head, summoning a smile. "It's alright. Despite the pain, I am fortunate to have grown-up children who now have families." Reflecting on them brought a subtle but welcome joy to my heart.

In the quiet aftermath of my revelation, the crackling of the dwindling fire underscored the delicate nature of the moment. Sensing the shift, Kathleen gave me a moment before gently prodding, "Would you like to tell me about them?"

I smiled. "Well, I guess I'll start with my oldest son. He's a determined young man, carving his path as a successful lawyer. And when he's not in the courtroom, he enjoys writing food reviews."

Kathleen's eyebrows shot up in genuine surprise. "A trial lawyer?"

I nodded affirmatively, allowing a moment for the weight of the profession to settle in.

"That's impressive! Must be an incredibly stressful job?" Her curiosity lingered in the air, eager for a glimpse into my son's challenges.

"Absolutely. He commands attention in court with his razor-sharp wit and bold, compelling arguments. It's fascinating to witness how he dissects complex legal issues, weaving a narrative that captivates judges and juries alike."

Kathleen leaned in, her interest piqued. "Tell me more. What kinds of cases does he typically handle?"

A thoughtful smile played on my lips as I delved into the specifics. "He specializes in corporate law, often dealing with high-stakes litigation. From intricate contract disputes to navigating the complexities of business transactions, he navigates the legal landscape with finesse. His tenacity and meticulous approach have earned him a reputation for being a formidable force in the legal arena."

As I spoke, the crackling fire seemed to dance in rhythm with the excitement in Kathleen's eyes. "It must be quite a rollercoaster," she remarked.

I nodded, acknowledging the highs and lows of my son's profession. "Indeed, it is. The thrill of victory and the weight of responsibility go hand in hand. But he thrives on it, always seeking justice and fairness in every case he takes on."

Kathleen's curiosity persisted. "And you mentioned he also has a passion for writing about food?"

I chuckled, the contrast between his legal prowess and culinary pursuits making me proud.

"Yes, quite the unexpected combination. Outside the courtroom, he channels his creativity into food reviews. It's his way of indulging in the sensory pleasures of life, meticulously dissecting flavors and ambiances, much like he does with legal cases. It's a delightful contrast that adds a unique layer to his multifaceted personality."

Kathleen's eyes softened as she gazed at me, her voice filled with warmth. "You must be so proud of your son. He's carved out such an impressive career."

I nodded. "Yes, he has."

Kathleen's eyes danced with inquisitiveness, lit up by the crackling fire, as she held onto a mug of hot coffee, warming her hands.

"So, tell me," she asked, her voice a gentle undertone to the crackling fire, "what does your daughter do for a living?"

I sipped my coffee. The soothing warmth filled me as I

gathered my thoughts. "My daughter is a speech-language pathologist. She works with children, helping them find their voices and communicate effectively. It's truly remarkable to see the impact she makes."

Kathleen's eyes lit up with admiration, a soft glow dancing in the flickering firelight. "That must be so rewarding! Making a difference in those children's lives. It's a beautiful thing."

I smiled. "It is. Watching her guide children through self-expression and witnessing the transformation in their confidence is a beautiful dance of compassion and growth. She has a way of connecting with them, unlocking their potential in ways that extend far beyond the confines of words."

"It's not just about teaching language," I continued, the warmth of the fire echoing the warmth in my heart. "She instills a sense of belonging and empowers these young souls to navigate the world with newfound clarity. Each small step forward is a triumph, and in those moments, you witness the pure magic of her work."

The night air seemed to carry the weight of my story, blending with the peaceful crackle of the dwindling fire. Kathleen's gaze remained fixed, captivated by the beauty of my daughter's profession.

"Children can be resilient beyond measure," I continued, a soft sigh escaping me. "And with her gentle guidance, my daughter helps them unfold their wings. She has a natural talent for understanding their struggles and guiding them through them. She's always had a kind, empathetic nature."

As I struggled with my children's absence, I took a moment to gather myself. Waves of emotion surged through me, and I drew in a deep breath, attempting to deal with their absence in my life.

"Collin, you don't have to continue if it's too difficult. I can see this is taking a toll on you. Let's shift the topic," she suggested, concern etched on her face.

"No, it's alright. I need to get this out," I responded, determined to share the burden weighing on my soul. After a brief pause, I spoke about my daughter's deep love for the outdoors.

"She cherished nature, especially the Smoky Mountains. The cozy crackle of a fire, the smells of pine and cedarwood, and the allure of log cabins captured her heart. It was as if she had discovered her utopia in those serene moments."

I brought my mug to my lips, inhaling the sweet aroma of roasted beans before taking a slow sip. The creamy liquid swirled across my tongue, flooding my mouth with warmth and pleasure. I savored it briefly before setting the mug down and continuing.

"Just like she loved being outside, she relished her time at the gym. The pulsating music infused her with energy and ignited a shared enthusiasm among her group of friends. She described how they developed an ideal training regimen to push each other to reach new fitness benchmarks."

Kathleen reclined, a gentle smile gracing her lips. “Your daughter seems to lead a fulfilling life, effortlessly juggling her professional commitments and personal passions.”

I chuckled, a soft undertone of pride in my voice. “Yes, she keeps herself occupied, but she’s struck a balance. It’s been a journey, but she’s found her way.”

Kathleen nodded thoughtfully. “That speaks volumes about her commitment and love for both her career and family. Achieving harmony in today’s world isn’t easy, or, at least, not in the world that used to be.”

“Absolutely. She always puts family first, ensuring they know they’re cherished and teaching her young daughter strong values.”

The fire blazed, and the heat embraced us as we celebrated the beautiful moments of my children’s lives. I was grateful to share these joys with Kathleen, feeling pride and love as I thought of them.

“And what about your grandchildren? How old are they?”

A smile stretched across my face as I shared the ages of my grandchildren. “Well, I have two grandchildren in high school, ages 17 and 14. The youngest is in elementary school, at the tender age of...” I paused, furrowing my brows as I struggled to recall the exact age of my youngest grandchild.

“Oh dear, I can’t seem to remember. My mind can be so

forgetful."

Kathleen giggled, placing a gentle hand on my arm. "Don't worry. It's completely normal. I'm sure their age is not the most important thing. What matters is the love and joy they bring to your life."

A sense of relief swept through me as Kathleen's empathetic words resonated. "You're absolutely right. They are remarkable kids, and I couldn't be prouder of them."

With a sparkle in her eye, Kathleen encouraged me to share more about my grandchildren. "Tell me about their accomplishments, their hobbies, and the things that captivate their interests."

My heart swelled with pride as I painted a vivid picture of my oldest grandchild, John Henry. "He's an extraordinary young man, just seventeen, but possessing a maturity well beyond his years," I expressed with genuine affection.

"One of his passions is weightlifting, and he's taken it to a whole new level by creating a series of tutorial videos. I remember the day he made his heaviest lift, sharing the triumph on his YouTube channel, where it swiftly went viral."

"Wow, that's truly impressive."

"He's not only a stellar student but also a genuine history aficionado. He delves into wars fought centuries ago and royal scandals with such enthusiasm as if he had witnessed them firsthand. He can keep you engaged for hours."

Kathleen's laughter bubbled up, a warm and delightful melody in the crisp air. "He sounds like quite the character. The way you describe him, he seems larger than life."

I couldn't help but grin. "Indeed! I remember him showing up at a family gathering in a sharp, stylish suit, looking like he had just stepped off a magazine cover. He had everyone gravitating towards him, weaving through good-natured jokes and captivating stories that left us all in stitches."

Maggie barked in agreement as if adding her approval to John Henry's charismatic nature.

"But there's more! He's also a key member of the high school rowing team. Watching him glide gracefully across the water, stroke by stroke, is nothing short of breathtaking. He's a living paradox, embodying both power and elegance, a history enthusiast, and a party aficionado, all seamlessly blended into one."

Kathleen's laughter resonated, dancing among the trees. It was a contagious sound, echoing endlessly with pure merriment. "A weightlifting, party-hopping scholar? That's quite the combination. You must be bursting with pride."

"I am," I confessed, feeling the warmth of pride spreading through me. "I am incredibly proud of the young man John Henry has become. He's out there, embracing life with all its opportunities and challenges. And I can't wait to see what he achieves next."

As Kathleen and I savored our coffee, the focus shifted to my second eldest, Caitlin.

"Kathleen, you won't believe this! At just 14, she's an extraordinary chef. Her culinary skills are beyond phenomenal, rivaling those of top-level master chefs. I'm not exaggerating!" My words brimmed with excitement.

"But that's not all. Caitlin is also a standout in volleyball, bringing an electrifying energy that seems to fill the entire court. She's a remarkable leader, commanding attention whenever she speaks. A talented athlete and a supportive friend, she brings out the best in her teammates."

Kathleen beamed, her eyes sparkling with delight, and released a contented sigh. "Collin," she said, "she sounds like an absolute joy. I'm sure having her around brings you immeasurable happiness."

I nodded in agreement. "Absolutely. Witnessing her growth and success in her passions brings me immense joy."

At that moment, the rustling leaves heralded Maggie's arrival from the dense forest. Bursting forth with boundless energy, she pranced through the clearing. Her tail, a blur of ecstatic movement, wagged back and forth in pure joy as she leaped towards me. She nuzzled against my leg with an exuberant zeal, radiating a tangible delight that only a canine companion could express.

"Oh, Maggie, aren't you proud of Caitlin too?" I chuckled, giving her a gentle pat on the head.

It intrigued Kathleen, her tone eager and curious. "Go on. Is there anything else that makes Caitlin unique?"

A warm chuckle escaped me as I considered the question. "Well," I responded with a grin, giving it some thought, "she's quite the go-getter. She spends hours glued to her phone, cruising through social media hotspots like Snapchat and TikTok, staying in the loop with all the trends and pop culture. And when she's not dominating the digital domain, she's deep in discussions about dating and boys with her friends."

"Ah, pursuing teenage romance. It takes me back to those good ol' days."

"Yes," I said softly, "back when life was simpler and carefree."

Then, like someone flipped a switch, Maggie turned into a furry whirlwind. Her tongue hung out, and her tail swung like a canine metronome on caffeine.

It seemed like her body had received the message that we were throwing a party, and she had returned to her puppyhood. She raced around in circles, a furry flurry of unbridled joy.

Laughter bubbled up from my chest, blending with the steady thumping of Maggie's tail against the air. Her playful energy was contagious as if she were performing a stand-up comedy routine for our amusement.

It was impossible not to join in on her infectious joy, and any lingering negative thoughts quickly got pushed aside by her exuberance. It seemed like happiness radiated from every strand of fur on her body, outshining any remnants of gloom within me.

Kathleen and I both gave a round of applause for Maggie's stellar performance. With the grace of a seasoned actress, she exited the stage and went back to sleep.

As the cool evening air settled over us, Kathleen wrapped her warm blanket tightly around her shoulders before breaking the silence. "What about your youngest?"

"Allow me to introduce you to my nine-year-old granddaughter, Maia, a little fireball always seeking fresh adventures."

"I remember a family camping trip to the Smoky Mountains. While everyone else was gathered around the fireplace inside the cabin, talking and joking, Maia was the exception. Instead, she braved the cold outdoors, clad in a vibrant puffer jacket zipped up to her chin, joyfully running around and laughing."

"When we called her for dinner, she responded from afar, her voice carrying through the mountain air. 'I'm not hungry.' However, mentioning graham crackers, marshmallows, and chocolate bars caused her to abandon her exploration. She raced to the campfire, ready to partake in the joy of crafting s'mores."

Kathleen's laughter erupted, accompanied by an enthusiastic clap of her hands. Her eyes twinkled with amusement as she exclaimed, "A genuine camping enthusiast, indeed! That's delightful!"

My face beamed with joy as I spoke about Maia's soccer prowess. "She can make the ball do whatever she desires! The other kids nickname her 'The Dancing Dynamo' because she is outstanding with the ball at her feet. She puts on a show each time she plays."

Kathleen erupted into laughter once more. "That's amazing!"

"But like so many other little girls, I'm sure Maia's favorite activity is shopping with her mother. Those two can wander from store to store for hours, and you can be sure that Maia has something new in her hands by the end. We even joke that if you gave her twenty dollars to spend, it'd be gone before the car had pulled out of their driveway."

"And you know what really warms my heart? Seeing her all cozied up with her beloved panda bear, clutching it to her chest like it's the key to the universe. There she is, looking like a picture of serenity, sprawled out in her bed. Her pint-sized self all tucked in under the blankets, lost in the embrace of blissful dreams."

"Sounds like grandchildren keep you on your toes. I bet they bring so much energy and liveliness to your family gatherings."

"They're the spark that lights up the room, the laughter that echoes through the house. I cherish every moment with them."

Kathleen's eyes sparkled with understanding, and she gently reached for my hand, intertwining her fingers with mine. "Thank you for telling these beautiful stories to me. It's quite clear how your family has filled your life with abundant love and joy."

I smiled, feeling a sense of kinship with Kathleen. "Yes, they've been my guiding light, my source of strength. They continue to inspire me with everything that has happened."

"I'm glad to see that," Kathleen whispered, a hint of tears shimmering in her eyes. "These connections and mementos keep us going in the darkest times."

I gently squeezed Kathleen's hand, showing my agreement with her sentiment. "Without a doubt. It is the love and bonds of family that sustain us, giving us the determination to endure."

The weight of our shared experiences settled upon us. We sat in companionable silence, finding comfort in each other's presence. At that moment, surrounded by flashbacks of the past, we found a glimmer of confidence despite the shattered world.

After a few minutes, I built up the courage to ask, "Are you married? Do you have any children?" I wanted to know about

Kathleen's life before the catastrophe.

Her gaze shifted away, and I couldn't help but notice her hand tracing circles on her left ring finger before responding.

"No," she sighed. "I'm not married and don't have children."

There was a touching pause, a momentary veil of sorrow dimming her features.

"Actually, I'm divorced," she admitted. Her fingers were anxiously playing with the edge of her jacket, revealing the emotional weight behind her words.

I sensed this was a delicate subject, so I attempted to change the matter. "What about your work as a nurse in the intensive care unit?"

Kathleen's expression changed from sad to jubilant in an instant. Her voice intensified as she portrayed the sights and sounds of the ICU. The beeping machines, nurses scurrying around, and physicians barking orders.

"It was an incredible experience! Every day brought a new test. I never knew if my effort would make an impact or not. But when it did, the feeling of success was electrifying. It changed me profoundly to observe the struggle for survival and to be part of that fight."

"Tell me a little more."

Kathleen's hands trembled as she recalled the struggles in the ICU. She relayed the episodes of joy and grief, of successes and failures that took place daily. With newfound clarity, she spoke of how life could alter instantaneously, how delicate it is, yet how resilient the human spirit remains.

Each phrase she uttered paid homage to her work, a solemn tribute to the significance and impact of her role during those times of need.

As I heard her speak, her dedication to the cause overwhelmed me. She radiated an aura of confidence that put a flame of hope into my heart. Amid all the destruction, it was a reassuring reminder that our world still has heroes.

Our conversation began as just a simple exchange, but it quickly grew into something much more substantial. We talked for hours, both of us seeking comfort in the company of another who could understand our pasts.

As the sunrise timidly painted the sky with soft hues, we nestled in our sleeping bags, seeking rest from the world beyond. I lay there, immersed in the tender embrace of the night's darkness, overcome by an unavoidable desire to reclaim a life now in ruins.

A profound ache, both intangible and all-encompassing, gripped me, reaching from the tips of my fingers to the depths of my soul. But those memories of my family were like flickering stars, guiding me toward hope and resilience.

At that moment, I vowed to take small steps towards healing, knowing their light would forever guide me toward a brighter future.

CHAPTER TWENTY-TWO

Sparks of Inspiration

Another fruitless day passed in our quest for supplies. The search concluded just as it began, empty-handed. We trudged along the cracked asphalt roads, shadows lengthening under the relentless sunlight. The boundless sky stretched above, a bright blue expanse devoid of clouds.

Exhaustion weighed us down, each step carrying the burden of fatigue and disappointment. The world had transformed drastically since the incident, leaving us stranded and yearning for the once-taken-for-granted comforts. Time seemed to have lost all significance, the days blending together in this desolate landscape.

At my side, Maggie trotted faithfully, her fur matted and dirty from days of scavenging. Despite her appearance, her spirit remained unbroken. A gust of wind swept through an old, abandoned building, causing Maggie's tags to jingle.

Kathleen's eyes widened, a smile forming as she spotted an abandoned Ford-150 hybrid truck behind the pharmacy, its rusted edges peeking out.

"Collin, if we connect this truck to our small generator at the police station, we could breathe life back into it! And oh, the adventures we shall embark upon once we get a larger generator from the Home Supply Store!"

Respect and skepticism mingled as I looked at Kathleen. Her excitement was contagious, yet I couldn't help questioning the feasibility of her plan. Still, the hopefulness in her eyes, a spark absent for so long, was undeniable.

"You really think it's possible?" I asked. Kathleen nodded emphatically.

"I do," she replied. "We've scavenged spare parts and tools. With a little ingenuity, we can make it work. And think about it, Collin, with a functioning truck, we won't be confined to this small town anymore. We could explore the untouched regions beyond."

Skepticism slowly morphed into an unexpected surge of excitement. The monotony of familiar streets and stores had worn me down. The prospect of venturing into uncharted territories rekindled an adventure I thought had long been extinguished by our harsh reality.

Her energy was palpable. As she shared her vision, I watched the excitement flicker in her eyes. The corners of her mouth curled upwards in anticipation. I felt my heart leap in response as I considered her ideas and a smile tugged at my lips.

"Kathleen, you never cease to amaze me!"

We worked in unison, each digging our hands into the dirt to free the old truck from its deep bed of weeds and sticks. The rubber tires squeaked as they rolled over rocks and debris, with a dust cloud rising behind us.

Despite our combined efforts, we could barely move the rusted monstrosity forward an inch at a time. We exerted ourselves, gripping the bumpers tightly, until we got it rolling on the cracked asphalt with one last heave.

The generator took forever to attach, sparks flying as we ignited it. The old Ford pickup truck slowly roared, smoke billowing from its tailpipe.

The rusty hood of the truck glimmered like a treasure trove of jewels, catching and reflecting the rays of light that filtered through the quiet streets. Our laughter rang out in the stillness, breaking the long silence over this abandoned town.

With determination and excitement coursing through our veins, we climbed into the old truck, Maggie already in the back, searching for a larger generator.

The worn seats creaked under our weight as we eagerly

planned our next move, ready to conquer any obstacle. The old truck rattled and groaned as we revved the engine, eager to venture into the unknown.

The scent of gasoline filled the air, mingling with our excitement. We were on a mission to find a larger generator to bring life back to our desolate town.

Our eyes scanned the dilapidated buildings as we drove through the quiet streets. Moss-covered walls and shattered windows told tales of lost dreams and faded hopes. Nature had reclaimed its territory, weaving vines through broken structures, a reminder that life continued to thrive even in the absence of humanity.

As we zigzagged through the abandoned streets, our tires kicked up clouds of dust and rocks, evidence of the destruction in this area.

We finally arrived at the outskirts of town, where a massive industrial complex stood tall and imposing against the skyline. The massive industrial complex, which once had a shiny exterior, now appeared faded and weather-worn, symbolizing a bygone era.

The truck rumbled to a stop in front of the Home and Lumber store, its tires crunching on broken shards of glass scattered across the pavement. We stepped out of the vehicle, careful not to step on any sharp debris as we approached the entrance.

The air was thick with dust and the smell of sawdust and paint.

We walked past wrecked shelving units piled with power tools, paint cans, and ladders leaning against the walls. Squinting, we strained our eyes to make out the chipped and faded signs that would guide us through the wreckage in the direction we needed to go.

We scanned the vast warehouse. Then, we found an 8,000-watt generator built of thick steel parts with a rubber-coated cord. After some quick calculations, we took it with us. With the help of a manual forklift, we slowly lifted the majestic machine off the ground and eased it into the truck's cargo bed.

The weight of it caused the vehicle to dip slightly, but we knew that this hulking behemoth would save our lives when we most needed it. We rumbled back to town, our truck rattling from the rough terrain.

When we pulled up to the gas station, we connected a power cable from our generator to the pump. With a few twists of knobs and switches, the pumps' engine roared to life, and fuel flowed like sweet nectar into our tanks. It felt like a miracle as we watched the fuel gauge climb steadily higher.

The sound of gasoline flowing out of the pump was like a beautiful melody, signaling that our journey had reached a triumphant victory. We had worked for hours, our arms tired as we filled the truck's tank with gas. We encouraged each other and laughed at jokes, knowing we were progressing.

The engine rumbled, shaking the truck as it sputtered and coughed out a cloud of black smoke. Finally, it roared to life with a deep roar, vibrating the metal and rattling the windows.

"Collin," Kathleen said enthusiastically, "Let's do it!" No sooner had she finished speaking when Maggie instinctively sprung into the back of the truck.

The truck rumbled beneath us like a caged beast, its engine vibrating and roaring in anticipation of the journey ahead. A gust of dusty wind blew through the open windows, bringing the scent of fresh adventures. We felt ready for whatever lay ahead, our excitement palpable as we embarked on our journey.

"Woof, woof!" Maggie barked, her tail wagging vigorously as she hung her head over the side of the truck bed, excited about the upcoming adventures. I grinned, my excitement mirrored in Maggie's wagging tail.

"Hold on tight, girl! We're about to embark on the adventure of a lifetime! Just remember always to keep your head inside the vehicle." Maggie barked in agreement before plopping back onto the truck bed, her tongue lolling out of her mouth. She looked ready for the journey as we were. She always knew when something exciting was about to happen.

The truck moved as we drove through the empty streets. The wind whipping our hair into a wild frenzy. It felt like being thrust into an alternate world. It's one that some whimsical director could have crafted for a post-apocalyptic rom-com flick.

"Collin, can you believe it? We're like Lewis and Clark, seeking a better world! Except without the questionable fashion choices. But the spirit is there!"

I laughed as I shook my head in agreement. "Yes, our journey may lack the dangerous allure of a vast wilderness duo, but we can still make an impact. We'll be the dynamic duo of innovation!"

Kathleen chuckled, her hands gripping the steering wheel with grit. "Absolutely, and who knows? Maybe we'll stumble upon a hidden treasure or two along the way. There must be more to this world than just ruins."

We drove for hours, navigating broken roads filled with vast stretches of nothing but dust and ruin. The sun blazed down on us from a cloudless sky, its relentless heat determined to defeat us before reaching our destination. Everywhere we looked were crumbling structures and dismembered machines. We pressed on despite the bleakness, hoping there might be a beacon of light in this dismal scenery.

"Collin," Kathleen said, breaking the silence, "remember the days when we worried about mundane things like paying bills and sitting in traffic? Sometimes, I miss those simple problems."

"Indeed. But this new world has allowed us to embrace our true potential. We're not just survivors anymore. We're pioneers, forging a path towards a brighter future."

Kathleen smiled warmly. "You're right. Together, we'll rebuild one ingenious idea at a time."

Our truck rumbled along, the engine purring like a contented cat. Amid the destroyed terrain, the sound of the engine and our laughter breathed life back into the city's forgotten corners.

"You know," Kathleen said, her fingers tapping on the steering wheel, "we could be the heroes that people talk about in legends. 'Collin and Kathleen, the pioneers who brought light to the dark, laughter to the silence, and a damn good generator to the world!"

I laughed, picturing us with capes flowing behind us as we swooped in to save the day. "Yes, yes! And they shall know us as the Legion of Ingenuity! Fighting despair, one invention at a time!"

Kathleen joined in my laughter, her joy infectious. "Oh, Collin, I couldn't have asked for a better partner on this adventure."

I reached over and squeezed Kathleen's hand, a surge of gratitude filling my heart. "And I couldn't have asked for a more brilliant and tenacious friend. Together, we'll conquer this new world."

The road stretched before us, a path of challenge and uncertainty. But I felt optimism with Kathleen by my side and Maggie's tail wagging in the back. No matter what lay ahead, we were ready to face it head-on.

The sun sank below the horizon, glazing the sky with a radiant array of oranges, pinks, and purples. As nightfall crept over us, our headlights flickered to life, straining against the darkness ahead.

The stars danced overhead, their twinkling rays piercing through the gloom like beacons in the dark. Occasionally, a sliver of moonlight would illuminate our path, casting an ethereal glow on the surrounding countryside. There was a quiet rustling sound as the wind brushed through the leaves and branches.

"Collin," Kathleen said softly, her voice filled with exhaustion and determination, "let's find a place to rest for the night. Tomorrow is a new day, and we have much more to discover."

I nodded. My eyelids were heavy with fatigue. "You're right. Let's find a safe spot to settle down for the night."

Discovering an old barn just off the road, we eagerly settled in for the night. Our hearts pulsed with excitement and expectation, our imaginations running wild as we drifted asleep.

In the tender cradle of sleep, dreams of the morning's untold possibilities whirled through our minds, stirring and stimulating our senses. The soft night air cloaked us in a mysterious serenade, weaving a web of anticipation around fantasies that whispered of captivating adventures awaiting us.

As the sun prepared to unveil its tender glow upon our journey, an elusive air of mystery clung to the dawn, leaving us to wonder what secrets the daylight would reveal.

CHAPTER TWENTY-THREE

Frantic Search

Clad in her favorite faded jeans and a plaid flannel shirt, Kathleen stood in the doorway. Her hair, still wet from the shower, featured a light dusting of freckles on her cheeks. Tucking a few stray strands behind her ears, she stated, “I’ll take the truck and get some groceries while you two have your fishing trip.”

I studied her eyes, and she nodded in confirmation. “I won’t be gone too long. Just have fun without me.” She grabbed the truck keys, patted Maggie quickly on the head, and vanished out the door.

I smiled and observed Kathleen’s purposeful strides toward the beat-up truck in the driveway. The morning sun cast a warm glow on her freckled face, accentuating the mischievous glimmer in her eyes. Despite her attempt to conceal it, I sensed a flicker of anticipation in her voice.

Climbing into the driver's seat, Kathleen's damp hair clung to her forehead. There was a refreshing quality to her casual charm and effortless beauty that added meaning to my life.

Kathleen, always independent and adventurous, fearlessly embraced new experiences, a trait I valued in our friendship.

Maggie wagged her tail and whimpered softly as she observed Kathleen disappearing down the road. A fishing trip meant hours of exploring the great outdoors, a prospect that excited both of us. With a gentle pat on Maggie's head, I grabbed my fishing gear and headed toward the old wooden boat by the dock.

Taking the path to the lake near the police station, Maggie and I, familiar with the area but never for an extended period, basked in the sun filtering through the trees, creating spotted lights on the water's rippling surface.

Maggie darted between the trees, her tail wagging with uncontained excitement. Possessing an unquenchable curiosity, she always sought something new and mysterious. I felt a similar sense of wonder in the dappled sunlight filtering through the canopy above.

Deeper into the woods, the air cooled, carrying the scent of damp earth and pine needles. The path guided us past a babbling brook, its crystal-clear water tinkling with an almost musical rhythm. I paused momentarily, scooping a handful of water and playfully splashing it on my face.

Maggie noticed my antics and bounded back towards me, her tongue lolling out in a canine grin. Her eyes sparkled with mischief as she nudged me with her wet nose, urging me to continue our adventure.

Laughing, I obliged, joining her in running around, chasing each other, and having a blast. Maggie's energy and joy were infectious, making me happy to partake in her antics until we reached the lake. There, we climbed into the small wooden boat for our day of fishing.

Casting my line and waiting patiently, hoping for a big catch, Maggie stood on the boat's edge, her nails gripping the rough surface as she leaned over. The sun glinted off the water, its rippled surface teasingly hiding any signs of life beneath. Undeterred, Maggie peered into the depths with doggie tenacity, ready to reel in her fish.

After a few hours, I felt a tug on the line, and a massive fish was on the other end. Maggie watched as I reeled it in, and I gripped the fish with a firm yet gentle hold, feeling its slimy scales against my palm.

Carefully removing the hook from its mouth to avoid harm, I marveled at the silvery rainbow scales glistening in the warm afternoon sunlight. With a final admiring gaze, I gently lowered it back into the cool water below, watching it swim away gracefully.

As the orange hues of the sun cascaded over the lake, signifying the end of our day on the water, I swiftly stowed away the fishing rods, lures, and bait in the tackle box. The smell of the lake and the sound of the water lapping against the shore created a peaceful atmosphere.

Eager to share our adventure, I was sure Kathleen would love to hear about it. I could already imagine the joy on her face when I told her of our successful trip.

The late afternoon brought a sudden coolness, a stark contrast to the earlier warmth, signaling the shift of seasons. Nature's harmonious melody quieted down, preparing for bedtime, until a lone bird's song shattered the stillness, filling the air with a haunting melody. The crisp air and the bird's tune created a serene atmosphere, wrapping the day's end in tranquility.

Arriving at the police station, I found Kathleen's truck absent from the parking lot. Shielding my eyes, I scanned the horizon, but there was no sign of her. With a shrug, I assumed she must be sightseeing and continued inside.

I closed my eyes for a brief nap, but when I opened them, the evening had arrived. A cold gust of wind blew by, causing me to shiver. I called out for Kathleen, but she didn't answer. Fear crept into my mind as I realized several hours had passed since she left.

My heart hammered as I searched the building. My pace quickened, anxiety weighing heavy in my chest with each passing moment.

Stepping outside, I walked the familiar city streets in the oppressive darkness. The sun had set, and my calls for Kathleen went unheard amid the wind's eerie howling and scattered debris.

My stomach knotted with worry. Minutes dragged on with no sign of her. Ignoring negative thoughts, Maggie led me down old back roads through winding streets and alleys. Hope and fear battled within as we stood there.

I navigated along a dangerous, winding path that clung tightly to the edge of a deadly cliff. I battled against the unrelenting wind and its constant threat to push me over the brink. In the distance, I spied twisted metal glinting in the moonlight, and my stomach lurched with revulsion. It was Kathleen's pickup truck, horribly mangled and resting against a massive boulder at least fifty feet below.

Adrenaline surged as I hurried towards it, hoping she had somehow survived. Hurtling down the hillside, my heart pounded like a drumbeat. Each step echoed through the steep hillside, a symphony of urgency.

Every muscle throbbed with apprehension as I approached the wreckage. My mind raced, replaying memories of our shared adventures. Fate seemed cruel, ripping her away in an instant.

Slipping on loose gravel, I slid into the side of the truck. A sharp hiss of vapor split the air. An immense boulder wedged the mangled frame, and Kathleen was still inside. My heart raced as I ran to her door.

"Kathleen!" I cried out, my voice trembling with urgency. "Can you hear me? Are you hurt?"

Kathleen's weak voice reached me. "Collin... I'm trapped... I can't move."

My heart sank, but I couldn't afford to dwell on it. "Don't worry. I'll get you out of there. Just hold on."

Frantically, I shook the unyielding door handle, desperation mounting with each futile attempt. Anxiety overwhelmed me as I faced the grim reality of not being able to rescue her. Thoughts raced through my mind, a barrage of questions. What can I do? How can I save her? My mind raced as I searched for a solution.

In a desperate sprint, I tore back to the firehouse beside the police station. Each step felt like a sprint against time, my heart hammering in my chest. Hope flickered that karma wouldn't make me search only to find nothing.

Reaching the fire truck, I scanned frantically for the Jaws of Life. Sweat beads formed on my forehead, dripping into my eyes as I finally spotted them tucked away in the truck's corner. With trembling hands, I snatched them and raced back towards the trapped truck, determined to defy time and rescue Kathleen.

As I returned to the location of the accident, a heart-wrenching scene unfolded before me. I saw Kathleen slumped against the mangled remains of her vehicle, her once flawless face now smeared with dirt and streaked with blood. She was barely conscious but lifted an arm when she sensed my presence.

My hands shook as I tried to pry the driver's door with the tool. My determination wavered against the sheer weight of the twisted metal. Every passing second felt like an eternity, and I feared I was doing more harm than good with each movement. Yet, I had to try. I had to save Kathleen.

With a loud screech, I pulled the door off its hinges and let it fall to the ground. A cloud of dust engulfed me as I stumbled forward, desperately reaching for Kathleen's petite body. She felt light in my arms as I struggled up the steep hill, my boots struggling for footing on the loose rocks and gravel.

Every step was a struggle. It drenched my entire back in sweat when we reached the top. With shaking hands, I laid her on the stretcher from the firehouse and wheeled it along the uneven road towards the police station.

Kathleen's breathing was shallow, and her skin was as white as a corpse, causing me to shiver. She fought to lift her heavy eyelids, revealing two glistening green eyes in the low light.

"Doctor Collin, don't worry. I'm doing great," she whispered. Her voice was barely audible beneath the flood of pain coursing through her body. Here she was, fighting for her life, yet still considering my well-being. It showcased her innate compassion and underscored why I knew she was exceptional.

Checking her body for broken bones, I found none but a deep

cut on her calf. With care, I wrapped the wound with a clean bandage before inquiring about other pain. She nodded in affirmation.

Reaching out, she grabbed my arm, guiding me to a cupboard stocked with various medications. The pain in her eyes was palpable as she communicated what medication she needed. I trembled slightly as I retrieved two small white pills and handed them to her. Within moments, the agony in her expression faded, and she slipped into a tranquil slumber.

Throughout the night, I was at her side, observing her every movement until morning light filled the room. Now and then, she would open her eyes and ask for a glass of water or something to ease the pain.

Sadly, as each hour passed, Kathleen's condition continued to worsen and became more agonizing. Her once vibrant complexion drained of life, and the lines of pain etched deeper into her delicate features. I observed as her chest rose and fell in a disjointed rhythm, breathing labored and shallow. Sweat glistened on her forehead, a glaring sign of an escalating fever.

Desperate, I rushed to gather damp cloths to cool her burning forehead, but the relief was short-lived. The once peaceful room was now filled with an air of desperation, interrupted only by her occasional moans of agony. A knot formed in my stomach as a deep fear took hold of me. The pills that had provided some relief before were now mere drops in an ocean of unrelenting suffering.

A mixture of fury and sorrow cascaded through me at the

cruelty of life. We had so much fun only days before until we stumbled upon that stupid truck. Now, all I could feel was regret, wishing we had never taken that road.

A chilling wind swept through the desolate police station, mirroring the emptiness that had taken root within me. The vibrant colors of life, once vivid, now faded into somber shades of gray, reflecting the bleakness of my soul. The accident had stolen the physical joys of existence and extinguished the flickering hope that once burned brightly in my heart.

Each night, as Kathleen lay in bed, fragmented memories haunted me, and despair covered me like a suffocating cover. In the recesses of my mind, I replayed that fateful day incessantly, tormenting myself with what-ifs and if-onlys that gripped my consciousness. The weight of guilt bore down on my shoulders, burdening me with an unbearable responsibility for the tragedy that unfolded.

Days turned into an endless cycle of self-blame and anguish. As faithful as ever, Maggie would curl up at my feet every morning and refuse to leave my side. She would nuzzle her head against my hand as if sensing my pain and would stay with me until I felt strong enough to face the world again. Her warm presence offered a small but significant measure of comfort.

One early morning, with the sun's soft glow filling the room, I made my way back to Kathleen's bedside. I brought a steaming mug of coffee, its rich aroma wafting through the air.

Kathleen's eyes fluttered open as I approached, a light

flickering in the previously heavy darkness that had blanketed the room for weeks. Her voice, though barely more than a whisper, shattered the oppressive silence, resembling a ray of hope piercing through a dark storm.

Turning her gaze toward me, her eyes scanned my face before fixing on the mug of coffee in my hand. With a half-smile, she asked, "Where's my coffee?"

Joy overwhelmed me, and I burst out laughing, narrowly avoiding spilling the coffee on Maggie, who wagged her tail excitedly by my side.

"So, now you think you're the nurse?" she whispered, a faint smile playing at the corner of her lips.

I chuckled, a nervous tremor in my voice. "Well, I'm giving it my best shot, but let's be real, I could never match your expertise."

She chuckled, wincing at the pain it caused. "You've done a stellar job keeping me company, though. That's just as crucial, if not more."

Reaching for her hand, I gripped it tightly. "I just wish there was more I could do. It hurts to see you like this. You deserve better."

She squeezed my hand, gratitude in her gaze. "You've done more than enough. Your care and companionship have given me strength. I'm grateful to have you by my side."

"Kathleen, I can't imagine losing you. This world is already a lonely place... I can't bear the thought of losing another person I care about."

She sighed. "Let's not dwell on what we can't change. I'm just grateful to have had you by my side."

As the days passed, Kathleen's vitality returned, and she shared the details of the unfortunate accident with me.

"The brakes failed. I couldn't stop the truck, no matter what I did."

My heart sank at the realization. It wasn't just a simple accident; it could have been a tragedy. Yet here she was, alive and fighting. And for that, I was grateful.

Once I felt Kathleen was strong enough to be left alone, I returned to the crash site. My mind raced as I tried to comprehend what had just occurred. The realization hit me like a ton of bricks, shattering the illusion of invulnerability clouding my thoughts.

Life's fragility had just once again unfolded before my eyes. Why do I always seem to go about my days unaware of the preciousness of each moment? I took so much for granted until it teetered on the edge of being taken away. How had I become so blind to this truth?

While standing there, the weight of my carelessness pressed upon me like a leaden cloak. How many aspects of my life had I treated with such disregard? How many potential tragedies lurked in the shadows, waiting for a momentary lapse in judgment or an unnoticed detail to turn them into grim realities?

Staring at the wreckage, my mind wandered, reflecting on the countless things I overlooked daily. It's remarkable how easily I became blind to the surrounding wonders, a vibrant sunset, the soft touch of a loved one's hand, or even the aroma of freshly brewed coffee in the morning.

But what about the veritable treasures in my life, my loved ones? I assumed they would always be there until they were not.

For years, I threw myself into my work, keeping my nose to the grindstone. I punched in day in and day out, chasing the dream of making a decent living. It was all about putting in the hours, meeting quotas, and making ends meet. The constant hustle consumed my days, and I figured success at work meant happiness at home. My family, well, I just thought they saw it the same way.

Staring at the wreckage, my heart heavy with grief and regret, it became painfully clear that this pursuit had closed my eyes to what truly mattered. It took another person's suffering to shatter my façade, tearing down superficial walls and revealing life's fragility.

Sadly, I recognized I had become the Ebenezer Scrooge of my life, neglecting what was truly important until it was too late.

CHAPTER TWENTY-FOUR

Kathleen's Plans

Having spent the morning chopping wood, I returned to the police station. With the weight of the hefty pine logs on one arm, I tried to turn the brass doorknob with my free hand, but it wouldn't budge. Stepping back, I kicked the door with my boot, which swung open with a loud creak.

As the door opened, a cloud of dust billowed into the air, making me cough. The room was dimly lit, with feeble rays of sunlight struggling to penetrate the grimy windows. Inside, the air carried the weighty scent of ash and burned timber.

Kathleen occupied a worn desk in the corner, her nimble fingers dancing across the buttons of an ancient battery-operated CD player we had salvaged. No particular melody guided her, just a journey through the individual tracks, each press releasing a soft tune that enveloped the room.

"Collin!" Kathleen looked up, mischief gleaming in her eyes. "You're back! I thought you got lost among the pines."

With a thud, I dropped the bundle of firewood on the floor and chuckled softly. "Wouldn't want to miss out on all this excitement, would I?"

Leaning back in her chair, a mischievous grin played at the edges of Kathleen's mouth. She stood, approaching me with sparkling eyes.

"Sometimes I can almost feel the warmth of the summer air on my skin and hear the laughter from those nights of long ago. When I would go out to five-star restaurants and dance until dawn."

My curiosity piqued, eyebrows raised at Kathleen's revelation. How much of a clubber was she before in this chaotic world?

A slow, playful smile spread across her face. "Wouldn't it be fun to do all that again? Here! Now?"

"What?" I asked.

"Fix this place to look like a fine restaurant and nightclub, silly."

The unexpected proposal hung in the air. Turning the old police station into an upscale restaurant and nightclub? It felt akin to transforming a battleship into a luxury cruise liner.

I chuckled, appreciating Kathleen's wild imagination. "You're always full of surprises, aren't you?" I said, my grin mirroring hers. "But how on earth will we turn this dusty old place into a five-star restaurant?"

Kathleen's eyes glinted with determination as she surveyed the room. "With a little bit of magic and some good old-fashioned creativity."

"It could be fun. Why not?" I shook my head, amused and skeptical at the idea of us transforming the crumbling ruins.

Kathleen's laughter echoed a vibrant and infectious sound. Excitement lit up her face, accentuated by the sparkle in her eyes. She smiled warmly at me and clapped her hands together.

"Oh, this is going to be amazing! I have some grand plans brewing. Just wait and see."

Standing in the center of the dilapidated police station, Kathleen stretched her arms out, declaring firmly, "Let's make this place our Club Inferno!"

"Club Inferno? Like the club on Miami Beach?"

I couldn't believe it. Decay surrounded us, broken windows, crumbling bricks, and disrepair everywhere.

"You think we can turn this site into something... like that?"

Kathleen grinned, her voice unwavering. "Of course we can! With a bit of imagination, anything is possible. We'll hang up blinking lights, set up a makeshift stage, and create a haven away from the desolation outside."

A spark ignited as I surveyed the worn walls and chipped paint. A vision of breathing life back into this place filled my mind. I considered the potential of what this room could become with hard work and love. Glancing at Kathleen, a warm smile stretched across my face.

"Alright, Kathleen, count me in. Let's bring Club Inferno to life."

Kathleen's eyes sparkled with delight, and her feet lifted off the ground as she bounced on her toes. She clapped her hands with an exuberance reminiscent of a cheerleader celebrating a game-winning touchdown.

"That's the spirit!" she exclaimed. "Together, we'll transform this forgotten space into a haven of creativity and joy."

With renewed determination, we embarked on our mission. My mind delved into the realm of creativity, birthing visions for the club's distinctive aesthetics. Walls once marred by time were reborn in vibrant hues, bold strokes of reds, purples, and golds replacing the worn, chipped paint.

Meanwhile, Kathleen explored every nook of the desolate buildings, salvaging the forgotten relics of the place's former grandeur. Old wooden crates found a new purpose, fashioned into a makeshift stage. Strings of blinking lights hung from the ceiling, creating a magical ambiance that danced with every flicker.

Our voices echoed through the vacant room, harmonizing with the rhythmic beat of hammers against wood. Dust swirled as we brushed off cobwebs and unfurled long-forgotten rugs.

Laughter filled the air, bouncing off bare walls, mingling with our animated conversations about plans for the upcoming event.

The atmosphere crackled with anticipation. Each flickering light breathed life into the space, casting a warm glow that dispelled the shadows of the past. Their shimmering colors whispered of joy and merriment.

Side by side, we toiled, exchanging bittersweet smiles and enjoying peaceful pauses. This transformation wasn't merely about the physical space but a rejuvenation of our emotional well-being. It was an opportunity to craft fresh memories. To weave a narrative of affection and joy that would drown out the echoes of past sorrows.

After days of hard work, we unveiled Club Inferno. Cheers reverberated through the destruction, revealing a dazzling refuge.

Kathleen twirled gracefully, reminiscent of a ballerina lost in the joy of movement. Laughter spilled from her like a melody, notes dancing through the air as she twirled around the room. Her appearance was a portrait of delight, her face aglow with happiness and her emerald-green eyes shimmering with pure joy as they locked onto mine.

"Can you hear it? The faint whispers of music, the distant rhythm of joy? We did it!"

My lips curved into a proud smirk, and my chest tightened with satisfaction. I looked over at Kathleen. Her body vibrated with joy, and her face was beaming. Somehow, we turned the old police station into a nightclub from scratch.

"Yes, we did it," I said, gesturing around us. "Our Club Inferno may not look the same as the one on Miami Beach, but it has its unique energy now."

"Now we need the perfect refreshments," Kathleen suggested.

"Refreshments? Seriously?"

"Yeah, for our night of dancing."

"Well, you go get some refreshments." I grinned. "But let's keep an eye on the budget," I added with a hint of caution.

Kathleen and I scoured the devastated streets, hunting for supplies for our upcoming Club Inferno extravaganza. We strolled down the sidewalk, eyes scanning the debris like treasure hunters on a quest.

"Collin, can't you see?" Kathleen's voice sparkled with excitement. "This night will be a beacon of light in this dark world. We're bringing joy back, one flickering bulb at a time!"

Kathleen's contagious enthusiasm was rubbing off on me. Creating a temporary escape from the harsh reality seemed more than worthwhile.

"You're right," I replied. "Let's turn this wasteland into a party that would make even The Gatsby proud."

As we rummaged through the rubble of an old grocery store, we collected cans of beans, stale crackers, and a pack of half-crushed soda cans. It wasn't a five-star cuisine, but desperate times called for a touch of culinary creativity.

"Voila!" Kathleen held up a rusty can of peaches. "Our pièce de résistance! Peach cobbler may be off the menu, but canned peaches will transport our taste buds straight to Club Inferno's imaginary paradise."

I surveyed our meager food supply and scratched my head. "I'm not sure how successful a nightclub can be without a decent drink selection. No party is complete without a gin and tonic or a margarita. But all I see here are some sad cans of soda. We need a miracle, Kathleen."

A glint sparked in Kathleen's eyes. "Collin, a miracle is what we shall have! Remember that abandoned liquor store a few blocks away? I saw a bottle of dusty tequila sitting on a shelf as if waiting for us. Let's go on a boozy scavenger hunt!"

We walked through the desolate streets, our excitement building like a chorus of heartbeats. Until we reached the shell of a building that once held the promise of intoxicating liberation. We cautiously pushed open the door, half-expecting a zombie bartender to greet us. But we found ourselves surrounded by rows upon rows of dusty bottles, each filled with the sweet nectar of possibility.

Whiskey, rum, vodka, all waiting to be resurrected for our extraordinary night. "Collin, pick up your jaw from the floor," Kathleen teased, delight dancing in her eyes. "We've hit the boozy mother lode! They will know Club Inferno for its legendary drinks. We shall mix, shake, and stir until we've concocted the elixir of dreams!"

I couldn't help but laugh at Kathleen's infectious enthusiasm. With every impossible challenge we faced, her spirit remained unyielding, almost defiant. She was a force of nature, pulling me out of my grief's darkest corners. We returned to our makeshift Club Inferno with tequila, whiskey, and vodka bottles in our backpacks.

The weight on our shoulders felt lighter, as if the very act of unified purpose was transforming our broken world, one step at a time. As Kathleen sprinted ahead, her excitement too fantastic to be contained, I marveled at how she brought life to everything she touched.

Each shadowy corner we walked through appeared to radiate

new life as if the universe celebrated her infinite spirit. Finally, we arrived at the police station, our haven filled with dreams of escape and possibility. We set the bottles on a battered table, the clinking sound echoing like a symphony of resilience.

Kathleen turned to face me, her eyes shimmering with determination and mischief. "Collin, it's time to dress the part. Let's find the perfect outfits to dance the night away and amaze the ghosts of this forsaken world."

I couldn't help but chuckle at her ever-creative mind. "Amaze ghosts, huh? We'll need attire fit for both the living and the deceased. Perhaps a little black dress for you and a dapper suit for me?"

Kathleen winked. "Oh, Collin, you underestimate my fashion prowess. We'll make heads turn even among the rubble."

Amidst the thrift store remains, we stumbled upon some hidden gems as fashionable clothing. Every discovery felt like a victory, a chance to breathe life into forgotten memories.

"Look what I've found!" Kathleen held up a dazzling blue satin dress with delicate beadwork that seemed to shimmer under the faintest light. "The night sky graces Club Inferno."

I gazed at the dress, marveling at its beauty. "Kathleen, you look like a shooting star. The sky itself would weep with envy."

We emerged from the remnants of a forgotten clothing store,

our arms laden with treasures to wrap ourselves in. As we approached our Club Inferno oasis, the transformation before our eyes took our breath away.

The twinkling lights we had hung sparkled like a sky full of stars. The makeshift dance floor, covered in worn-out rugs stitched together, looked inviting and alive. And in the corner, the vintage jukebox stood like a time traveler, ready to spin melodies that would carry us away.

"Kathleen," I whispered, awe coloring my voice, "we've created a little piece of magic in this forsaken place. It may not be the club on Miami Beach, but dear friend, it's our slice of heaven."

She giggled, her eyes gleaming with mischief. "Who needs Miami Beach when we have Club Inferno right here? We may make our dance floor of old rugs, but it holds the promise of joy, of forgetting the horror outside, even if it's just for one night."

We threw open the doors of our Club Inferno, our laughter echoing through the once desolate police station. The dust danced in the air, giving the illusion of confetti falling from a long-lost celebration.

"Welcome to Club Inferno!" I announced, holding open the door with a flourish. "Tonight, we dance, we laugh, and we let the magic of our imaginations carry us away."

Kathleen's eyes alighted with joy. "Collin, my partner in hope, let's disappear into the music, into a world that only exists within these walls. For one night, let's be more than mere survivors. Let's be alive!"

And so, the night of our grand escape began, with the old police station pulsating with newfound life. We danced as if no tomorrow existed, twirling and spinning to the rhythm of the old songs that filled the air. Our past sorrows seemed to melt away with every beat, dissolving into the music that swirled around us.

Tonight, all that mattered was the infectious laughter, the sparkling eyes, and the promise of a new beginning. I watched Kathleen twirl across the dance floor, her dress billowing like a burst of color in a monochromatic world.

Her laughter resonated in my ears, and suddenly, the weight of the past lifted, leaving only the shimmering dance of possibility. As the night wore on, we invited the ghosts of the past to join our festivities. They watched from their forgotten corners, their faces filled with longing and joy. It was as if, for a moment, they, too, had found peace in the enchantment of Club Inferno.

"Collin, my partner-in-escape," Kathleen whispered, her voice carrying the weight of countless memories. "I can almost hear the whispers of the music from our past, mingling with the joy of tonight. They remind me of the laughter, of the stolen moments once cherished."

I pulled Kathleen's hand close, our bodies swaying to the sentimental melody. "Let's dance for them, for all those who couldn't make it to tonight's celebration. Let's weave a new story filled with laughter and the hope that life can blossom even amidst destruction."

And so we danced. We danced for every lost dream, broken heart, and future that would never come to be. We danced to honor the resilience of the human spirit and show that even in the darkest times, a sliver of light can still flicker.

The night carried on, and the walls of our Club Inferno grew warmer with the memories we created. Each step we took, each spin, held the power to wash away the sadness that had weighed us down for so long. As dawn broke on the horizon, casting a gentle glow on the remnants of our Club Inferno, we knew we had accomplished our mission.

Though the world outside remained a desolate wasteland, we had found comfort in each other and the power of imagination.

"Collin, we've created something beautiful here, something that defies the ashes of this world. Our Club Inferno may be a whisper in time, but it will forever echo in our hearts."

I held Kathleen's hand in mine, a smile on my lips. "It may be a fleeting oasis, but it's our oasis. A place where we dared to dream even amidst chaos and pain. A reminder that even when everything falls apart, love and laughter will always find a way."

And so, we stepped out of Club Inferno, the morning sun casting a hopeful glow on our tired but content faces. As we closed the doors behind us, we knew that within those walls, a lifetime of memories had been born.

Our adventure wasn't over, and the world outside still held its share of challenges. But armed with the magic of Club Inferno, we faced each day with renewed hope, believing that joy and love could shine through, even in the darkest nights.

From that day forward, Club Inferno became our beacon of resilience. No matter what life brought our way, we knew we could turn our struggles into triumphs and our pain into strength.

So, let the world crumble. Let the chaos scream its endless symphony. We had our Club Inferno, our place to dance, laugh, and remember the power of hope. And as long as we held onto that, the destruction would never truly win.

CHAPTER TWENTY-FIVE

Cupid's Aim A Miss

It had only been a few weeks since our enchanting night of dancing beneath the glittering stars. Kathleen sat calmly in a weathered, creaking chair, tears pooling in her eyes as they sparkled in the dwindling twilight. The chair moaned softly, resonating with the melancholy that cloaked her form.

Her trembling fingers delicately caressed the silver locket dangling from her neck, its surface adorned with an intricate heart design. Kathleen's thumb traced the etching with profound reverence. Although I had never inquired about its origin, Kathleen kept the memories of the person who had given her the locket securely tucked away in the recesses of her heart.

In the quiet room, I could feel the memories swirling in her mind, like fall leaves caught in a gentle breeze. "Kathleen, you seem troubled. Is everything alright?" I asked, sensing the weight of her emotions.

She hesitated, her toes gripping the floor, lips bitten in contemplation. Finally, she met my gaze and spoke with a raw vulnerability.

"Collin, there's something about me I need to share. And please, don't brush it off." Her voice quivered with emotion.

I nodded, my intrigue heightened. "Of course. You have my word."

With a deep breath, her voice just above a whisper, she confessed, "I loved him, Collin. With all my heart. But he didn't love me back."

Kathleen's hands quivered, delicately twirling a strand of her hair between her fingers. As she began recounting tales of her ex-husband, a noticeable sadness seeped into her voice, prompting her to avert her gaze.

A solitary tear traced a path down her face, swiftly banished by her hand. Her chest rose and fell in a struggle to gulp a deep breath before she could continue. Intrigued and sympathetic, I probed, "Oh, I'm sorry to hear that. What happened?"

She unfolded memories of nights entwined in each other's arms, the echoes of laughter still vivid in her mind. Together, they spun hopes and dreams into a delicate web. Yet, as she spoke, it became clear that love, too often, proved fleeting.

Kathleen's eyes reflected a blend of pain and yearning, haunted by the remnants of a shattered relationship, lingering like stubborn specters refusing to release their grip on her fragile soul.

"The night before our wedding," Kathleen resumed, her voice holding a bittersweet cadence, "we sat on the porch swing, gazing at the twinkling stars above. He reached into his pocket, producing a small velvet box. My heart fluttered as he unveiled a delicate silver locket with a tiny heart etched into its surface."

She described the tender act of fastening it around her neck, his lingering touch against her skin.

"This symbolizes my endless love for you, he whispered before a soft kiss. The weight of the locket against my chest became a constant reminder of his promise. Until it wasn't."

A pause lingered, her eyes fixed on the floor. After a deep breath, she spoke hushedly, "Life was a dream before our wedding. He made me feel like royalty; I thought it would last forever. But somehow, our marriage changed everything..."

Confusion etched my face as I sought clarification. "What do you mean? How did he change?"

"It started as a gradual unraveling, his return home growing progressively later each night. At first, he brushed it off as overtime, but the pungent mix of liquor and perfume on his clothes betrayed a different story. When I confronted him, he erupted into a fiery rage, accusing me of smothering him. He even hinted that my interactions with wealthy physicians might warrant suspicion."

"Collin, I stood in disbelief, his words hanging heavy like a toxic fog. The accusations sliced through the layers of trust we had painstakingly built over the years. How did we go from a deep, unbreakable connection to this vast, distant separation? I gazed into his eyes, desperately seeking the man I once knew, but all I found was anger and resentment."

"His late-night escapades became routine, accompanied by increasingly implausible explanations. With each passing day, my heart sank deeper. Suspicion, fueled by his insidious words, gnawed at me. Was he truly toiling away at work, or were darker forces at play?"

Kathleen wiped away her tears and then went on. "Our first anniversary was supposed to be the perfect evening, with a lovely dinner at our most beloved restaurant. I'd looked forward to it all day, excitedly imagining our fun together. Sadly, he called me at 7:30 PM, half an hour after our reservation. To tell me he had gotten held up at work and couldn't make it."

Realizing the depth of her pain, my heart sank. "I am deeply sorry," I whispered. A part of me wanted to convey that this guy seemed like a total jerk, but I refrained, not wanting to add to her sadness.

Kathleen nodded, a tear slipping down her cheek. "It was. It still is. It wasn't just his actions but how he made me feel. Like some displayed object, he expected me to be this aesthetically pleasing wife around his friends. He didn't care about my thoughts or feelings, just how I appeared to others. It was suffocating and dehumanizing."

Kathleen's stillness filled the air, suffocating in its own right. Her lips pressed together in a tight, pale line. My mind raced, desperate to find the right words or actions to ease her agony. Something, however, trapped my voice in my throat like a caged animal. Self-hatred burned within me as I fumed with frustration at my helplessness. It was torture to witness her suffering, knowing there was nothing I could do to ease her pain.

"But Collin, do you know the most painful moment? It was when he confessed he was leaving me for someone else. And to make matters worse, he had a child with her despite always telling me he didn't want kids!"

Kathleen continued, "I stood there, frozen in a sea of emotions tearing through my chest. The words resonated in my ears, each carving a deeper wound into my shattered heart. How could he? How could the person I loved with every fiber of my being abandon me for someone else?"

"Collin, I could hardly make out his face through the haze of my tears, but I saw no remorse or regret in his eyes. Instead, they glistened with a cruel glimmer of satisfaction. As if he reveled in delivering the final blow to our once beautiful relationship."

Kathleen's hands balled into tight fists, the knuckles turning white under the strain. Kathleen clenched her jaw, her muscles tensing as she fought to contain the anger and hurt bubbling inside her. I could see the trembling of her body as she struggled to maintain control of her emotions.

"In that moment, Collin, time seemed to stand still. Every memory we shared flashed before my eyes, each cherished moment now stained with the bitter truth. All the whispered promises and dreams we had woven together evaporated like mist on a winter's morning. How easily he discarded them all for another woman and a child he claimed he never desired?"

My hands trembled as I reached for Kathleen's hand, cherishing the warmth of her touch. Desperation fueled my desire to convey the profoundness of my feelings for her. Yet, as I locked eyes with her, a sense of inadequacy crept in.

Deep down, I cared for Kathleen, but articulating my empathy proved challenging. Was it because of the absence of a role model to teach me, or had I perpetually kept myself at a distance, never truly letting anyone know me? This moment wasn't about me; it was about Kathleen.

"Kathleen," I uttered, my voice wavering, "you are amazing. You deserve someone who can appreciate all your wonderful qualities."

She closed her eyes, took a deep breath, and leaned closer to me. The faint streaks of tears adorned her damp eyelashes, and as our eyes met, I sensed the weight of her sorrow.

"I want to trust again. To open my heart up to someone else and feel safe knowing they won't hurt me like before. But I can't bring myself to do it. Every time I let go of the fear, a part of me holds back, remembering how much pain I felt before. How can I rebuild trust when I still feel so scared?"

Time appeared to freeze at that moment. I grappled with the profoundness of her words. It was as if the universe had conspired to hold its breath, anticipating my response. My mind raced, searching for the right words to convey my swirling emotions.

Her eyes bore into mine, their intensity piercing through any lingering doubts. The moment's gravity seeped into my bones, sending tremors through every fiber of my being. How could a mere string of words possess such power?

Yet, there they were, suspended between us, poised to change everything.

I felt the weight of my hesitation pressing down on me, making it difficult to move or speak. But beneath it all, I knew this was a pivotal moment. It was a moment where I had to decide whether to embrace the unknown or retreat into the familiar comfort of what it once was.

A fierce desire to sweep her into my arms and shelter her from the world surged through me, but fear paralyzed me. Her eyes, filled with raw vulnerability, pierced through me, and I saw the harsh reality of life, messy, unpredictable, and utterly terrifying. No amount of fairy tale wishes or romantic notions could shield me from its cruel grip. So, I retreated to the safety of words.

"Kathleen, entrusting someone with your heart is like taking a leap of faith. You hope that their words and actions will stand the test of time. It's a waiting game; it feels like an eternity before you can completely believe in them. We yearn for it to be easier, but we understand that true trust is a precious gift we cannot rush or force. It requires patience, vulnerability, and a willingness to let go of past hurts."

She sighed, her shoulders sagging with the weight of her emotions. "It's just so hard to believe that after everything, there could be someone out there who truly cares. And now, in our hellish world, I'll never find love again."

"I understand. You deserve to discover happiness and love, even in this world."

Kathleen sniffled, a faint smile playing on her lips. "Thank you, Collin. Sometimes, it's comforting to hear those words. To know that someone believes in me."

I wrapped her in a reassuring hug, drawing her into the warmth of the embrace. "Believe in yourself. You're resilient and capable of finding love again. And when you're ready, I'll be here to support you every step of the way."

She nestled against my chest. "You're a genuine friend. Thank you for always being there for me."

"Well, what are friends for, if not to offer a listening ear and a shoulder to lean on?"

Kathleen gently released the embrace and leaned back. A blush tinted her cheeks, and she bit her lip, a coy smile playing on her lips as an unmistakable sparkle lit up her eyes.

"Hmm, true. But I have one question, Collin. How did you become such a wise old sage?"

I chuckled, shaking my head. "Well, it comes with age and experience, my dear Kathleen. I've lived a thousand lives in a few decades."

She nudged me lightly and smiled, her mouth curving into a mischievous grin. She tossed her head back and let out a quick chuckle.

"Alright, Mr. Sage," her eyes sparkling with mischief. "I'll accept your wisdom only because I trust you."

My face stretched into a wide grin, and my chest filled with warmth, like a cozy fire glowing in winter. I looked at Kathleen and said, "Thank you. It means the world that I have your trust."

With that, we sat together in comfortable silence, the weight of Kathleen's past slowly lifting with each passing moment. In the darkness of our shared existence, we found support in being there for one another, even without uttering a single word.

The gentle rustle of leaves outside the window provided a soothing symphony as if Mother Nature knew of the healing within those four walls.

Once filled with sadness and torment, Kathleen's eyes now held a glimmer of hope. In the soft glow of candlelight, I could see her shoulders relax, the tension she had carried for so long dissolving. It felt like I had become her refuge, where she momentarily forgot her troubles.

I reached out, my hand finding hers in the vast darkness. Our fingers intertwined, creating a silent bond that spoke volumes without explanation. We were two lost souls, finding solace in our shared journey through life's hardships.

In that instant, I realized just how intertwined our lives had become. Our encounter may have been fate, but our bond ran more profoundly than mere chance. We were both struggling to mend ourselves, and we had found each other by some stroke of luck.

Until then, we may not have realized it, but we were searching for the same thing. And in each other, we found it. At that moment, I fully grasped the immense power of human connection.

Kathleen's breath hitched in her chest, and she leaned back, her eyes fixed on mine. "You know, Collin," she whispered, "these moments mean everything to me. To have someone who truly understands, who selflessly cares for me." Her voice trembled with emotion as she looked at me, tears glistening in her eyes.

I gently placed my hand on her arm, reassuringly squeezing it. As our eyes met, I could sense the depth of our bond, our friendship, something truly extraordinary. It was like an invisible thread connected us, weaving our souls together in an unbreakable bond. At that moment, I knew we were in each other's lives forever.

"I'm glad I have you," she said.

A sudden surge of warmth flooded my cheeks, spreading like wildfire and causing the corners of my lips to curl upwards. It felt like an invisible force was pulling them, making it impossible to contain the delight bubbling up inside me. Despite my best efforts, I couldn't hide the infectious joy that blossomed on my face, radiating outwards like rays of sunshine.

"You flatter me with your words. But I truly meant what I said earlier. You deserve nothing less than pure happiness, an abundance of love, and everything that your heart desires."

Her eyes, a deep emerald green, softened at my words, revealing a mixture of gratitude and vulnerability. They were like pools of liquid emotion, reflecting the depths of her soul.

"Thank you," she whispered, her voice trembling slightly with emotion. At that moment, I knew my words had touched her deeply, and I felt grateful for the opportunity to bring a smile to her face.

She squeezed my hand, her grip firm and comforting. "I don't know what I did to deserve you as a friend, but I'm forever grateful."

The night whispered its approval as gentle winds carried our dreams into the universe. Amid our shattered reality, we found consolation in believing something extraordinary could be born from the ruins.

Time slipped away, unnoticed and unimportant, as we sat there, uninterrupted by the chaos of the outside world. In those stolen moments, I realized how precious our bond indeed was.

Kathleen yawned, her eyes heavy with fatigue. "I should probably get some sleep. Tomorrow is another day, after all."

I smiled, releasing her hand. "You're right."

She stood and stretched her tired limbs. "Thank you. For being here, listening, and reminding me that there is hope even in the darkest times."

I stood as well, mirroring her actions. "Always. I'm here for you, no matter what. And remember, even in the gloomiest of nights, the stars still shine."

She gave me a grateful smile, her eyes reflecting the trust we had built between us.

"Goodnight. Sleep well, my friend."

I returned her smile, a sense of contentment settling over me. "Goodnight, Kathleen. Sweet dreams."

And with that, we parted ways, retreating to our separate corners of the old police station, finding peace in its shelter.

I slumped to the rough floor below me. My tired eyes could not look away from the broken ceiling above. Even though my body was exhausted, my heart refused to let go of the optimism that things could improve soon.

That we could make it through this challenging life. That Kathleen might find peace with herself. A comfort that will sustain her and guide her through these difficult times.

As the comforting, velvety embrace of darkness encircled me, I closed my eyes and surrendered to the endless possibilities that awaited in my mind. A world of love and harmony filled my thoughts, seamlessly intertwining with my deepest desires.

Like a vibrant kaleidoscope, images of fulfillment and joy danced before me, casting a hopeful light on the canvas of my dreams. In this tranquil moment, I felt at one with the universe, connected to the flow of abundance that allowed for endless growth and happiness.

CHAPTER TWENTY-SIX

Garden of Life

As the sun ascended, casting its golden glow upon the waking garden, I witnessed a spectacle of nature bursting with vitality. Kathleen's indomitable spirit and my steadfast belief in her echoed through the vibrant dance of colors, each leaf and bud bathed in the sun's soothing warmth.

Venturing through the lush rows of vegetables, I marveled at the abundant harvest sprawled out before me. Each plant shared tales of tenacity and rebirth, their leaves swaying in a rhythmic celebration as if nature applauded our journey. The once-barren soil had transformed into a fertile haven, pulsating with life and the promise of a thriving future.

From behind a thicket of tomato vines emerged Kathleen, her hands adorned with streaks of soil yet emanating a profound sense of fulfillment. Her radiant and spirited eyes met mine with a joy mirrored in my heart. We had overcome the desperate days of hunger, now standing amidst the lush bounty we had collectively nurtured.

Observing Kathleen gracefully navigate the garden, I couldn't help but be awestruck by her commitment to preserving the land's beauty. Sweeping her auburn hair behind her ear, she cast a warm smile my way, and at that moment, a surge of admiration swelled within me.

"Care to lend a hand?" Kathleen asked, her voice as gentle as the breeze rustling through the trees.

Feeling a surge of motivation fueled by her presence, I nodded eagerly. We worked side by side, our hands synchronized in harmony with nature. Kathleen's skilled touch and knowledge of plants made it seem almost effortless as she taught me the subtleties of tending to a garden.

Underneath the vibrant petals and lush foliage, we delved into conversations that flowed effortlessly. She spoke passionately about her love for gardening and how it comforted her soul. Each word she uttered was like poetry, awakening a newfound appreciation within me for the intricacies of nature.

"Collin, I never dreamed I'd witness this day. We turned desolate land into a garden. It is nothing short of a miracle." Kathleen beamed.

I nodded in agreement. "It's all thanks to your green thumb.

Your dedication and passion have truly worked wonders."

We worked in the morning sun, its gentle rays increasing in intensity as it rose higher in the sky. Its warmth caressed my skin like a warm blanket, soothing my tired muscles. We worked silently, enjoying the natural harmony between us.

We started a garden to ensure we had enough food to get by. But over time, our garden became something more substantial. It became a lighthouse of optimism amidst the world's weariness. It showed us that things could bring us joy and peace, even in adversity.

We would enter its welcoming embrace each morning, eager to witness the miracles nature bestowed upon us.

The fragrant scents of lettuce and peppers danced under the caress of gentle breezes, filling the air with their intoxicating perfume. Delicate butterflies flitted from petal to petal, their wings painting the garden with elegant beauty. Bees hummed in a harmonious symphony as they diligently pollinated the blossoms, ensuring the continuation of this life cycle.

The garden was our sanctuary with its kaleidoscope of colors and perfumes. We spent countless hours tending to its needs, nurturing each plant like a precious child. Our hands became thick with the earth's embrace, calloused and weathered from the tireless work we put into cultivating this haven.

Immersing myself in the invigorating fall breeze that caressed the garden, I reveled in the orchestrated dance of leaves gracefully falling to the earth. The slender cornstalks swayed elegantly, their bright yellow tassels adding to the enchanting sounds of nature's symphony.

Above, birds serenaded the peaceful scene with cheerful melodies while squirrels engaged in playful pursuits around tree trunks.

"Like watching magic!" I exclaimed, my voice resonating with amazement. "Every seed we plant holds the potential for life, for nourishment. It's a beautiful thing."

Kathleen's eyes lit up with excitement, a contagious enthusiasm infusing her words. "It is. Observing it all grow and thrive gives me purpose in this chaotic universe. Like I'm making a difference, no matter how small."

I nodded in agreement. Together, we knelt in the embrace of the rich soil, our hands adorned with the earthy remnants of the plants we had just picked.

Kathleen's smile deepened, revealing the dimple on her left cheek as we worked through the rows of tomatoes, peppers, and other vegetables. We handpicked each plump piece and placed them in our basket, ensuring they did not bruise or damage.

The soil caked our hands with earthy orange stains from digging through the fertile soil to unearth our treasures, freshly grown carrots. We grinned at each other, proud of our dedication and hard work, as we held up our stained hands for proof. Afterward, we headed over to the tomatoes.

I took my knife and sliced a tomato down the middle. I handed half to Kathleen. I felt an unexpected sense of accomplishment as juice pooled around my fingertips. We both marveled at the tomatoes' juiciness while our excitement bubbled over. We couldn't help but cheer like jubilant warriors celebrating victory.

"We've done it again!" I shouted. "Another successful harvest in the books."

Kathleen's face beamed excitedly, and she threw her fists into the air like a champion savoring victory in the ring. Jumping up and down, her ponytail swayed behind her, capturing the essence of her jubilant celebration.

"Well, when life pushes you to the brink, sometimes you discover hidden talents. Who knew we'd become survivalist farmers?" She said.

As the sun dipped below the horizon, casting shadows across the garden, we gathered our baskets and ventured toward the police station. A brisk breeze tousled my hair, and my stomach grumbled, eagerly expecting the forthcoming dinner.

"You know, back in the day, I couldn't stand the taste of vegetable soup," I admitted.

Kathleen shot me a mischievous smile, her eyes sparkling with a secret. “Oh, but you haven’t savored my vegetable soup yet. It’s like a warm hug for the soul.”

Around the flickering campfire, we settled into our spots as the pot simmered. The aroma of roasting vegetables mingled with the crisp evening breeze, captivating our senses and enticing our appetites. It was a symphony of flavors promising to soothe our bellies and rejuvenate our weary spirits. With each passing moment, our anticipation heightened, the air buzzing with the promise of a comforting and flavorful meal.

As the steam billowed from the pot, my mind whisked me back to simpler times when life unfolded leisurely. My gentle stirring of the simmering soup filled the air with a fragrant aroma, evoking memories of my grandmother’s kitchen.

As I thought back to her kitchen and the old wooden table, my mind was captivated. That table's surface bore witness to countless memories of our family coming together for meals and sharing in each other's lives. In my mind, I could hear echoes of conversations and laughter.

My thoughts journeyed to a summer day from my childhood, the kitchen pulsating with anticipation as my grandmother concocted her renowned beef stew. She possessed the knack for transforming ordinary ingredients into extraordinary dishes, weaving love and a dash of magic into every creation.

Perched on a chair, wide-eyed and eager, I observed her skilled hands deftly seasoning the meat. Her movements were swift and confident, as if she inhabited her world, wholly engrossed and content within the rhythm she had mastered.

Anticipation bubbled within me as the stew's tantalizing aroma encircled her kitchen. I could hardly wait to savor it, akin to a child on Christmas Eve, anticipating the joyous unveiling of a unique gift the following day.

Breaking free from my reverie, my gaze shifted to Kathleen. Her fingers delved into the contents of her well-worn backpack, a testament to the adventures it had weathered. Unfazed by the chaos, she unearthed various items, each carrying a unique memory or practical utility from her travels.

After a while, she extracted a small, weathered notebook from her bag, its pages bearing wrinkles from countless outdoor escapades. Concentration furrowed her brow as she perused the contents, the words bringing her joy clear in the smile gracing her lips and the sparkle in her eyes.

"So, Collin," she said, her voice tinged with excitement, "I've been researching preserving our produce. I think it's time we take our skills to the next level."

I glanced at her, my curiosity piqued. I was used to Kathleen's enthusiasm for our small garden, but something about her tone today felt different. There was a glimmer in her eyes that she had stumbled upon, a secret that held the key to our future.

“Preserving our produce?” I echoed, studying Kathleen with a mix of concern and curiosity. I admired her dedication to our sustainable lifestyle, but I couldn’t help but wonder what she had discovered during her research.

Kathleen nodded, her smile widening. “Yes! I’ve been reading about ancient preservation methods used by our ancestors to store food for long periods without refrigeration. It’s like unlocking a hidden treasure trove of knowledge!”

This unexpected turn intrigued me. “Tell me more,” I said, leaning closer. “What have you found?”

Gingerly, she turned the worn notebook around and placed it before me. Different ink colors covered the pages, lined with neat handwritten notes. She pointed out other techniques for food preservation, explaining each one as her finger moved across the page.

“With canning, drying, and fermenting, we can preserve our harvest and have plenty to eat all winter,” she explained, pointing to each method as she spoke.

“That’s brilliant. With our stockpile of vegetables, we won’t have to worry about the unpredictable world outside these walls.”

Kathleen smiled. “Exactly! We’ll bottle up summer’s taste and the freshness of our garden and savor it all year round. We’ll be able to enjoy our garden, even when it’s cold outside. It’ll be a reminder of warmer days to come.”

"Let's do it!" I said. So we gathered the ingredients and got to work.

The sweet aroma of ripened fruits filled the air, mingling with the earthy scent of freshly cut herbs. Time seemed to slow as we labored in harmonious silence.

In this age-old tradition, each of us had our role to play. With an artist's precision, Kathleen diced the cucumbers, her nimble fingers moving like a conductor's baton, guiding symmetrical cubes onto a waiting platter. Meanwhile, I took charge of the firm tomatoes, their vibrant red skin yielding effortlessly under the skilled strokes of my knife.

A captivating array of spices and condiments surrounded our large wooden table, a culinary battlefield where ginger, garlic, cloves, mustard seeds, and coriander joined forces. Their heady fragrances mingled and danced in the air as we blended them with measured care, crafting a medley of flavors that would elevate these humble ingredients into an extraordinary taste.

As the last jar found its place on the shelf, the room brimmed with anticipation for the coming months. Summer's bounty, carefully preserved, would continue to grace our tables long after its warmth had faded.

Kathleen, wiping her hands on her apron, took a moment to bask in the aroma. The tangy scent of vinegar intertwined with hints of dill and garlic, promising flavors that would dance upon our taste buds in the dead of winter.

Gazing at the rows of mason jars, their glass surfaces were a kaleidoscope of colors, and our hearts swelled with memories. Each jar held a precious fragment of our past, preserved like time capsules waiting to be opened. The vibrant hues in each glass vessel symbolized moments of laughter, love, and a sentimental yearning for days gone by.

"Done!" Kathleen exclaimed, her eyes gleaming with satisfaction. "Look at them. Our cherished treasures of goodness."

In the aftermath of our creative endeavor, we took a moment to revel in the beauty and permanence we had crafted.

"It's like bottling sunshine," I marveled. "We'll always remember the taste of summer."

Stepping outside into the crisp night air after completing our task, we approached the blazing campfire. The heat embraced our icy bodies as we ladled generous portions of piping-hot vegetable soup into our bowls.

Seated around the fire, we immersed ourselves in the dance of flames that illuminated the dark sky above. Each spoonful of comfort was a celebration, a masterpiece of flavors gracing our taste buds.

The stars twinkled overhead, as if nodding in approval at this moment of peace and contentment. Closing my eyes, I released a satisfied sigh, feeling the weight of my worries dissipate with each flavorful bite.

Taking another spoonful, I couldn't help but compliment Kathleen on her culinary prowess. "This is absolutely amazing!" I exclaimed. She blushed and grinned, clearly pleased with the praise.

"Thank you. It's a labor of love, just like our garden."

As the last mouthful of food passed my lips, a warm feeling of delight washed over me. I closed my eyes, allowing myself to fully savor the peace and contentment that filled the air after such a delicious meal. My gratitude towards Kathleen and our flourishing garden overflowed from within, bringing a smile to my face.

"You know, Kathleen," I said, leaning back against a log, "sometimes I think this garden is more than just food for our bodies. It's food for our souls, too."

Kathleen gazed into the dancing flames, her eyes reflecting a mix of curiosity and amusement. "Food for our souls? How so?" she asked, her voice tinged with intrigue.

I pondered her question, allowing the crackling fire to lull my thoughts. "Well, think about it," I began, a smile tugging at the corners of my lips. "When we tend to the garden, when we sow the seeds and watch them grow into vibrant plants, it's as though we're nurturing a piece of ourselves. A certain satisfaction comes from seeing nature respond to our care."

She nodded thoughtfully, her gaze drifting towards the rows of vegetables bathed in moonlight. "You're right. It's like we're connecting with something deeper, something primal."

"Exactly," I replied, feeling a surge of enthusiasm in my words. "There's a sense of purpose in cultivating life from the ground. It reminds us of our connection to nature and the delicacy of life. It gives us a sense of hope in a time when so much is uncertain. And it's a reminder of the resilience of the human spirit."

She smiled. "I agree. Nature does have a way of healing and grounding us. It's a reminder of the beauty and strength within us all."

I nodded. "And in this garden, we've found our sanctuary."

We sat side-by-side as we gazed into the fire. Flames licked hungrily at the logs, and occasional sparks flew up from the blaze, twinkling briefly before fading into the night sky. The warmth of the fire filled our faces with a pleasant tone while the sweet aroma of smoke surrounded us like a comforting embrace. The beauty of it all mesmerized us, and we felt connected that words could never explain.

After another hour, the fire had nearly died out, casting the clearing in a soft orange glow. A gentle breeze blew through the campground, rustling leaves and carrying the scent of an excellent night. We returned to the police station to our sleeping bags, grateful for the warmth of our shelter.

The fire in the stove sparked and roared, casting a vibrant glow across the room as we gathered closer to its warmth. I reached for a few logs from the neatly stacked pile beside us and tossed them into the flames.

As they crackled and blazed, our sleeping bags and blankets covered us in a cocoon of comfort. We settled down for the night, immersed in the dancing flames and the symphony of popping embers. Eventually, exhaustion took hold, and we drifted into a peaceful slumber, surrounded by the comforting scent of burning wood.

In the midst of a calm silence, our celestial beings intertwined with the boundless cosmos, connecting us to the timeless essence of nature and filling us with a tangible feeling of peace and harmony.

CHAPTER TWENTY-SEVEN

The Tempest

My eyes blinked open to the soft tone of the pre-dawn sky stretching over the worn police station. Cozy in my sleeping bag, I shrugged off the chilly air weaving into the morning.

Those moments of quiet seclusion, wrapped up in warmth, were a sweet indulgence. A gentle breeze outside whispered a call to embrace the day while the winter chill slipped through the window cracks, leaving a frosty touch on my skin. Goosebumps rose, and my breath hung in the air like white clouds.

Snuggling deeper into my sleeping bag, I tried to ward off the cold. The air carried the scent of frost and pine, with a hint of wood smoke from a distant stove.

Lying still briefly, I gathered the will to shake off drowsiness. With a sigh, I traded my sleeping cocoon for a faded flannel shirt and worn jeans, pulling on a tattered jacket. Inhaling deeply, I hardened myself against the cold and stepped into the front room, ready to face whatever the day had in store.

For the past three days, I'd been crafting a shortcut to the lake, a project aimed at sparing us the labor of hauling water for miles. The effort had left my limbs sore, hands blistered, and clothes caked with dirt.

Initially, a seemingly straightforward task, it had unfolded into a maze of challenges, pushing my determination and creativity to their limits. Clearing trees, moving rocks, and battling thick shrubbery became a complex dance. I only hoped to finish before it drained me entirely.

Entering the room, I found Kathleen already there, her troubled expression evident as she gazed out the window at the sky.

I couldn't fathom the source of her distress. Silently, I followed her gaze to the window, and the sight that unfolded before me sent a shiver down my spine. Brooding black clouds hung heavily in the sky, casting a foreboding shadow over the landscape below. The distant rumble of thunder echoed like a cautionary note in the air.

Her voice trembled, and she shifted her gaze to the ominous sky. With a gentle touch, her hand landed on my shoulder, a silent plea urging me to reconsider stepping outside.

"Collin, I truly think you should stay here today," she implored, worry and fear in her eyes. The dark clouds on the horizon seemed to reinforce her words, warning of potential peril.

Despite her earnest pleas, an unexplainable urge compelled me to defy her warnings and forge ahead with completing the path. I grappled with conflicting loyalties, between being there for her and seeing through the construction of the lake path to ease her burdens.

The wooden floor creaked beneath my feet as I moved toward the door. Kathleen stood before me, hands wringing, lips bitten. I embraced her gently, feeling the tension in her frame.

"Don't worry," I reassured her with false confidence, my stomach churning with nerves. "I'll have this pathway finished in no time." Grabbing my ax leaning against the doorframe, I strode toward the incomplete trail.

Contrary to my strict orders for her to stay behind, Maggie pranced alongside me with an energetic trot. Her soft paws left delicate imprints on the damp earth, and her vigilant eyes scanned the surroundings for potential threats. Despite my attempts to dissuade her from joining this difficult trek, I couldn't help but appreciate her steadfast companionship.

Years of neglect had weathered the cobblestones lining the road to our new pathway, rendering it uneven and treacherous. Moss-slicked stones challenged my footing as I navigated toward the looming trees of the forest ahead.

A heavy weight of guilt tugged at me as I turned my back on Kathleen, who stood in the doorway with a look of longing and disappointment. She was the only one I had left in this world, yet I was leaving her behind. But I knew our future would be brighter and more manageable if we cleared this path.

As I made my way down the winding road, I couldn't help but think about all the obstacles we had overcome together and how this path would be another challenge we would conquer.

The storm brewing seemed to swallow the sky, casting a deep blue hue while the ozone carried its metallic tang on the wind. I watched a brilliant flash of light illuminate the darkness, casting razor-sharp shadows across the trees. A loud boom thundered overhead, followed by a long rumbling that made my bones shudder.

The raw fury of nature held me captive. The air crackled with an electrifying tension, every breath charged with anticipation. A palpable sense of foreboding hung thick in the atmosphere as if the storm itself were a living entity poised for something ominous.

The rain, initially a gentle drizzle, morphed into a relentless downpour. Each raindrop felt like a tiny explosion against my skin, leaving a tingling sensation in its wake.

The heavens opened up, unleashing a deluge that soaked me to the bone, my clothes clinging like a second skin. A howling wind swept the landscape, accompanied by thunderous echoes that dwarfed my existence in the face of nature's relentless power.

I stumbled through the storm, the unyielding rain blurring my vision. Each step became a fierce battle against the wind, a force determined to impede my progress.

But my resolve remained unbroken. The storm, seemingly mocking my determination, intensified its assault with each passing moment. Raindrops fell like liquid bullets, slashing against my face and stinging my skin.

As I pressed forward, a majestic oak tree stood defiant against the raging gale. Its towering branches swayed dangerously, entwined in a dangerous dance with the storm. The tree, weathered by countless storms, stood as a testament to the relentless passage of time.

Then, with a sudden, gut-wrenching crack, the air echoed. My heart raced as I instinctively turned toward the sound. Eyes widened in terror, I watched a colossal branch tear free from the oak, hurtling toward me with a malevolent force.

Time stretched into a sluggish crawl as the massive branch hurtled menacingly toward me, its descent laden with impending doom. Adrenaline surged through my veins, sparking lightning-fast instincts that kicked my mind into high gear.

In a heartbeat, I flung myself sideways with a desperate lurch, narrowly escaping the deadly trajectory of the plummeting branch. The earth quivered beneath an earth-shattering thud as the colossal limb crashed onto the spot I had just vacated. Splinters of wood and leaves erupted into a chaotic dance, painting the air with the aftermath of destruction.

My heart pounded relentlessly in my chest as I staggered backward, breaths escaping in ragged gasps. The harrowing brush with disaster left me rattled, my body shivering with the lingering tendrils of fear. My gaze drifted toward the massive oak tree, its imposing presence etched against the darkened skies.

My chest heaved with each breath as I frantically sifted through the debris, eyes darting anxiously for any sign of Maggie. Gasps escaped my lips in sharp intervals as I delved into the tangled mess, sending bits of twigs and leaves flying in my desperate search.

Finally, amongst a pile of branches, I spotted her trembling form. A wave of relief crashed over me, washing away the fear and panic that had gripped me moments before. My hands trembled. I carefully removed the twigs and leaves from her coat and assisted her in crawling out from under the tree branches. A sense of relief washed over me when I realized Maggie wasn't injured.

The atmosphere shifted instantly, plunging into a deep and foreboding darkness. The relentless rain stopped abruptly, leaving an unsettling stillness that cloaked everything in its grasp. A thick shroud of blackness enveloped the sky as if it were the dead of night. All movement ceased, and a sense of impending doom hung in the air with no sound.

The hairs on my neck stood upright as the low hum filled my ears. I didn't need to see it to know a tornado was coming. The frightening sound grew in intensity, like an angry beast coming closer and closer, eager to devour me whole. My heart raced as I darted my gaze across the horizon, searching desperately for escape.

Dread gripped my heart as a colossal funnel cloud bore down, its dark base swirling with malevolence. The thunderous winds unleashed an ear-splitting roar, a force that reverberated through my very core. Its sheer might manifested as it rampaged across the landscape, mercilessly uprooting trees and obliterating everything in its path.

Approaching like a ruthless predator, the tornado flung chunks of tree bark and swirling dust into the air, orchestrating a chaotic dance of destruction. Havoc loomed in every direction, a nightmarish scene unfolding before my eyes.

The wind's biting cold stabbed at my exposed skin, each gust feeling like icy fingers clawing at me. Time hung precariously in the balance, and I knew I had mere moments to seek refuge from the unforgiving beast.

Maggie whined beside me, her body quivering with fear. She was straining against her collar, trying to escape the surrounding danger. I tightened my grip on her leash and ran towards the town's safety behind us as quickly as possible.

The wind whipped my hair across my face and stung my eyes. I pulled Maggie along. Her tiny paws barely touched the ground as she struggled to keep up. The menacing funnel cloud trailed closely behind, tearing through the trees and leaving a path of destruction.

I frantically searched for a way to outrun the relentless storm that pursued us. Every breath burned in my lungs as I pushed myself harder, willing my legs to carry me faster and farther away from the impending danger.

In our frantic escape, my eyes locked onto the silhouette of an old church standing ominously in the distance. Its doors, worn and weather-beaten by the relentless wind, stretched open like arms offering sanctuary. Urgency propelled us towards it, a desperate bid to find shelter from the relentless onslaught of nature's fury.

Determined, I propelled myself forward, my body hurtling through the entrance like a speeding bullet. Close behind, Maggie followed, her breaths strained and ragged.

As we burst into the ageless church, the worn doors slammed shut behind us with a loud boom, as if attempting to barricade us from the encroaching darkness outside.

The air within was thick and musty, saturated with the scent of aged wood and the echoes of centuries-old incense. The dimly lit sanctuary offered a brief refuge from the tumultuous storm, its eerie stillness providing a surreal contrast to the wild chaos we had just escaped.

I squeezed my eyes shut and prayed for safety within these hallowed walls, hoping they would shield us from the horrors lurking just beyond. As I stood there in the dim light, I couldn't help but wonder what terrors awaited us on the other side of those solid doors.

The storm drenched me from head to toe, every inch of my body coated in freezing water that sent sharp shivers through my nerves. The rain drenched Maggie's fur, leaving it matted down. The cold droplets seeped into every fiber of our being, causing us to shiver uncontrollably.

Maggie and I frantically scrambled towards the far corner for shelter, our bodies trembling with fear and desperation as we prayed for safety from the fierce storm. We huddled together to keep warm. While the wind continued to howl like a pack of wolves, threatening to tear down our fragile haven.

It felt like the flurry would never end. The wind roared like a freight train, slamming against the walls and rattling every window and door. The sheer force of it threatened to shatter me into a million pieces as if I were nothing but fragile glass in its wake.

Each gust felt like a physical blow, leaving me breathless and disoriented. I could almost feel the walls of the church trembling under the relentless assault of the storm outside. It was as if Mother Nature herself had unleashed her fury upon us, and I was just a speck caught during it all.

The tornado's thunderous roar seemed interminable until, abruptly, it ceased. In its aftermath, what had once been resilient homes now lay reduced to twisted wreckage. Once steadfast, towering oaks and majestic maples were now uprooted, their roots exposed as if desperately clutching at remnants of life.

I stumbled through the shattered front doors of the church, my legs trembling beneath me. Pausing, I surveyed the devastation that unfolded before my eyes.

It felt as though Mother Nature, in a fit of wrath, had unleashed her fury upon this small town. Her immense power stood evident, a stark reminder of our insignificance in the grand scheme. I pondered whether she sought to erase every trace of human existence from her landscape or merely intended to underscore our vulnerability and mortality in the face of her relentless fury.

A surge of panic and anxiety gripped my chest at the thought of Kathleen's safety within the storm-ravaged police station. Visions of her trapped and defenseless, buried beneath debris or confronting an unknown peril, flashed in my mind. Without hesitation, I propelled myself into a frantic sprint towards the station, desperate to uncover her fate before it was too late.

But as I drew near, my steps slowed, struck with horror at the sight of destruction before me. Nature, in a relentless fury, had decimated this once-sturdy fortress. Once a formidable barrier, the metal gates now twisted and bent as if a colossal force had gripped them in its fist, crumpling the resilient steel like paper. The walls, marred with cracks and missing bricks, told the tale of a relentless assault that had battered the very foundations of the building.

A sense of paralysis gripped me as I stared at the crumbling building, my heart speeding up with every ticking second. A thick white fog of smoke coiled into the sky like a venomous serpent, an ominous testament to the chaos before me. Was this a nightmare from which I couldn't escape?

"Kathleen, are you there? Say something!" I screamed.

Each breath became a struggle, the oppressive silence stretching endlessly, devoid of the response I yearned to hear. With each passing second, my heart throbbed in pain as though a piece of me was being torn away, hope fading like a distant echo.

"Please, be here. Answer me."

My hands, driven by desperation, clawed at the rubble, bits of wood snapping between my fingers as I cast aside the broken pieces. Pausing, I scanned every direction, eyes frantic in the search for her.

A sudden realization hit me like a weight, stealing the air from my lungs. The thought that Kathleen might never return burdened my heart, aching with sorrow.

Sharp edges of debris cut into my skin as I dug through the wreckage, ignoring the stinging pain in my hands. Sweat mingled with tears streaming down my face as I desperately sought any sign of life in the devastation. Fingers clawed at the rubble with raw desperation, fueled by a faint glimmer of hope that Kathleen might still be alive beneath it all.

Terror consumed me, gnawing at my soul and leaving me frozen in fear. I prayed for a miracle, scouring the wreckage for any hint of her presence amidst the destruction.

With every tick of the clock, my heart grew heavier, sinking into the depths of my chest. I felt utterly powerless, like a fragile vessel tossed mercilessly in a raging ocean, unable to withstand the onslaught of my deepest fears. Still, I pressed on despite the anxiety coursing through my veins and the nagging apprehension that clung to my thoughts.

Hours of fruitless searching left my body limp, drained of vitality. Collapsing onto the cold concrete floor, the weight of guilt settled upon me like a heavy cloak, as if I were Atlas bearing a lifetime of sins.

I could feel the chill of defeat seeping into my bones. Gazing into the darkness, a sense of powerlessness and helplessness engulfed me. I had failed, and the cost weighed heavily upon my shoulders. Closing my eyes, I leaned against the wall, the grip of despair tightening with each passing moment.

Trapped in an unending cycle, I seemed fated to receive losing hands despite my efforts. The crushing weight of life's unfairness pressed upon me, snuffing hope and joy. Why was fate so cruel? What sins had I committed to deserve such unrelenting punishment?

Amidst the depths of despair, a glimmer of clarity slowly dawned on me. It wasn't some murky past misstep that sentenced me to this sorrow; it was the unrelenting nature of life itself. I had to come to terms with the ceaseless ebb and flow of birth and death, joy intertwined with pain, triumph shadowed by failure. The outcome of life lay beyond my control, but my response to it was firmly within my grasp. I needed the courage to face it head-on and keep pushing forward.

This realization settled upon my weary heart like a dense fog. With its unpredictable twists and turns, life had finally unveiled its true nature to me. It wasn't a gentle sail on calm waters but a turbulent sea where moments of happiness pirouetted fleetingly with moments of despair.

In that moment of clarity, I understood that sorrow was an inseparable companion to the human experience.

Once I embraced that truth, fear loosened its hold on me. I realized my life wasn't any worse than anyone else's, and perhaps, just perhaps, it was even a bit better than some. Life isn't just about facing obstacles; it's about the opportunities they bring for growth and learning. We can welcome those challenges with open arms or give them the cold shoulder, but they'll always be a part of our journey.

Yet, tonight, my heart weighed heavily with worry and the emptiness of solitude. The mere thought of never seeing Kathleen's face again was unbearable. I clung to the belief that, against all odds, I would find her.

Otherwise, I feared my heart would shatter into a million pieces, never to be mended.

CHAPTER TWENTY-EIGHT

The Pens Drops

As the colors in the sky blended into a mesmerizing mix of purples and oranges, I couldn't help but be fascinated by the long shadows cast by the trees. The calmness of twilight mirrored the scattered thoughts running through my mind as I stood alone in the abandoned fire station.

Inside that dimly lit room, the dancing shadows seemed to possess a life of their own, enchanting me with their movements. The only sounds that broke the heavy silence were the occasional creaks of the floorboards beneath my feet. This place had been left untouched for what felt like an eternity, a relic from when courageous firefighters patrolled these halls, always prepared to combat any fires that threatened our town.

The walls, worn and weathered with age, bore the marks of time and memories from days long gone. The cracked paint, peeling away like ancient parchment, unveiled layers of history etched into every inch. Amidst the emptiness, a faded mural depicted a tranquil scene with rolling hills and vibrant flowers, starkly contrasting the desolation surrounding it.

A tremor coursed through my hands as I reached into my coat pocket and retrieved a crumpled photograph. It captured Kathleen on her graduation day from nursing school, her radiant smile frozen in time. It had been a playful gift from her, but now it remained as my sole memento of her presence.

As I smoothed out the creases on the photograph, a lump formed in my throat, and my eyes welled up with tears. My heart felt like it was being wrung out, twisted with grief and longing for what it once was. Kathleen's once luminous smile now haunted me from that faded image. The mischievous glimmer in her eyes that used to brighten my world now brought forth a surge of pain instead.

Questions consumed my mind as I grappled with Kathleen's sudden departure. It felt like a storm followed me everywhere I went. Is happiness merely a fleeting illusion that slips away when we try to hold onto it? Why does everything I hold dear seem snatched away against my will? Am I destined never to know true happiness?

A malevolent presence seemed to sit on my shoulder, hissing that I was unworthy and urging me to surrender. My mind incessantly replayed my past failures and mistakes like a broken record. My gaze dropped to the floor, my once confident strides now reduced to a shuffling gait. Glimpses of myself in the dust-coated mirrors brought on waves of self-loathing as I looked upon the husk I'd become.

Lost in this labyrinth of uncertainty, I yearned for a glimpse of clarity. What lay beyond the horizon of my understanding? It felt like existence itself had been woven with enigmatic threads, concealing truths beyond my reach.

In this uncertainty, one question lingered prominently in my mind. What was the purpose behind all of this? Was there a grand design hidden within life's chaotic tapestry? Or were we merely wandering amidst the cosmic symphony of chance and circumstance?

"Why?" I angrily erupted, my voice echoing off the cold stone walls surrounding me. My gaze shifted to Maggie's tattered red collar lying lifeless on the desk before me. Holding onto it served as a cruel reminder of how swiftly life can change.

I looked back at Kathleen's photo next to Maggie's collar. A tsunami of anguish and isolation crashed over me with an intensity that threatened to engulf my entire being. I whispered her name, the woman who had brought light into my darkest days.

Maggie loved her so dearly. Both now rested in peaceful slumber in the cemetery over the hill behind the station. Each visit to their gravesites served as a reminder of the happiness we once shared and how quickly it vanished.

As these thoughts consumed me, I wondered if I was looking at the situation from the wrong perspective. Maybe life didn't intend for us to experience constant happiness. Perhaps we needed a balance of joy and sorrow, light and darkness, to truly appreciate life's beauty. This realization settled within me, bringing a newfound acceptance that washed over my weary soul.

I had spent years pursuing happiness, endlessly seeking that elusive state of constant joy. But now, standing at the precipice of this newfound understanding, I realized that life was not meant to be an uninterrupted, joyous affair.

The moments of sorrow and despair that punctuated my journey suddenly held a different meaning. They were not failures or obstacles to overcome but essential components of life's grand tapestry. Each moment of darkness served as a stark contrast, allowing the light to shine even brighter.

With this acceptance, a weight lifted off my shoulders. I no longer saw happiness as a destination to be reached. Instead, I understood that the inevitable trials were integral to my growth.

I took a deep breath and exhaled, feeling my chest rise and fall with every ragged breath. It felt like I was sinking into the earth, the unforgiving surface pushing against my weary limbs. Yet even in this desolate wasteland, surrounded by darkness, I couldn't help but smile.

Memories flooded my mind, days filled with life and laughter. They consumed me as I gazed at the sparkling stars overhead, resembling millions of tiny diamonds. In the distance, faint traces of a city destroyed by cataclysmic forces came into view, yet its presence comforted me.

A smile formed on my lips as mementos of joyous celebrations, gut-wrenching pain, and hard-earned victories flashed through my mind. The highs were euphoric, the lows almost unbearable. But through it all, there was love. Love in all its forms—passionate and tender, fierce and unconditional.

Love wove its thread through the tapestry of my existence, connecting me to others and myself. It was my anchor and guiding light, making even the darkest nights bearable. Now, as mortality tightened its grip around me, I found myself letting go, each breath drawn with less resistance than before.

Life was a beautiful symphony, with its highs and lows, crescendos and decrescendos. I had played my part and added my notes to the melody, and now it was time to let others take the stage. In this silence, in this solitude, through my experiences, I have come to realize that life is not just about achieving a final destination but instead cherishing every step of the journey.

It was about the choices we made, the lives we touched, and the love we shared. As my final breath drew near, before whispering farewell to this mortal coil, I could feel a strange sensation wash over me, acceptance.

My eyes shifted upwards to the glimmering stars, and a gentle grin spread across my face as I turned to the final page of my diary. The once-empty pages now overflowed with words and memories. With one last firm stroke of my pen, I signed my name before my hand released the pen, marking the end of this incredible journey.

And so, dear reader, I leave you with this, seize the chaos, embrace the uncertainty, and live a life that fills your heart with joy. We come alive when we dance with life's ebbs and flows.

With that thought in mind, I embarked on a new journey, one filled with gratitude for the imperfect, messy, utterly breathtaking gift that is life.

The End

CHAPTER TWENTY-NINE

Epilogue

Collin was never truly alone, even though he felt isolated. His journey and reflections were a symphony of human experiences, echoing through the annals of time. His legacy will linger in the hearts and minds of those he encountered, a testament to the beauty of existence.

Years of joys and sorrows, successes and failures stitched together Collin's life. His deep love for his children and grandchildren, the bond of friendship with his childhood buddies, The Backyard Brawlers. He honored those who'd fallen in battle before him and the fresh faces he encountered in the coal mines. They braided each thread with the next, eliciting an affirmation of the power of our life and how it enriched the lives of everyone around us.

The climax of Collin's story is the understanding that life is a tapestry meant to be shared and experienced. The purpose of existence lies not in the answers we seek, but in the connections we forge along the way.

The last strokes of his journey, painted with the brush of his choices, left a lasting impression on the universe's canvas. The legacy of Collin, a man who dared to embrace life's mysteries, lives on in the hearts of those who remember.

And as the story of Collin fades into the annals of time, fresh stories unfold, new souls beginning their cosmic dance. Their essence entwines with Collin's, gently reminding us we are never truly alone.

The room where Collin sat, pen in hand, remains frozen in time. But the energy of his spirit, the essence of his being, lives on in the fragile heartbeats of those who carry his memory.

The story of Collin, the writer who dared to seek meaning amidst the emptiness, becomes a testament to the resilience of the human spirit. In the end, the connections we make, the love we give and receive, leave an indelible mark on the world.

As the last strands of Collin's essence dissipated into infinity, a sense of completion washed over him. He played his part in the grand tapestry of existence, a small but vital thread that wove together a story of love, loss, and the inherent joy of being alive.

And so, dear reader, as you close the book on Collin's tale, may you carry his story in your heart. May it serve as a reminder that life's purpose lies not in grand resolutions or tidy endings but in the connections we forge and the love we share.

Embrace the beauty of the tapestry that is your own life. Let the highs and lows, the moments of laughter and tears, mold you into the person you are meant to be. And remember, always remember, that your story, no matter how humble or extraordinary, is a masterpiece in its own right.

Every ending gives way to new beginnings, and every journey holds the promise of discovery. So, let your pen dance across the canvas of existence, painting your unique story in vibrant hues that will echo throughout eternity.

www.ingramcontent.com/pod-product-compliance
Lightning Source LLC
LaVergne TN
LVHW091025080826
845145LV00002B/355

* 9 7 8 0 9 9 6 9 9 0 0 2 8 *